I0670897

MAPS

M A P S

L.J. Garrod

Maps

Maps is a novel, a work of fiction. Any resemblance to actual events or persons, living or dead, is purely coincidental.
Depictions of locale and period history are fictionalized.

ISBN: 978-0-578-54348-2

CHAPTER 1

SAN FRANCISCO

MONDAY, OCTOBER 23, 2000

Tick. Tick. Tick. RRRRIIIINNNNGGG!

The mound of covers on the bed across the room elevated. Covers flying, Titania Ariel (TA for short she'd tell people, and shortened it once again by dropping the middle space) leapt across the floor. She slapped her hand down on the turn off button of the old wind up alarm clock on her dresser and stood quivering from the shock of the sudden awakening.

Brain catching up with her startle reflex, she started to strip. Off with the bed sweats, on with the sports bra and running sweats--bright red University of New Mexico sweatshirt and gray baggy shorts over her long legs. Staggering into the bathroom she grabbed her toothbrush, applied paste and brushed enthusiastically. Finishing, she put up the brush and grabbed a washcloth, mopped her face with cold water and ran a comb through her curly brown hair. She paused to check her face for toothpaste, none, but yes, the freckles were still there, scattered across her nose and cheeks. She grinned at herself, laughing at her childhood fantasy–the hope that somehow the freckles would disappear in the night.

Entering the small living room she flopped into her old recliner, a lucky street find, and bent down to grab the running shoes she kept parked beside the chair. She slid her feet in pulled the laces tight and double knotted the bows.

Snatching up her house keys she slipped them over her wrist as she went out the door and leapt down the stairs. Pushing out the front door she paused at the base of the stairs for a few stretching exercises. As she straightened up, her eye was caught by a car parked against the curb in front of the apartment building. It was facing the wrong direction and the driver was leaning against the window, peering at her, his mouth slightly open. He had been watching her do her stretches. Gross! A peeping Tom! She threw him a finger and started running down the street. At least he didn't start the car and follow me, she thought.

As stiff muscles started to limber, her run turned effortless. Smooth joints rolling and light steps springing, she allowed her mind to drift. Her annoyance at the peeping Tom shifted to annoyance at the male race. TA worked in a shop that specialized in antique maps. At twenty-eight, with a master's in archival and restoration cartography and halfway through her doctorate she felt her chances of advancement were minimal because of her gender.

Friday, she had been doing research on a map of 18th century Boston, when a Japanese gentleman, Mr. Kamakura, had entered the shop. He wanted someone to travel with him to New Mexico to verify an old map he was picking up in a small town north of Santa Fe. TA's boss and mentor, Ezekiel Feather, who was severely crippled with arthritis, confined to a wheelchair, had offered TA's services. Kamakura had refused a 'woman' and requested the names of male archival cartographers. TA's usually root beer- colored eyes turned to what her grandmother called her camera eyes, a dark red tinge added to the brown color. She was so tired of not being accepted into the male world! Not only did she want equality but she had decided that she needed a Grand Adventure.

TA was annoyed and a bit wistful. It would have been fun to finally be accepted as an archivist and a blast to travel back to New Mexico, the state where she had been born and where she had gone to the University.

She had run a full circle through the park and was approaching her street so she dropped her pace for a cooling off period as she ran toward home. Ahead of her she could see the car still parked in front of the apartment. She'd just ignore him.

She jogged to the apartment steps to do her cool down stretches. As she extended her leg she looked back over her shoulder at the car. The man was still peering out, his mouth hanging open. "Sick!" she said. She straightened and, jogging in place, looked back at him, shaming him into looking away, only he didn't. He stared straight at where she had been stretching on the bottom steps of the apartment stoop.

She jogged over to the car window and knocked on it. "Get lost, get out of here or I'll call the cops." He kept staring. She knocked harder and to her horror his head started to slide slowly down the window, eyes and mouth still open.

"Oh God, he's dead! Oh God, oh God!" She turned and ran up the steps, slammed through the door, and ran down the hall to her landlady's apartment. Pounding on the door, she yelled, "Mrs. Maisel, Mrs. Maisel. It's me, TA."

"Just a minute, TA." Mrs. Maisel called as she struggled with her multiple locks.

"Never mind the locks, call 9-1-1 and tell the police that there's a dead man out in front in a car. I'll go out and wait." She could hear Mrs. Maisel talking to herself as her footsteps retreated toward the phone.

"A dead man in front of my apartments, who could it be? Why me? Why me?" Mrs. Maisel's usual refrain was Why me? The cares of the entire world all pressed on Mrs. Maisel's frail shoulders.

TA turned, ran down the hall and out the front door. The car was still parked in front but the man wasn't there. She ran over to

3

the car. Yes he was, he'd slid down beside the steering wheel. There was dark, drying blood smeared down the back of the seat, drawing her eyes to the large blood patch on the man's exposed back and side. Ugh, ugh! TA had never seen a dead man before and she was unconsciously jogging in place, her teeth chattering both from early morning chill and from the shock of what she was seeing. Continuing to jog, she turned away to face the building. Any view was better than what was at her back.

It must have been a slow morning because she heard the sirens almost as soon as she had jogged to the stairs.

Two police cars pulled up and disgorged multiple stern-faced men. The youngest one officiously moved her back to the front of the building. He pulled out his notebook, "All right lady, name?"

"TA Mc..." She stopped when she saw his expression. "Titantia Arial McGovern." She gestured over her shoulder, "I live here, in 2A."

He wrote it down. "When did you find him?" he asked.

"I came down around 6:00 this morning and I thought he was a Peeping Tom. I threw him a finger and went jogging, but when I came back he was still here." TA continued jogging in place. She was cold both from the temperature and from watching the police leaning into the car as they inspected the body. Just like CSI, she thought. Flashes were going off from all angles as they photographed the crime scene.

"I thought he was staring at me," she said, looking away. "When I was doing my exercises, so I yelled at him." She paused and gulped, yelling at a dead man! Her teeth chattered.

She wrapped her arms around herself. "He just kept looking," she continued, "so I went over and yelled at him and I knocked on the window when he ignored me and then he started slipping down the window." She paused as she relived it in her mind. Oh God, oh gross! "And then I told my landlady to call 9-1-1."

"Geeze lady, can't you hold still, I can hardly write with you bouncing around like that." He slapped his notebook against his leg.

"I'm freezing!" She found herself screaming in his face. Oh Lord, now she was yelling at cops. She kept jogging up and down, up and down, her arms wrapped around her chest.

An older man, plainclothed, came over. "What's going on over here?"

"Awwww, Lieutenant, she won't hold still while I'm questioning her!" whined the uniform.

"Fuck! Pardon me, Miss. D'Angelo, you better hope she doesn't. She'd freeze to death out here and then we'd have two corpses. Did you get everything you need?"

"Yeah, I guess so." He made a production out of checking his notes. "You can go now, lady, but don't leave town," he added pompously, eyeing his superior.

She spun on her heel and jogged up the steps and out of the cold.

It took ten minutes in a hot shower before she started feeling warm. After the shower and wrapped in her warmest robe she made nursery tea with lots of sugar and milk, curled up in her recliner with all its comforting lumps and valleys and thought about her morning.

She mentally traced her complete run and then started to think about the man and his car. Had she seen anything that would help? He had looked fairly young, Asian, she now remembered. Hmmmmm. He must have been shot from the street side of the car, stabbing would have been too awkward. Besides, the window she had looked in had been rolled up and unbroken, so the attack would have to have been from the street side. Had she seen anyone else on the street when she came out of the apartment? No, the street had been empty of people. TA, as did most of the country, enjoyed the weekly crime dramas that ran on TV. She felt mildly disappointed that she couldn't solve, or at least furnish telling clues in this mystery that was sitting right at her front door.

She could hardly wait to tell her boss what had happened this morning. She finished her tea and went in to dress.

When TA arrived at the shop Ezekiel Feather was already in his office. He owned the building. The top floor was his apartment and the ground floor was the shop. The basement, hermetically controlled, held a large safe, storage and workrooms. He was pulling out a selection of maps for the two sets of clients with scheduled appointments. Each was interested in maps from different eras and areas.

As they discussed the maps' good and bad points, TA told him about her early morning activities; he listened and gave her the comfort she needed.

The morning went quickly with all the clients arriving simultaneously completely disregarding their scheduled appointment times.

When TA left for a late lunch she hurried across the little Poets' Park that the shop faced. She loved the park with its four statues of poets placed one on each side. Her favorite was Robby Burns, probably because of his tartan and tam, though she admired the other three--Poe, Frost and Elizabeth Barret Browning.

She looked around for Gentleman Friend, a big scruffy yellow tomcat she had met several months before. It had been a mild, sunny day and she had been sitting on a park bench eating a sandwich and reading a particularly atrocious gothic novel she had bought for ten cents at a small bookstore around the corner. The book had attracted her because the cover showed a smiling Irish setter leaning on a beautiful woman. Unfortunately, that was the whole role that the setter played as he had not yet appeared in the book and she was halfway through it. The heroine had a tall, dark, handsome man panting after her, however. The man had no name and was referred to as 'my gentleman friend'. It was just as 'gentleman friend' was holding the panting, heaving heroine to his broad chest that TA felt a presence beside her. She glanced over to see who was invading her space, and more to the point, who was sitting close enough to see what truly atrocious taste she had in books. A large yellow cat, of great presence, was sitting beside her. His gaze was not on her reading material but riveted pointedly on her tuna sandwich. "Well, hello, my gentleman friend," she had laughed. They shared the sandwich and struck up a friendship. She called him Gentleman Friend but soon shortened it to Friend. The friendship had continued for many months and many sandwiches.

She found Friend pursuing his favorite pastime--stalking the yarn shop poodle.

A thoroughly obnoxious yapping miniature poodle inhabited a tiny yarn shop on the far side of the park. The poodle spent a good part of its day jumping around in front of the shop, tethered by a neon pink leash, a color repeated in his collar and on the ribbons tied into his curly top knot and tail puff.

Friend had a quest, one he pursued with single-minded fanaticism. He lusted after the poodle's pink ribbons. TA, with a true researcher's dedication, had at various times offered Friend ribbons of different colors, widths and lengths but he had spurned them all. She had finally decided that his ribbon quest had something to do with the challenge, similar to the Plains Indians counting coup in battle, the tapping of an enemy warrior with the coup stick to bring honor to the tribe.

Friend's modus operandi was not to confront the poodle. He always approached from a blind side and with a deft stroke of an extended claw he would hook the ribbon from the poodle, never scratching flesh but almost always removing a few kinky white poodle hairs in the process. He would be gone before the beleaguered creature had time to change from yap to screech, leaving the poor beast spinning in circles until it was completely wound in its leash and rolling around the pavement screaming.

Once Friend had the ribbon, he could hardly wait to get rid of it. He would immediately carry it to the nearest street grate and drop it in.

Sure enough, there he was, draped over a branch, tail lashing, eyes intent on the heedlessly yapping dog.

"Gentleman Friend!" yelled TA. He turned his head and looked at her. Friend could never be startled and guilt wasn't in his vocabulary. "Yes?" he seemed to say. "You screamed?"

"Friend," she coaxed, "Come down. See, I brought you a hard-boiled egg." She held up the egg she had brought from home.

He cocked his head and then rose slowly and elegantly. Balancing delicately, he stretched and then leapt down and came to her.

"Meowrr?" he asked. "Your bench or my tree?"

"Yes, a good egg. Yum, yum. Much better than poodle hair. Come on. Let's go eat." They went to their bench and TA broke the egg apart on the paper sack, after first extracting her lunch of low fat yogurt. They ate companionably, while she told him about her morning.

"It was awful, Friend, but I need to run and I'll go again tomorrow. She gave him a forehead scratch and rose to return to the shop and soon buried herself in restoring a garden map from rural England across which someone had evidently spilled an entire English tea.

CHAPTER 2

SAN FRANCISCO

TUESDAY, OCTOBER 24, 2000

She woke at six and slipped into her running outfit. It wasn't raining, but the morning was cold and there was a brisk wind. It felt good to run this morning, just a bit of yesterday's stiffness left, so she upped her distance to two miles.

Running back toward her apartment building, she was almost to the entry stairs when she noticed the bum lying across the middle step, right where she was planning to stretch. He was blocking her access to the door.

She paused at the bottom of the stairs, jogging in place. "Pardon me…Excuse me?…" He didn't move.

She reached out and touched his shoulder. At least he was clean looking, from the back anyway. "Hey!" She prodded his shoulder and slowly, reluctantly, he rolled over…and over…and down until he sprawled across the lowest step, his hand, his dead hand, flopping out across her foot.

"Yeesh!" she screeched as she jumped away, falling back across the curb and into the street, her bottom coming down hard on the dew-damp gritty pavement. TA sat there, legs sprawled, looking at him. He was dead alright, no noticeable holes in him but dead, dead, dead.

TA jumped up, wiping street grime off her hands onto the hips of her shorts.

She ran toward the stairs, gave a leap, cleared the body and landed on the third step. Not pausing, she ran up the steps, through the door and down the hall.

Pounding on Mrs. Maisel's door, she called to her. Mrs. Maisel was already opening the last bolt before TA could stop yelling.

She threw open the door and face-to-face with TA, said, "Well, TA? Another body? Ha, ha." She laughed at her own humor.

TA snapped out of her shock as she got a good look at Mrs. Maisel's night attire. Mrs. Maisel was a tiny seventy-two-year-old widow and thin as a stick—but there she stood in a black babydoll nighty. There were waving ostrich feathers around the neck of the gown and on the high-heeled mules that she wore on her gnarled feet. Two red hearts were embroidered over her breasts. It was obvious that while age might be advancing on Mrs. Maisel, it hadn't caught her yet.

"Wow, Mrs. Maisel," admired TA. "That's some cool outfit."

Mrs. Maisel preened for a moment and then, "TA, I hope you didn't get me up to admire my nighty. What's all the yelling about?"

TA shifted back to reality, "Call 9-1-1, Mrs. Maisel. There's another dead body. He's on the front stairs." To her horror she found herself snickering. "They're gaining on us!" She put her hand over her mouth and tried to stop laughing but she couldn't. She leaned weakly against the wall, tears streaming down her face and laughter wracking her body.

Mrs. Maisel looked disapprovingly at her and then TA's laughter caught her. She chuckled, then hoo-hawed, gave TA a horrified look and turned to run to the telephone. TA burst into new gales of laughter as she watched Mrs. Maisel's back. There were two red hands appliqued on the seat of her nightgown.

By the time TA had reached the outer door her laughter had died to giggles and when she went outside and saw the body, all laughter left.

She stood at the top of the stairs, blocked from going down by the corpse. There was nothing that would make her vault that body again. There she stood, waiting and freezing. She started jogging in place. "Geeze, cold, cold, cold. Where are they?"

A man and woman came out of an apartment down the block, looked at TA and the body and hurried off in the other direction.

A taxi cruised down the street, the driver leaning out his window looking at addresses but when he saw the body he sped up and turned the corner.

She could hear a siren in the distance but it seemed to be going in the other direction.

More and more people came out on the street on their way to work but after one quick glance in TA's direction, they all hurried away with eyes averted.

Behind TA, Mr. Farmer, from 3B, came down the stairs, looked through the glass in the door and retreated down the hall and out the back into the alley. One by one the rest of the tenants arrived and retreated.

Another siren sounded but it too was going away rather than approaching.

TA was getting tired of jogging but it was too cold to stop. She found she was getting bored with the whole thing and thoroughly sick of the body. Now she knew how the ancient mariner felt with the albatross swinging from his neck.

She heard two sirens this time and they got louder and louder. Then two police cars came hurrying officiously up the street and parked at the curb. "Thank you God," she murmured. "Now I can get out of here."

The plainclothes detective from yesterday got out of the first squad car and stood looking up at her, hands on hips, coat pushed back and whipping in the wind. "Holy Toledo, lady, not you again!"

TA, jogging, freezing, waved weakly, "Just lucky, I guess."

"D'Angelo," he yelled over his shoulder, "Get your book and talk to the lady." The young cop scurried around the end of the car and paused at the base of the corpse-draped steps. He looked as if he were considering jumping but instead he stepped around to the side of the stairs and stood looking up at TA.

He held his notebook in front of his chest, shield-like, and called, "Name?" They went through the whole question and answer thing again with TA leaning over the side railing. She suddenly remembered her high school play of Romeo and Juliet and felt the giggles rising.

The lieutenant jumped lightly over the corpse and mounted the steps. "Let's go inside, I want to talk to you." Her urge to giggle left immediately.

She turned and led him upstairs to her apartment. The young officer followed, carrying his notebook and pencil in front of his chest at attention.

When they arrived, she offered them coffee, quickly switched on the coffee maker and then excused herself for a moment.

She removed her headband and ran a comb through her hair, kicked her running shoes into the closet and pulled on her warm slippers and a heavy robe. By the time she returned to the living room the coffee was ready.

The men had taken the two chairs so she curled up on the couch and warmed her hands around her cup as she sipped.

The lieutenant, leaning forward, his hands holding the cup between his spread knees, said, "I'm Lieutenant Samson. Ms. McGovern, I have a few questions." He paused and pulled out a small notebook. Expertly balancing cup and notebook, he continued, "Do you know a Mr. Wang Bo?

12

"No, is that the dead man downstairs?"

"No, it's the man from the car yesterday. You might know him under another name. Would you mind looking at a photo of him?" He pulled a picture from his pocket, adroitly adding it to his balancing act. He leaned forward and handed it to her.

She took it reluctantly, having no desire to look at a dead man ever again. She forced her eyes down and found herself looking at a smiling face of a young man. It seemed to be a passport photo.

She looked at him carefully. How sad, he had a nice face. She shook her head and handed the photograph back to the lieutenant. "Sorry, I don't recognize him. Who was he?"

"You'll be reading about him in the paper this morning so I'll fill you in. He's a Chinese national and a cultural attaché at their embassy. They have no idea, they say, what he was doing here in front of your apartment's door. Now, do you know anything about him?"

TA paused to think for a moment. "No, the only Chinese national I know was someone I went to school with my freshman year at college and she left to go to MIT after our first year. We really weren't close friends and we never wrote. I know a few Chinese Americans, but they're more American than Chinese. I don't think any of them even speak Chinese. It was probably just an accident he was here.

"How come you're questioning me? I found them, but only because I went out early. Why aren't you questioning the rest of the people who live here?"

The lieutenant was checking his notebook and looked at her from under his brows. "I don't think it was an accident, especially after today. Accidents like that don't happen. Wang wasn't robbed and the body today is a Chinese male who wasn't robbed either. His billfold shows that he's also a cultural attaché at the embassy. If this keeps up, the Chinese aren't going to have any culture left."

TA managed a weak smile. D'Angelo laughed dutifully and falsely. He was sitting on the edge of his chair, balancing his notebook on his knee, looking alertly from one person to the other as each spoke.

Samson continued, "We know you work in a shop specializing in antique maps, have you recently been approached by the Chinese Government or by anyone of Chinese descent regarding maps?"

"No, no Chinese at all recently and no new maps from China. In recent years the Chinese haven't been selling anything old. They're doing a good job of protecting their heritage."

"Perhaps your boss hasn't told you everything."

TA laughed, "If Ezekiel had gotten a new map, he'd be waiting at the door to show it to me. We love maps and we love sharing them."

Putting his cup down, Samson stood. "We'll probably be around to talk to him today. Please don't leave town. Thanks for your cooperation."

TA felt his thanks weren't sincere. He walked toward the door, almost tripping over his assistant, as D'Angelo leapt toward the door to get it open before his superior arrived.

After they left she hurried into the shower and then dressed for the shop. It was going to be another busy day. She was surprised that she wasn't nearly as upset today as she had been yesterday. Finding bodies must be something you started getting used to, at least after the initial shock.

As she arrived at work, she glanced across at the park and saw Friend, crouched pigeon-like on the head of the Robby Burns bust. For some reason Friend preferred Robby over the other poets' statues and spent a good deal of his time draped, or crouched as the spirit moved, on Robby's tam.

"But for the glorious privilege, Of being independent," she called to him, quoting from Burns' poem, Epistle to a Young Friend.

Friend blinked sleepily but other than a twitch of his left ear, he remained motionless.

When she entered the shop, she went directly to Ezekiel's office, flipping lights on as she went. He hadn't come down yet so she started the coffee, turned up the heat and checked the appointment book. They had one 11:00 appointment, two corporate appointments in the afternoon, and one collector coming at 8:00 that evening.

She spent the morning telling Ezekiel about her early morning adventure, going over the books and vacuuming. She always enjoyed doing the housekeeping because it gave her a chance to admire the room. It was so Dickenseque. The front door of the shop was heavy carved wood with an oval beveled window and a brass door pull. The entryway held a small table with a large glass ashtray and a small brass no smoking sign. On one side of the table was a straight chair and on the other was a large blue gray ceramic umbrella stand in the shape of an octopus. It had large bulging black eyes with a small chip in the upper area of one of the eyes giving the octopus a zany welcoming expression. There was an ornate brass coat rack and an elevator door on the other side of the entry. The elevator led to Ezekiel's apartment above and to the workrooms below. Straight ahead was the inner glass door that led to the shop.

The main room had a bay window with two armchairs flanking a table holding a brass lamp and the latest copies of Connoisseur, Architects Digest and the Wall Street Journal. A round Duncan Phyfe table with four chairs sat in the middle of the room with a lamp suspended above it. A magnifying glass and two weighted rods sat on the table. Two more straight chairs stood against the walls. The lower walls of the shop were dark green brocade; the upper part painted cream, the better to display matted and framed maps. The maps were highlighted by lights recessed into the ceiling. There were also lights set into the molding that ran around the ceiling edge, giving the room a gentle glow.

Behind the main room were two smaller rooms decorated similarly, one was Ezekiel's office and other a small room with a smaller table for the 'shy' buyer (as Ezekiel referred to those quiet anonymous people who prefer to keep their buying very much from the public eye.

Off the main room was a small powder room, and a tiny kitchenette with a utilitarian circular stair at the very back, which led up to the apartment above and down to the basement below.

After the few housekeeping chores TA was ready for their first appointment which was a couple who wanted 'beautiful' maps to decorate their library, which, as far as TA could surmise, was without books.

They selected three English maps of estate gardens from the early 1800's and left with a list of reference books on maps and gardens that TA suggested they get for their empty library.

Lieutenant Samson came in at 12:30 and asked to speak with Ezekiel alone. `TA went to lunch.

She and Friend shared a gyro from the deli around the corner, and then strolled around the perimeter of the park together. She returned to the shop when she saw Samson's car pulling away.

Ezekiel was sitting by the door waiting for her and looking worried. "TA, this is very serious," he said as soon as she walked in. "The Lieutenant says that these men were connected and he says they have a direct connection to you."

TA laughed. "Ezekiel, get real, how could they have a connection to me? I don't know anyone at the Chinese Embassy. There're hundreds of people living on that block, why me?" She shrugged out of her coat and turned to hang it up.

"Because Wang Bo and Zhang Honghui both had a picture of you in their pockets, that's why."

TA stopped dead, holding her coat suspended inches from the coat rack. She turned slowly, clutching the coat to her chest. "What do you mean; they had picture of me?"

"Just that, Samson didn't tell you earlier because he was running a background check on you to see if you were into anything like drugs or smuggling artifacts."

16

She turned and hung up her coat. "Ezekiel, this is nuts," she turned back to him. "I don't have any idea what's going on."

"You don't have to defend yourself to me, TA. Remember, I know you. He's running a check on me, too, and he wants us both to be very careful for the next few days. He says the State Department is going to lean on the Embassy a little bit and maybe they'll come up with something."

TA turned and stalked across the room, she stopped when she realized she had nowhere to go. She turned. "This is crazy," she repeated.

Just then the outer door buzzed and three men entered the vestibule. TA and Ezekiel froze and then relaxed when they realized that the men were their next appointment.

The men were looking for, what they called 'classy' maps to decorate their new boardroom. They happily settled on four maps of early San Francisco. One map was drawn around 1850, another was pre1906 earthquake, the third was 1920 and the fourth was 1940. When they were matted and framed they would make a handsome collection.

The next appointment was a man who announced bluntly that he needed to curry favor with a Japanese automobile company. I want a map that'll knock the socks off the little bastards." TA winced but kept a poker face. They hadn't done this much business in a month. "I want," he continued, "a map of early Japan, or maybe something of China. They invaded China, didn't they?"

TA glanced over at Ezekiel and could tell he was ready to explode. "Mr. Feather, why don't you go on with what you were doing and let me handle this," she said. They needed the money even if the guy was a jerk.

Ezekiel excused himself and rolled into his office. TA turned to the man, "I think that they might be more interested in a map of early Detroit. After all, you want to give it to an automobile company and Detroit was thought of as the automobile capitol of the world for many years. We have a beautiful map from 1905 and after

17

we have it matted and framed it would be a handsome presentation piece."

After offering the man some refreshments, TA excused herself and went to the downstairs archives to retrieve the map. Wearing cotton gloves to protect the map from any oils on her hands, she carried it carefully upstairs and spread it across the table, placing the long weighted brass rods on either end. He reached for it but she forestalled the reach with a protective arm and withdrew cotton gloves from the table drawer and handed them to him. He grumbled over being asked to put them on and said he didn't need to touch it, nor did he need the magnifying glass she offered. "He could see fine without help." He inspected the map and pronounced it satisfactory. He paid and left with the promise it would be delivered to his office in five working days.

TA called their framer and made arrangements for the eight maps to be picked up and then went into Ezekiel's office. He had calmed down and was working again on the Napoleonic map.

"I hate to disturb you, Ezekiel, but do you want me to get anything from the vault for this evening? Mr. Frompton is due at 8:00, do you want me to stay?"

Ezekiel swung his chair around, "No, no, TA. He's interested in seeing this map and we can pull any others ourselves. He'll probably stay quite late; we have a lot to discuss. He's not really buying, anyway. It's more a get together for a drink and to enjoy the maps." Ezekiel's face lit. "Did I tell you he's just back from Barcelona and has been researching there? I'm really looking forward to seeing him. It's been months.

"You go home, TA," he continued. "This has been a long day and I want you home before dark. Take care, my dear."

TA gave him a quick hug and peck on the top of his head. "You're a sweetheart, Ezekiel. I'll see you in the morning."

TA let herself out of the shop and looked across the street, but Friend was not visible. The bus was just pulling up at the corner and she was home in twenty minutes.

CHAPTER 3

SAN FRANCISCO

WEDNESDAY, OCTOBER 25, 2000

It rained in the night but by morning it had stopped and turned cold and cranky with running gutters, puddles, dripping trees and tendrils of mist twisting around buildings and street lights like diaphanous kudzu vines. TA woke to the screaming alarm but chose to ignore it and snuggled down into her pillow wishing for a downpour so she'd have an excuse not to run. No such luck.

She rose and slapped the alarm clock to silence. She pulled on clean underwear, socks, clean shorts; the ones from yesterday were covered in street ick, and then sniffed her sweatshirt and decided that it and her headband would do for one more run before hitting the wash. Hanging her keys on her wrist she did her warm up exercises in the living room and then jogged down the stairs, praying that today would be normal.

She hit the sidewalk moving easily, with none of the stiffness of the last two days, the fog twisting and ebbing, swirled around each leg as she moved.

The street lights were still on and despite the fog the visibility was fairly good. In the second block she saw another jogger, an older man with whom she had a nodding acquaintance. He was coming toward her on the other side of the street and they waved as they passed.

She jogged on, waiting until she came to the park path to break into a run. As she entered an area of heavy fog, her feet disappearing in the swirling coils, she heard another jogger coming from behind. She moved over to the side so she could be passed, refusing to play the macho game of who can outrun whom that took place on most streets and tracks. The person behind her matched her stride and stayed a few paces behind. It felt ominous. The thought of Jack Palance, black caped as Mr. Hyde, crossed her mind. She had seen the old movie just a few days before and it was still vivid in her memory.

They broke free of the fog and she glanced back. The jogger was a man. She felt her muscles tighten and then an adrenaline rush.

They jogged on down the sidewalk, their footsteps muffled in the damp air. She sped up a bit but his footsteps still matched hers.

Pausing under a streetlight, she bent over, pretending to adjust her shoe. He almost fell over her but continued past. She glanced up as he went by and saw that he was young and Asian. He continued a few paces down the street and paused to jog in front of a store window. She fiddled with her laces for what seemed an eternity. Should she go the other way? Scream? What? Her brain felt like mush. Is this what rabbits feel like when they're hiding from the coyote? Finally, she rose, and rabbit-like, sped past him and down the street toward the park. She was probably overreacting to nothing. There would be people at the park; she be safe if she kept moving.

She came to a yellow stoplight and immediately, with just the switching of a light, there was traffic and she felt suddenly safe and just a bit embarrassed, surely she had overreacted. She jogged in place, feeling foolish. He came up behind her and she turned, jogging, looking at him. He didn't threaten. He stared at her. Expressionless. They jogged in place waiting for the light. Suddenly she wasn't so sure, maybe he was following her. She stared back at him, trying to look tough and threatening and not in the least intimidated.

The light changed to green and she spun around and went into high gear. Feet, go faster. Oh God, don't let me get a stitch. They pounded across the street, he just a few paces behind. She leapt the curb and passed a newspaper delivery man, bent over the newspaper machines, inserting the morning papers. She was past him before she could stop to ask for help.

She raced around the corner, only one more block and one more street to cross and she'd be in the park. He was keeping up with her. There was more and more traffic, surely she was safe with people driving by.

Suddenly, there was no more traffic; it was as if someone had thrown a switch. Without thinking, she swerved between two parked cars and darted across the street. She was too quick for him. He overshot her and had to cut around two more cars before he started across the street. She was farther ahead now and almost to the other side of the street.

She heard a car accelerating toward them. Oh God, please. Don't let me get hit. She jumped toward the curb. She could hear the car going faster and faster. She turned her head as she sailed through the air. It had no lights! It wasn't aiming at her! It hit the other runner with a hollow smacking noise. It must have been going 50 mph. He went flying through the air, over a parked car, landing on the top of another and then spinning like a propeller, his arms and legs, twisting and flopping like arms and legs were never meant to move, he ricocheted off the car and sailed, oh so slowly through the air landing with a sodden, splushy sound at her feet. She could hear the car retreating into the distance.

Where there had been no people, the sidewalk became populated: people that had been jogging in the park, people going to work, a derelict sleeping on a hot air vent, and suddenly a policeman, shooing everyone back.

"Do you know this man, Lady?"

"No, no, I never saw him before." She backed away and turned and pushed through the crowd.

"Lady, wait, I need a statement."

She kept going, pretending she hadn't heard him. The crowd closed in behind her, trying to get a better view.

She circled back toward home, running flat out, never repeating a street until finally she cut up the alley behind her apartment. She came to the back door, her hand shaking, looking back over her shoulder, key missing the lock twice before it slid in. No one was behind her and she scrabbled in through the door, throwing the dead bolt, dropping the night safety bar, not caring if another tenant tried to enter from the back. Safe! Maybe.

Up the back stairs, two at a time, pulling herself up by the railing, hands sweaty and slipping on the metal banister, down the hall, key sliding into the lock of her door. Throwing the door open, entering, panting, trembling, slamming the door closed, flipping locks faster than she had ever thought she could move.

She stepped to the middle of the room, chest heaving, dripping sweat, shivering. She stood, head cocked, listening. All she could hear was her heart pounding, her lungs heaving. Was anyone following? Be still, she told her body, trying to control her breathing, her heart. She stood, poised for flight, listening, projecting her mind into the hall, envisioning it, the other apartment doors, the entrance to the stairwell, questing for threats. Nothing.

Slowly, her breathing returned to normal, her heart pounding in her chest, subsiding until its thud was unnoticed. She walked over and flipped on the TV news, more for human sounds than for any information about the...accident? Was it? No, the car had accelerated when it had seen them crossing the street. It was murder, another murder.

Her attention was suddenly caught by the traffic report. "The three intersecting streets will be closed for at least another hour, as the police interview people who were jogging in the area of the park. We have been asked to announce that the police request anyone with information about the accident to call them at this number." The announcer than gave a phone number which was repeated across the bottom of the screen.

"No way," muttered TA. She left to get ready for work.

A long shower, dressing, eating a piece of toast, brought her a long way back toward normal. She switched off the TV and headed out the door. Out into the hall, away from her apartment, her sanctuary, which might not be as safe as she had supposed.

She would talk it over with Ezekiel. Perhaps together they could figure out what was going on. As she went down the stairs she had a sudden thought--maybe there was something in their past files that pertained to China. She would also check their entire inventory just to be sure that there wasn't something she had forgotten.

CHAPTER 4

SAN FRANCISCO

WEDNESDAY, OCTOBER 25, 2000

At precisely 11:05 am Lieutenant Samson slammed through the shop door with D'Angelo panting behind. Samson turned, brushed D'Angelo aside as if he were an annoying fly, threw the bolt on the outer door, tossed the "closed" sign haphazardly at the window in the door and stormed into the shop.

"Okay, let's talk," he said. TA stood frozen, just inside the door to Ezekiel's office. "Hey, Ezekiel, come on out here and join us," he called as he drew out one of the chairs from the central table. He turned the chair around and straddled it, not looking up, never doubting that they would come. He drew his notebook from his pocket and laying it out on the table, began flipping through it.

D'Angelo pulled a chair out and turned it also. He tried to do it one-handed in one motion, just as Samson had. The chair was heavy and he ended up having to put his notebook on the table and taking the chair in both hands he lifted and positioned it. When he tried to straddle it as Samson had he discovered he had picked a chair with arms. He looked at it a moment and then sheepishly turned it back around and sat. Head down, he gathered his notebook and pen and prepared to take notes.

TA came forward and pulled out a chair and sat. Ezekiel rolled in from the back and came to the table, sliding his wheelchair in between TA and the last empty chair. There they sat; TA, Ezekiel, and D'Angelo, looking at each other. Samson ignored them, studying his notebook.

He looked up at TA, "Would you like to tell me everything that happened or do I take you to the station?"

TA blushed. "How did you know?"

"It wasn't hard to figure out. How many women are running around in red University of New Mexico sweatshirts and sweatbands in the vicinity of your apartment? If I had any doubt, when they found your photograph in his pocket, I might have guessed. Now, what happened?"

"My picture?" squeaked TA. She cleared her throat, it convulsed. "Does anybody need a drink? I'm going to get myself a glass of water. We have coffee, tea, pop." Ezekiel and Samson passed, D'Angelo asked for a Coke. She went to the back and returned with drinks and coasters.

When she was settled again, she looked over at Samson. He stared back, not blinking. She felt as if she were about to be dissected. He had pulled a small tape recorder out of his pocket and placed it on the table. He picked up the mike and gave the time and place and who was present and then set it down facing her.

"I started out for my run and this man started to follow me. I stopped to tie my shoe to let him pass but he just jogged in front of a store window until I started running again. I knew I couldn't outrun him, at least I tried and he didn't have any trouble keeping up. I figured there'd be people near the park so I kept going. When I got by the park there was a break in the traffic so I went across the street in the middle of the block. I swear, there was no traffic at all from either direction when I started across but just as I got near the other side, this car came out of nowhere and started accelerating. I thought it was after me and I made this huge leap toward the curb,

25

but it wasn't. After me, I mean. It was after him. He had overshot me on the sidewalk, and he went between a couple of cars past where I started across. He was out in the middle of the street. The car must have been going at least fifty when it hit him, and it never braked. It didn't pause, even. It just kept going." She stopped for a minute, reliving it.

"He sailed through the air. It was like slow motion, he just kept spinning toward me. Then he landed. There wasn't anything I could do for him. All the people came. I was afraid that there might be another one, another man after me. I ran all the way home by a different route." She stopped.

Everybody sat quietly. Finally Ezekiel turned to Samson. "Another Chinese cultural attaché?"

"Yes, the last. The San Francisco Chinese Consulate is out of culture." He snorted and then looked embarrassed.

"Look," he said, leaning forward over the table. "There's a connection, we just have to figure out what it is." TA studied him. There was a muscle on the side of his jaw that was bulging, he was grinding his teeth.

She pulled her attention back to the problem. "I was going to check the maps that we have on hand, just to see if any of them might relate to China or to any country adjoining it." She paused a moment, thinking. She turned to Ezekiel. "How about Russia? We had quite a few maps of various parts of Russia in the latest shipment. I haven't cataloged them yet. It's a shame, but they're really hurting there and some of the few things they have to sell are antiques and art. Of course, they're trying to hang on to the big stuff, but there're a lot of secondary things, things of lesser historical value, that're leaving the country. We received the maps from one of our European buyers."

D'Angelo, who had been listening, mouth open, eyes glazed, adenoidally attentive, decided he should say something. "How come Russia? I thought all these guys were Chinese."

26

"D'Angelo, think," barked Samson, "Russia is big, or at least what was Russia before they broke it up. Russia and China have a common border." He paused, thinking for a moment.

D'Angelo looked down at the table. He wouldn't be bad looking, thought TA, if he were a bit more intelligent. He had a thick head of curly dark brown hair, which was all she could see of him for the moment. Maybe it's just that he tries too hard. Samson would intimidate anyone.

She glanced over at Samson. He was wearing a gray tweed sport coat and pale gray shirt with a wine-colored tie. His gray hair was freshly trimmed. He had a square face with deep blue eyes. He could have been a banker or a business executive except that his expression was that of a hunter, a tough hunter.

He glanced up and caught her looking at him. She smiled with what she hoped was an innocently ingratiating expression. He didn't seem to notice, he was on another thought track.

"Why don't you check for any maps that touch China? By the way, have any Asian customers come to the shop lately?"

"Just one," answered Ezekiel. "We had a Japanese national, Norio Kamakura, who made an inquiry. He wanted me to go with him to New Mexico to look at a map he's planning on picking up. I refused and suggested TA's services. He didn't want a young woman so I gave him the names of several other qualified men."

"Okay, look," said Samson, stuffing his notebook and tape recorder back in his pockets. "You check your map inventory and get back to me. If this Kamakura shows up again get in touch with me, too."

He stood and turned to TA. "Miss McGovern, don't jog. Don't go out alone. Don't let anyone you don't know into your apartment. If you even think someone is following you, call me immediately. Here's my card."

He handed her his card, collected D'Angelo with the same dispatch he had collected his notebook and recorder, and left, taking time to put the "closed" sign back on the table by the door.

27

TA and Ezekiel spent a quiet day going through their archives. All the Russian maps they had were of Eastern and Southern regions and mostly 19th and 20th century city and estate maps. There were a few maps from India but none near the Chinese border. There was an 18th century map of Tibet drawn by an Englishman. There were several maps dating from WW II of Thailand and Burma, which was now named Myanmar, and quite a few nice maps purchased from an estate in England that were of Korea, mostly from 17th and 18th century. There was even an early map of Singapore. It was an interesting day but not productive in finding anything that the Chinese might be coveting, certainly nothing that they couldn't have walked in and bought.

TA called and left a message for Samson that they hadn't come up with anything of interest and then she left for the day. She stopped in the park to talk to Friend for a few moments and bought him some fish from the Yee Oldee Fishees & Chippees restaurant . Her bus came so she left him still munching at the base of Robby Burns and went home.

CHAPTER 5

SAN FRANCISCO

THURSDAY, OCTOBER 26, 2000

The next day Kamakura entered the shop accompanied by a young man.

Bowing slightly, he asked for Ezekiel. He did not introduce the second man. TA bowed back and gestured welcomely toward the armchairs by the window but Kamakura walked over and stood by the table. The man with him stood behind him. TA went to find Ezekiel.

Ezekiel was working at his table in the back. As he pushed his chair back he murmured, "Call Samson and tell him Kamakura's here." He turned and wheeled himself to the door.

TA called the number Samson had given them but he wasn't in so she left a message and hurried to catch up with Ezekiel.

When they arrived in the front room they found Kamakura and the man standing stiffly by the table. The men bowed to Ezekiel, who returned their bows.

"I wish to discuss your assistant," said Kamakura.

"Please be seated," returned Ezekiel courteously. "Would you care for a beverage?"

Kamakura refused for both of them and seated himself at the table. The man accompanying him remained standing behind him. Kamakura waited for Ezekiel to roll up to the table before he spoke.

"I do not speak English well enough to have a business discussion so I have brought an interpreter."

He drew a deep breath and began speaking slowly in Japanese with many pauses for the interpreter to translate. "I have contacted the men on the list that you gave me. They were not available. I also asked them for the names of anyone that they thought could help me. They all recommended TA McGovern, your assistant."

TA, who had retreated to the back had been listening intently. Yes! She thought. They know me. More importantly, they respect me enough to recommend me. Way to go! She gave a little two step as she listened.

In the front room, Kamakura continued speaking through his interpreter. "They said you trained her well. As my time is limited and I can spend no more of it in searching for another expert I am here to request the services of Miss McGovern. Is Miss McGovern available for a short trip? I will, of course, cover all expenses, besides compensation for her time. The retainer will be the down payment on her services." He pulled out a check book and wrote a check which he then tore out and passed to Ezekiel.

Ezekiel accepted the check and without looking at it he turned it face down on the table. "I will need to know more about your project before I can discuss Ms. McGovern's employment. Also, she needs to hear all of this. If we decline, we will of course return the retainer." He turned slightly toward the back of the shop and called to TA.

"TA, please come here." She came forward to stand beside him. "Please sit down, my dear. Mr. Kamakura wishes to discuss a project with us."

As TA pulled out a chair and sat down, Kamakura began. "There is a map that has been missing from my family for many years. It was brought to this country by my cousin, the son of my uncle. He lived in California before World War II and returned to Japan with his son just before the start of the war between the United States and Japan. He left the map with his wife and daughter for safekeeping as he planned to return to California as soon as his business in Japan was completed. The war started before he was able to return to his family. He and his son were killed during the war. His wife and daughter were interned and both died before the end of the war. Recently, I received a letter that leads me to believe the map may be in a small town in the state of New Mexico. I wish Ms. McGovern to accompany me and to verify the map when it is returned to me."

"I have no problem with Ms. McGovern accompanying you to New Mexico but it is not my decision to make, it is Ms. McGovern's. But surely it would be easier for you to just go get the map and bring it here for verification?" said Ezekiel.

"There are several problems with that," returned Kamakura. "First, the letter writer may be dead before we reach New Mexico. She is very old. Second, the head of the family has a great hatred of Japanese so he might not allow me to talk to the old woman but he might allow her to speak with an American. Third, the map is valuable and he might not give me the correct map and it would be easier to know this before I left New Mexico."

"How long do you think this will take?" asked Ezekiel.

"It will be at least two days but perhaps more. I will pay transportation and all expenses. I will also pay $500 per diem to your company, as I understand that is the standard rate. Of course, these fees will be paid above the retainer check."

Ezekiel turned to TA. "Do you wish to accept, TA"

TA looked at Kamakura. "I accept. When do you want to leave?"

"We fly out at 7:00 am tomorrow." He drew a ticket envelope from his pocket and handed it to her. "Meet me at the gate at 6:00 am." He rose and reaching across the table he shook hands with

31

Ezekiel. He nodded his head and gave a small bow to TA and, followed by his interpreter, he briskly left the shop.

"I don't like him," said TA. "He has a little mean mouth and his manners are rotten in any language. However, I wanted to be recognized as an equal player, or at least as a player, and here's the opportunity on my doorstep. How much is the retainer?"

Ezekiel turned over the check. He whistled. "It's made out for $5,000. I wonder who told him the retainer amount and the per diem of $500 a day. He does leave a bad impression wherever he goes. I guess somebody decided to stick it to him." He chuckled and then, turning serious, he said, "TA, you'd better call Samson again and make arrangements. Remember, he said not to leave town."

TA called Samson's number again and left a message that she would be going to New Mexico for a few days and that she'd be in touch with Ezekiel if they needed her.

They spent the rest of the day going over the resource books on pre-WW II maps of Japan.

CHAPTER 6

SAN FRANCISCO/NEW MEXICO

FRIDAY, OCTOBER 27, 2000

The next morning TA called a taxi to take her to the airport where she met Kamakura in the waiting room outside their gate. He was without his interpreter and was more interested in reading a Japanese newspaper then in making small talk.

When their flight was announced TA discovered that while her ticket was in coach his was in first class.

She had just settled into her aisle seat when a wet baby was plopped into her lap. He stuck out his lower lip; TA was repulsed to see a drop of spittle trembling from it. The mouth opened and he let out a mind-blasting scream.

She looked up as a leather clad woman swung a guitar case up into the overhead compartment. The woman then leaned down and snatched the baby. "Poor thang, did the mean lady scare you?"

TA looked more closely and found herself staring at Elvis Presley, a female Elvis Presley. The woman, still crooning to the baby, squeezed past TA's legs and plopped into the window seat. "Whooo-ie, Ah didn't think we'd make it. Hank, my main man, had too many beers las' night and Ah like tah nevah got him out ah bed."

She put her hand out, "Hi, Ah'm Elvas, with an A, Preistly. My momma named me after the King. This here is Elvis Priestly. Isn't that cute? The name was jis' meant tah be, even if Ah wasn't an Elvis fan." TA found herself shaking the offered hand. The baby glared.

"Yah know," the woman continued without pause, "Yah really should practice yah baby manners. Ah mean, it's obvious yah don't have kids, how yah act an' all, but some day yah might an' yah need tah be prepared."

Li'l Elvis gave TA a dirty look as he sat sniffling and drooling in his mother's lap. TA studied him. He was wearing a tiny black Elvis outfit made out of synthetic fabric made to look like leather. The upper zipper was open part way down and his naked chest was wet from drool. She felt at that moment that if she never came within a mile of a baby for the rest of her life, it would be too soon.

"Hello," managed TA. "Are you going to Phoenix or on to Albuquerque?" Phoenix, Phoenix, she prayed silently to herself.

"Oh, Ah'm goin' ta Nashville but Elvis here is jis' goin' ta Phoenix ta stay with his granmaw, aren't yah Elvis?" Elvis let out another scream as she bounced him on her knee. She seemed oblivious to the fact he needed a diaper change. The kid was making squishing sounds when her knee hit his diaper.

"Yah hush now, yah'll like yar granmaw. Here, take yar plug an' be quiet." She pulled a pacifier from her pocket and inserted it in his mouth. The back of it was a set of fat smiling red lips with a black mustache above them. The baby sucked frantically on it, never taking his malevolent stare from TA. The effect was unnerving.

TA tried to tear her gaze from the baby but found herself in a staring contest with him. The baby won when TA blinked first.

She shifted her gaze to the baby's mother, who was looking expectantly at her. Despite herself, TA was intrigued. The woman was dressed entirely in black leather. Her top was partly unzipped and her bosom bulged alarmingly through the opening. Her hair was dark and combed into an Elvis pompadour with one lock falling down her forehead. She had red pouty lips that looked very much like the pacifier her baby was sucking but minus the mustache. As TA watched, the lips smiled.

Elvas gave an excited bounce. "Ah've an audition in Nashville. Ah do Elvis impressions. When baby Elvis is bigger he's gonna be in ma act. Ah'm so excited," she continued. "This might be ma big break. Ah have another li'l Elvis on the way so Ah have ta git crackin'. My mama, when Ah tol' her, she said, shoot Elvas, yah better git crackin' before ya start showin'. Nobody wants tah see a pregnant Elvis, but if they like ya now they might be willin' tah wait for li'l Elvis II. Ah'm gonna call all my kids Elvis. Ah figure if George Foreman can call all his kids George, Ah can call all mine Elvis." She paused for breath.

TA, speechless until now, finally managed a question, "How old are you Elvas?"

"Why, Ah'm eighteen, honey. Ah've been on the road for three years but Ah always keep track of where my mama is. Sometimes Ah need her and sometimes she needs me. My mama tends bar in Phoenix, now. She says she's gonna lose fifty pounds and join my Elvis act. Think of that," she paused in wonderment, li'l Elvis sucked on, oblivious to his mama's dreams. "Three generations of Elvises, all up on stage together. Now that'd be a sight." She gave a heaving sign of pleasure and the zipper over her bosom descended three inches.

TA sat stunned, her mind full of pictures of fat momma Elvis, bosomy Elvas, and a whole chorus line of baby Elvises, all in black leather and strumming guitars.

"Does your mama play guitar?" she asked.

"Oh yah, she plucks a mean guitar," she pronounced it gee-tar. "Ah'm tryin' ta teach li'l Elvis ta play but his bitty fingers aren't strong enough yet." She bounced him on her knee and his diaper splashed out on either side as if she were hitting on a wet sponge.

"My goodness, Li'l Elvis, yah're all wet, and momma forgot tah bring any diapers. Ah'll ring for the stewardess." She pressed the call light and soon a steward appeared.

Elvas looked up at him and gave a heaving sigh, making her bosom rise a good five inches above it's starting position. She blinked her eyes. "My goodness, Ah have sich a problem. Ah went and forgot my diaper bag and this bad lil' boy of mine has gone and gotten all wet. Do yah'll have any diapers put away up there in yar li'l cubbyhole where yah keep all that good food." She slowly licked her lips and smiled wetly at him.

He looked like he'd been hit with a board. After a moment he straightened up, almost to attention. "I'm sure we have some diapers somewhere, I'll go check."

As he turned away, Elvas called sweetly after him "Do yah think ya could bring me a few extra, jis' ta hold me?"

He waved a hand weakly as he staggered off down the aisle. He soon returned with an armful of diapers and suggested that Elvas might want to bring Li'l Elvis up to the front to change him.

"No, Ah don't want ta disturb anybody. Ah'll jis' lay him out on this nice lady's lap and change him here."

At that, TA jumped up and announced she'd leave the steward to help KEEP HER SEAT DRY while she went to the bathroom. She left the steward, looking harried, shoving magazines under Li'l Elvis as Elvas flopped him down on TA's seat. Li'l Elvis, sucking on his lip pacifier, ignored the whole procedure and gazed vacantly up at the ceiling.

When TA re-opened the bathroom door, having loitered as long as possible, she met the steward returning to his den, bearing a barf bag brimming with the rejected diaper and an armload of soggy magazines. He gave TA a frantic look and a reflexive smile as he pushed past. TA returned to her seat feeling smug that she had avoided the great Elvis flood.

The rest of the trip consisted of Elvas unzipping almost to the navel and flipping one vast white breast out and attaching Li'l Elvis to it, as she discussed her plans for the storming of Nashville.

When Phoenix was announced, Elvas returned the breast to her jacket and dropped Li'l Elvis on TA while she prepared her hair and make-up for the arrival. After landing, she gathered up her son and guitar, "Now, if yah're ever in Nashville, yah look me up. An' don't forgit to practice lots with babies. Yah nevah kin tell when yah'll need tah know all about them."

No one sat by TA between Phoenix and Albuquerque so she had some blessed quiet and time to reflect about the Grand Adventure on which she was embarked. She dozed off but awakened abruptly as she seemed to hear her grandmother's voice saying 'Be careful what you wish for, you might get it.' Thoroughly awake she glanced out the window. She could see Albuquerque in the distance. It was noon and they were landing.

CHAPTER 7

NEW MEXICO

FRIDAY, OCTOBER 27, 2000

Kamakura and TA met in the waiting room and walked downstairs through the generically southwestern airport to pick up their rental car.

At Kamakura's request, TA handled the talking while he filled out the papers. They picked up the car and TA was surprised when Kamakura directed her to driver's side and even more surprised when he got in the back. Huh, guess that puts me in my place, the menial. She began to chuckle. Or makes me *THE ONE IN CHARGE*.

The sky was an infinite achingly deep blue that seemed to tug at her, the city and the rugged mountains. Her grandmother had annually brought her to the Albuquerque Balloon Fiesta that was always staged the first part of October every year. She had floated with friends, running the river, drifting along above it on the currents of air that followed the water currents below, floating just above the shallow water, playing 'dip' once when the teenage son of the owner was piloting it. He wanted to show off for the 16-year-old TA. He was grounded for the rest of the Fiesta by his apoplectic father after another pilot ratted on them.

They had also been repeatedly told not to attempt flying over the Sandia mountains which reached over 10,600 feet. Many people had made it but several more had crashed trying, tossed against crags by the aberrant wind currents shooting up from the valley some 5,000 feet below.

So, of course, the next year they decided to press their luck and try to cross the mountains. Luckily, that was the year the winds all blew west, away from the mountains, so they were never able to complete their plans. Her friend graduated from high school that year and went to Colorado Springs to the Air Force Academy. She still received an occasional e-mail from him. He was flying jets now, somewhere off the coast of Alaska.

She started the car and drove down hill to the freeway toward Santa Fe.

As TA drove, Kamakura read the map. They were on I-25 and it led directly to Santa Fe with no changes so TA could sit back, drive and admire the tall Sandia Mountains on their right and the deep blue New Mexico sky overhead. She remembered that in the evening as the setting sun lit the mountains, the Sandias turned as pink as the watermelons for which they were named. Now, however, in the early afternoon, the mountains were covered in a patchwork of fall-yellowed aspen and dark green pines.

They drove along the base of the mountains on their right and on their left she could see the Rio Grande River bottom ornamented by fluffy yellow cottonwoods with a backdrop of large pink hills.

They passed the upper edge of a small town snuggled along the river; a highway snaked through it and climbed a distant hill.

"That is Bernalillo," said Kamakura, "and to our right is Placitas."

He was reading the road signs from the back seat. He continued to read the names of small communities and Indian Pueblos as they came to them. He seemed to want to practice his English, blissfully unaware that the names he was phonetically sounding out in English were usually either Spanish or Indian in origin.

39

Further along they climbed a cut through a cliff, magenta walls shading to maroon, and on to a gently sloping plain where more mountains, short and conical, nippled up from the flat earth. Beyond them, in the distance, was Santa Fe, tucked against the foot of a long range of purple snow-topped mountains. There were more mountains, navy blue this time, further away on their left.

Surrounded by mountains reaching up through crystal air, saturated with color, the temperature brisk in 7,000 feet of altitude, it was easy to see why Santa Fe was favored by the rich and exclusive and the artists who catered to them.

When they reached the outskirts of Santa Fe, Kamakura unfolded a city map and they wound through narrow streets to the plaza at the center of town. After circling through tiny one-way roads they finally managed to arrive at their hotel parking lot. The antique hotel was situated on the corner of the plaza.

The La Fonda Hotel lobby was richly southwestern ethnic with a tall ceiling constructed of large beams, Indian rugs on the tile floor and heavy, carved furniture grouped about.

After they were shown to their rooms they returned to the lobby to meet for a late lunch. Kamakura pulled out another map and traced a finger north to a small town named Espanola. He tapped it, "This is where we are going. You will make an appointment to visit Mrs. Gabaldon. Her granddaughter, Eliza Roberts, wrote me her Email address and here's her phone number." He passed a slip of paper to TA.

When they were through eating, TA returned to her room and put a call through to Espanola. Eliza Roberts answered the phone and the appointment was arranged for the next morning at 10:00 am. She also gave detailed directions on how to reach her grandmother's house and cautioned that if her father were there, his blue Ford pickup would be in the driveway. If the truck was there, they were to continue on their way and return in an hour or so. Under no circumstances were they to come to the door until he was gone.

"I don't understand," TA said, "Does your father have something against strangers?"

"Oh, no. He has something against the Japanese. You see, he was in the New Mexico National Guard during WW II and he was stationed in the Philippines when the war broke out. You sound young, so perhaps you don't know about the Bataan Death March."

"I vaguely remember reading something about it, but I guess I really don't know anything. What happened?"

"After the Japanese invaded the Philippines in December, 1941, the American and Philippine troops withdrew to the Bataan Peninsula and Corregidor Island. My father was on Bataan. They fought for two and a half months and by the time General King surrendered Bataan, over two thirds of the force was either dead from wounds or had starved to death. He surrendered on March 9th and when the Japanese troops came in they tied the men's hands behind their backs, it didn't matter if they were sick or wounded, and they marched them for 85 miles to Camp O'Donnell without food or water. If a soldier fell he was killed. If one soldier tried to help another they were both killed. Our troops and the Philippino soldiers were imprisoned until MacArthur landed October 20th, 1944. They lived on rice and an occasional rat, if they got lucky. My father survived but he's never forgiven."

TA, horrified, "I didn't know. Why didn't they tell us about this in school?"

"I guess it wasn't politically correct", replied Eliza, bitterly.

"When Dad returned home and found out that my grandmother had given shelter to a Japanese national and that his brother had married her, he almost went crazy. By that time the poor girl had died and my uncle had joined the 10th Mountain Division and gone to Italy. He died there in 1944 but it didn't make any difference to my father."

"They should have told us all this in school—made it more personal," said TA.

41

"Maybe it was too long ago. You have to understand that though all this happened before you or I were born it's still fresh in my father's mind. He and the New Mexico survivors of Bataan still get together every Memorial Day. They'll go to their graves hating the Japanese."

"I'm sorry to burden you with all this, my dear, but I want you to understand that it's not that you're unwelcome, it's just that to my father the whole subject is unwelcome and Mr. Kamakura's presence, if he knew about it, would give him a stroke. He thinks all the items were destroyed long ago and that most of the family doesn't even know about it."

"I understand, Mrs. Roberts, thanks for being so frank with me," replied TA. "I just have one last question. How on Earth did you get in touch with Mr. Kamakura and why so late?"

"Oh, that was surprisingly simple. My 17-year-old nephew loves to surf the internet and he put in the names of the family members and bingo – all the information came rolling out. In no time at all, Mr. Kamakura got in touch with us and we started exchanging information. You know," she continued, "not letting the family know what happened and having the trunk with all the family things in it has always bothered my grandmother. But out of respect for my father she has waited all this time. The end is near and she wants to rest in peace. She's so pleased to finally be able to send all of Hana's things home. Especially as Mr. Kamakura says we have a map that the family has been searching for for a long time."

"Thanks for all the information," TA replied. "I'll caution Mr. Kamakura about your father and we'll be there at 10. Thanks again and goodbye."

After she hung up TA sat for a few moments going over everything the woman had told her. Wow, this is really something. I wonder how the daughter met Mrs. Gabaldon's son. It suddenly occurred to her that she didn't even know the names of any of the people involved. How did Kamakura's relatives end up in New

42

Mexico when they had been living in California? She knew that there had been internment camps in California but she had never heard of them anywhere else. I'm going to have to do some research, this is really interesting. I doubt old Kamakura is going to give me any more information than he has but perhaps I can find a library around here. I'd better call him and let him know our appointment time, first.

She dialed Kamakura's room. He picked up his phone halfway through the first ring.

"Why did it take you so long to call? When do we go?"

"She, the granddaughter, wanted to talk to me for a few minutes and to caution me. We are to be there at 10:00 am tomorrow. I need to talk to you about what she said."

"We can discuss anything you might need to tell me tomorrow in the car. I will meet you in the lobby at 8:30 am tomorrow, be ready to go then." He replied and hung up.

"Well," TA huffed out loud. "I guess I've got the rest of the afternoon off so I think I'll go exploring and try to find a book about the Japanese internments."

She grabbed her jacket and purse and quickly left the hotel.

CHAPTER 8

SANTA FE

FRIDAY, OCTOBER 27, 2000

As TA exited the hotel she could see the plaza on her left but on the right she saw an old cathedral at the end of the street that ran beside the side of the hotel. As she walked toward the church she could see a retaining wall along the sidewalk; the church had wide double doors and a rose window and was above street level. On either side were towers, the one on the left had a bell and was crenulated. The other was smooth on top and no bell. There was an old man pruning some bushes that grew along the wall. TA, intrigued, walked up and started a conversation. "This is a beautiful old church."

The old man looked up and with a gentle smile replied, "Yes, it is. It was completed in 1886 by Archbishop Jean Baptiste Lamy who built it on the site of an even older church. He turned and looked at the church, smiling. "The Cathedral Basilica of St. Francis of Assisi," he said reverently.

"I was wondering why the towers were different," asked TA.

The old man laughed, delighted. "Most people don't notice that the towers don't match. Back when the church was built, the diocese of Mexico still controlled this part of Catholic North America.

When you finished a church you had to pay a levy, so they never finished the church."

TA laughed, "I wish it were that easy now."

"Ahhhh. But the headquarters of the diocese was far away, to travel here to check up on the church and then to return would have been a long and difficult trip and cost a great deal. Now they would look at a fax of the church and just tell us to get on with placing the last few stones."

"I guess progress isn't always good," TA laughed. She waved to the man and walked on.

She was facing a cross-street with a row of specialty shops and a covered sidewalk. She crossed. The small stores displayed crafts, sweets, Christmas ornaments and native jewelry in their windows. A wide tunnel went between two stores and she could see a courtyard with more shops surrounding it. She walked through into a garden with a few late flowers, a tall fountain with water lilting over its lip, two iridescent pigeons drinking at the edge and old cottonwoods shedding yellow leaves onto the brick walks and the benches surrounding the courtyard. She paused to look and admire. The shops facing the courtyard displayed clothing and kitchen items and in one corner was a used-books store.

TA never even tried to resist kitchen stores with all their wonderful tools. In she went, to the astounding world of gourmet gadgets. She cruised narrow aisles admiring tin cookie cutters bent in the shapes of cactuses, coyotes, and roadrunners, copper pans from France, kettles from Scandinavia costing more than a week's pay, colorful placemats from Central America, batik tablecloths from India, chocolate whisks from Mexico, and hand carved ladles and spreaders in exotic woods. She settled on a small ladle made from olive wood. It felt wonderful to the touch, the grain of the wood was beautiful and it was small enough to fit in her flight bag.

Next she turned to the bookstore and as soon as she put her foot on the time-hollowed step and entered the old, high-ceilinged room, she was charmed. The room was small, with one narrow window letting in the last of the daylight. A golden ray shown on the old waxed wood floors. The bookcases were overflowing with books and there were chairs tucked here and there for weary customers to use as they leafed through books.

The shopkeeper welcomed her much as one would welcome someone into his home and when she inquired if he had any books about the Japanese internment camps he made a distressed sound. "That was such an awful thing. We had a camp right here in Santa Fe, you know. Not really a camp, per se, but they sent all the highly educated and verbal men here, separated them from their families. It was a sad time for America, a shameful time. They sent farmers and fishermen here first. They sorted all those poor folks out and sent some back to their families in regular relocation camps and others to prisoner of war camps and then they brought in educators, professors, doctors, actors and journalists; all the people who might speak out or write articles about what was happening. That was in 1943. They had almost 2000 men here. Poor souls. They made gardens of flowers and vegetables and taught classes in camp; anything to keep busy. The authorities kept them locked up. At the time there wasn't much written about it, too shameful, I guess. Even now, with the reparation payments and everything, there is still not a lot written. America needs to know, and to face its shame. So sad, so sad."

He shook his head and walked over to a bookcase by the door. He studied it for a few moments and then drew out two books that he handed to her. "Feel free to look through them; I hope they'll be of help." He smiled at her and left to help another customer.

TA leafed through the books, pausing to study the photographs of families trying to make new homes in barracks and pictures of sad puzzled faces staring into the camera lens. The books seemed to cover what she wanted to know. She made her purchase and returned to the courtyard.

She looked across the yard and noticed that the sweet shop had a back entrance on the patio and even at a distance she could smell chocolate scents coming through the screen of the open door. She couldn't resist. She tried to buy one piece but before she left she had a small box of chocolates, English toffee, pinion nut penuche and a pink marzipan pig.

Nibbling on the toffee she continued her walk to the right, past more craft shops, a weaving studio and finally to the plaza. Along the side of the plaza was an old building. She walked past Indian vendors with their wares spread on blankets and paused to read a sign mounted on the wall of the building beside the entrance. The Palace of the Governors, a sign said, was the oldest continuously occupied government building in the United States. It had been built in 1610 when Spain ruled this part of the world.

She entered. The Palace was a beautiful old adobe building, and she paused to see reproductions of rooms from early colonial times and then on to view stage coaches, printing presses and into a patio with a large concave stone matate that had been used by Indians to grind corn.

She returned to the Palace's front walk and inspected the vendor's jewelry, pottery and drums as she strolled. She continued on across the street to a large art museum. It was getting late and the doors were just closing but she promised herself that she would try to return before she left town.

She walked around the edge of the plaza peeking in restaurants, bars, a shoe store and jewelry stores all set up to attract wealthy tourists. The La Fonda was next and since the October sky was darkening and the evening chill was descending she decided to forego the last side of the plaza. She returned to her room with her candies and nested in her bed to read her new books.

CHAPTER 9

SANTA FE/ESPANOLA

SATURDAY, OCTOBER 28, 2000

When TA met Kamakura in the lobby the next morning she studied him. Did he know about the things she had been reading? Did he know how her country had treated the Japanese people living here during WW II? Did he know that the government had taken legal immigrants and those native-born United States citizens whose only crime was being of Japanese descent and put them in concentration camps and then euphemized those camps by calling then Relocation Camps? That they hadn't stopped there but had imported Japanese citizens from Central and South America and interned them also? That the United States Government had confiscated peoples' property and resold it and in some cases had even separated families?

Of course, Japan had done far worse in Asia. At least our Government didn't starve and murder people, but still, that didn't excuse the United States.

Kamakura acknowledged her arrival in the lobby by a brief nod and, pulling a road map from his pocket; he held it over his head and led the way to the car park. He's just like those Japanese guides who lead excursions through scenic wonders, bicycle flag waving, their flock scurrying behind, thought TA as she scurried along behind. As soon as she unlocked the car he got in the back seat and immediately unfolded the map and began giving directions as to how to get to the highway.

The drive led up over a hill, leaving Santa Fe behind, past the entrance to the Santa Fe Opera, past pink cliffs with balancing rocks, past a huge pile of rocks shaped like a camel, on past two Indian casinos and a road marked to Los Alamos and Bandelier National Monument and on into the town of Espanola. During the whole drive Kamakura gave directions and pronouncements and generally proved that a person can be an officious jerk in any language and from any country.

As they drove along TA tried to explain everything that Eliza had told her about her father's feelings but Kamakura dismissed them as not being relevant and by the time they reached the Gabaldon house TA had divorced herself from the whole mess. Let the bodies fall where they may.

The house, when they found it, was an old adobe with a wide covered porch. Rose vines twisted up the porch supports with a single late blooming rose, glowing like a garnet in the morning sun. The house had a pitched roof covered in gray corrugated metal sheeting; the walls a warm natural adobe brown, the window frames and door painted white, highlighted with a narrow line of blue. The house looked neat and well cared for.

They got out of the car and walked up to the porch. Kamakura knocked.

A woman in her mid-forties opened the door. TA didn't know what she was expecting, a housewife perhaps, but this was a businesswoman, a high-powered one at that, who had taken the time to return home to meet with them. She had black hair with a touch of gray at the temples. She wore a dark red suit that set off her golden skin and high heels on her tiny feet. She wore small gold cross earrings in her dainty ears and a gold pin in the shape of a heart on her lapel. Mom was engraved in its center and several different

49

birthstones were spaced around the edge. Incongruously, she was wearing a voluminous apron scattered across with bright orange and yellow flowers and virulent green leaves.

"Welcome," she greeted them. "I'm Eliza Roberts." She pronounced it Eh-lee-sah. They introduced themselves and she gestured them inside.

The room they entered was immaculate, simply furnished with a flowered couch, two armchairs and a floral area rug on a highly polished hardwood floor. The room's walls were white and on one was a large picture of the sacred heart and on another a large crucifix. A TV stood in one corner, a statue of the Virgin of Guadalupe standing on it.

"My Grandmother is resting right now. Before we go in I want to caution you. She is almost 97 and she tires easily, but she is alert and looking forward to seeing you." Eliza turned toward a hall. "Please come this way."

They walked down a short hall and entered a bedroom. The tall windows along one side of the room had lace curtains hanging from ornate wrought iron curtain rods, the shades were up and the room was flooded with light. Blue Maxwell House coffee cans stood on the windowsills with blooming geraniums of every color. It radiated into the room and as the lace curtains stirred slightly in a draft. TA thought of a kaleidoscope with constantly changing shapes.

The walls, the bed and its spread were white and across the foot of the bed was a pieced quilt in the colors of the geraniums. A pair of fuzzy pink bunny slippers was parked under the bed. A young woman was sitting in a rocker near the bed. Both patient and nurse were watching a Spanish language soap opera on a TV sitting on a dresser near the foot of the bed. The walls had religious pictures, another crucifix, and hanging beside the bed was a large bulletin board covered with school pictures and family photographs.

TA's attention turned to the old woman lying so still on the bed. She was so small that she hardly raised the spread from the mattress.

So old and frail that she had been reduced to her very essence, a translucent echo of all she had been through the years, child, daughter, mother, grandmother, the laughter, the tears, the strengths and the weaknesses, lying there quietly waiting for the inevitable next step on her path.

Eliza bustled them into the room, "Thanks, Annette," she said to the nurse. "Why don't you go do the grocery shopping now?"

The nurse stood, "Thanks, Aunt 'Liza, I'll be gone about an hour. Do you want me to take my beeper?"

"No, but please stop by my house and check Christopher, he's been running a temperature and I told him to stay home today. Just be sure he's drinking enough fluids."

"No problem, Auntie." The nurse gave her a quick kiss on her cheek. She squeezed the old woman's hand. "See you in a bit, Granny."

After she left; Eliza shook her head. "She doesn't know much Spanish. None of the younger kids do. What a pity. They go off to college and they don't want to be bothered. The only great grandchild that speaks any foreign languages works for the government and he speaks French and Arabic."

Kamakura, in all this bright movement, stood at the foot of the bed like a slender monolith, dark and rigid, his gaze fixed on the delicate old lady lying on the bed.

As TA glanced at him he seemed to come to a decision. He bowed more deeply then TA had ever seen him bow, and drew out his business card. He reached as far as he could from where he stood and tendered it with both hands.

The old lady had shifted her gaze from the TV to Kamakura. Her eyes brightened and her whole face came alive. She lifted her hand and received the card and held it up to her eyes. She gazed at it intently, turned it over and looked as carefully at the blank side, then she nodded to him and laid it carefully on her chest amid the ruffles of her nightgown.

"Grandmother," introduced Eliza. "This is Mr. Kamakura and TA McGovern." She nodded toward their guests, "My grandmother, Maria Gabaldon."

Then began a three-sided conversation between the old lady, Eliza and Kamakura. The lady spoke first, in a high, quivery, sighing voice. "She welcomes you. She's glad you have finally come and that she's not too late to tell you that she loved Hana, her little flower," translated Eliza. "That's what she called my uncle's wife. Her little flower. Hana is flower in Japanese," added Eliza in an aside to TA. Kamakura, standing stiffly at attention at the foot of the bed, replied, "It is an honor to meet you. We have often wondered about my cousin's wife and daughter."

"I never met your cousin's wife, Hana's mother," translated Eliza. "She was very sick when they put her on the train and sent her to Santa Fe. She should have never come here. Santa Fe was only for men, men brave enough to speak out. She died soon after she came. It was all a great mistake." She sighed deeply and shut her eyes, as if in pain.

Eliza spoke gently to her and stroked her hair back from her forehead. The lady answered softly. Eliza gave her a drink of water and patted her hand.

The old lady continued her story with Eliza translating, "Douglas was working in Santa Fe, it was summer and he had just graduated from high school. He was staying with my sister in Santa Fe because it was too far for him to come home. He was only seventeen, my beautiful Douglas Fairbanks. How I loved the movies. I named both my boys for movie stars. Douglas Fairbanks Gabaldon was my baby. His brother was named for William S. Hart. Oh, they were beautiful, my boys, just like movie stars." She paused a long moment, remembering, a soft smile playing across her mouth and around her eyes.

"It was summer," she repeated, "Hana was there. The guards didn't know what to do with her, she just walked the streets in the daytime. Douglas met her in the plaza and they got to talking. Every day they'd meet for lunch, there, under the trees in the plaza in front of the Palace of the Governors."

"She was so tiny," the old hands fluttered, showing how high Hana had been. "So tiny and young, just sixteen, and so alone, so sad to have lost her family and her home. They fell in love, there, under the trees."

She sighed and rested for a moment, her eyes going to the crucifix on the wall. She reached out and felt among the items on her bedside table; picking up a rosary of crystal beads and held it to her chest. Blue-veined hands wrapped in the rosary were at peace and a spot of sunlight fell across the rosary, scattering bright rainbow drops across the walls; sending shining spots up and down with each shallow breath.

She continued, "Finally, they said they'd send her back to California. Some guards were going to Manzanar and they'd take her there." A quiet sigh. "So the next day she ran away and Douglas brought her here. She stayed here awhile but they found her, those soldiers. They were going to take her right away but I cried." She smiled. "Oh-o-o-, I'm a good crier when I want to be," she chuckled proudly. "They went away and talked and talked. But in the end they decided to leave her with us. What harm could a little girl do? I remember when they came to tell us she could stay, they brought her trunk. She cried, she was so happy to have her family things. She showed them all to us, all her pretty things.

"Father Jose Maria married them a month later. She got pregnant soon after that, just a few months. But she was so tiny," a whispery sigh. "She died, she was too young, too small, she went to heaven to be with Mother Mary. The baby died too. And then Douglas joined the army. He went to Leadville, Colorado to learn to ski in mountains and then he went to Italy. He won medals, I have them still. But he lost his life. I lost them all, Hana, my little flower, the baby, my first grandchild, and my beautiful son, Douglas Fairbanks."

53

Kamakura broke in for the first time, "I wish to see the trunk. There are valuable things that belong to the family. I need to check for them."

"Grandmother," said Eliza, patting her grandmother's hand lovingly, she spoke to her in Spanish for a moment and then turned to them, "I told her I'd show you the trunk while she rests and then we can come back in and you can ask any questions you might have."

Kamakura bowed to the old lady and marched from the room into the hall. TA rose and took the frail cool hand in her young warm ones. She was overwhelmed by all the life this woman had experienced, the pain she had felt, the bravery she had shown. She clasped the hand to her breast for a moment and when she looked into the old eyes, there was a moment of communication where words weren't necessary. She saw compassion for all that TA had yet to experience, and warm caring for this stranger who the woman had never met before. She set the hand gently on the covers and followed Kamakura into the hall.

Eliza straightened the covers, gave the old lady a sip of water, and then followed them.

"Come this way, please." She led them back down the hall through a sparkling kitchen and out into the backyard. The yard was swept hard-packed adobe earth with a few rose and lilac bushes around its perimeter. There were some brown hollyhock stems still upright by the shed that she led them to. She turned to them, "The shed's dark and packed, I'll pull the trunk out to the door."

Kamakura stood back but TA followed Eliza into the shed. It was crowded with gardening tools, broken furniture, boxes, and in one corner an old stiff tarp, draped over some crates. Eliza shoved the tarp back and grabbed the handle of an antique leather trunk. TA reached out and together they pulled the trunk through the door into the bright sunlight.

Kamakura pushed forward and tried to undo the latches but they were rusted shut. He pulled out a pocketknife and using the blade as a pry he managed to get them loose and threw back the lid.

They stood looking down at carefully folded baby clothes lovingly sewn for the baby that had not lived. Kamakura reached down and stirred the contents with his hand. There was a woman's suit, a small hat with a feather and a veil, a soft blue kimono, a fan, chopsticks, nested lacquer bowls holding a rosary and two hair combs of silver stamped in a shell design and set with turquoise, some photographs of a Japanese family posed stiffly in front of a shrine, and a small book of poems in Spanish. TA picked up the book and a dried red rose fell to earth, broke apart into separate petals that blew away in the gentle breeze. She opened the book to the fly leaf and saw a handwritten inscription written in Spanish. She handed the book to Eliza.

"It says," translated Eliza, "'For my beloved wife Hana, these poems can never match our love.' Look, there's something written under it in Japanese." She turned to Kamakura and gave him the book.

"It says the same thing in Japanese," he said, and tossed the book carelessly back into the trunk. He turned to Eliza. "I wish a box to put these things in while I search the bottom part of the trunk."

Eliza went back into the shed and soon returned with an empty carton. He began tossing things into the box.

TA couldn't stand the desecration. "Wait, let me. You can watch." She knelt and started carefully transferring the things to the box. There were more clothes, two beautiful silk kimonos and then a scroll which Kamakura grabbed and opened. It was of peach blossoms with a small kitten batting at the falling petals, something a young girl might have in her room. He tossed it dismissively into the box. There was a tortoise shell comb and brush. The brush still had one long black hair twined among the bristles. And then, way at the bottom of the trunk, wrapped in a length of heavy striped silk, was a tube. Kamakura snatched it and, dropping the silk to the ground, he uncovered a black lacquer cylinder. It had a band of tarnished silver spiraling around and around its length. He pried off the cap and dropped it to the ground where it rolled toward TA, stopped by her knee.

She looked down; the cap was tarnished silver etched by tiny waves around the edge with frolicking fish. On top of it was a ball that looked like the world, the Japanese islands etched at the center, with a dragon surrounding it, holding his tail, eyes rolled up in his face, looking at her. The dragon's tail formed a loop with a silk tassel braided through it. The tassel was of soft aqua threads and the strands floated free like spilling water.

Kamakura stood over her, trying to pull the contents from the tube. Finally he had it free and dropping the cylinder to the ground he unrolled the maps, for that is what they were.

TA cringed to see him holding them without gloves, the oil of his hands impregnating the antique paper. He was practically ripping them apart in his eagerness to read them, the old paper cracking and flaking into the breeze.

He gave an impatient hiss, and turning, thrust them at TA. "Here, look at them. How old are they?"

TA pulled her cotton gloves from her pocket and slipping them on, took the maps. Still on her knees, she turned and closed the now empty trunk so she could use the top as a table. Wishing for a ruler or a flat stick to help her unroll the maps, she picked up the chopsticks and used them to carefully unroll the first map, resting the lacquer bowls on the top and bottom to keep it from curling. She scooted her body around to block the direct sunlight from damaging the ink. She gasped. The map was perhaps eleventh century Japanese. The earliest she had ever seen, surely classical. From her studies of Japanese maps with Ezekiel she could tell it was of Kyushu Island. It was beautiful. She couldn't even begin to give it a price. It belonged in a museum. It was a national treasure.

56

She carefully allowed it to roll back up and gently wrapped it in the heavy silk that was lying by the trunk.

Next she picked up the other map. She repeated her unrolling and shielding process. This was a new map, perhaps nineteenth century, of Kyushu Island. It was cruder than the first, but still beautiful. It looked as if it had been drawn by someone who had studied with the Americans, perhaps been attached to Commodore Perry's fleet. The blending of Japanese and American techniques was interesting and of historical interest but it didn't compare to the map resting in the silk by her leg.

Kamakura had been leaning over her shoulder the whole time. She turned and looked up at him, "The first map is a national treasure. Its value is incalculable. The second map is much newer, probably latter nineteenth century, surely after Perry arrived. It is valuable but doesn't compare with the first map."

"Neither is of the American coast!" he exclaimed, standing straight.

She looked up at him, speechless, her mind racing. "The American coast? What is this? I understood that these were antique maps that had belonged to your family for many years. How early are we talking about? The American coast in the 1800s when the Japanese started to immigrate? What are we looking for?"

He stood looking down at her, measuring her. "We are talking about a map that was drawn of the American coast sometime in the fifteenth century. It was made in the early part of the 1400s. He had it, her father. He left it with his wife when he returned to Japan. I want it and you are going to find it for me. It has to be here."

He spun toward Eliza. "Where is the other map?"

She took an involuntary step backward. "I don't know anything about another map. That chest had all of Hana's things in it and hasn't been opened since she died."

"I will ask your grandmother," he said. He turned and headed back toward the house.

Eliza sprang after him and TA was left kneeling by the chest with all Hana's treasures spread around her. She quickly scooped everything back into the chest except the maps and the map tube. She didn't take time to put the maps back but wrapped them and the tube with its lid in the heavy silk in which they were originally swaddled. She picked up the bundle and cradling it in her arms, she hurried after them.

When she entered the bedroom, Kamakura was again standing at the foot of the bed and Eliza, hovering protectively, was standing at the head.

"Thank you for giving me the trunk of my niece," he was saying. "One of the maps, the most valuable, is missing. Where is it?"

After the translation and a long answer, Eliza turned to him, "She says that they hid one map in a cave up near Los Alamos. They left it there because they thought the army guarding Los Alamos would protect it. Nobody knew what was going on up there but there was army everywhere."

Laughing softly she spoke again. Eliza translated, "The government told the people they were building a submarine base. Nobody was allowed in the area. It is in one of the many Indian caves. Indians lived there many years ago and they dug caves into the cliffs in some of the canyons. She isn't sure which cave it is. They called it their special cave. She will give you a map to the cave that Douglas left her."

The old woman pointed to her Bible, lying on the table by the bed. Eliza handed it to her. The old fingers carefully opened the cover and slid down along the inside edge. It opened slightly, where the glue had come loose, and from the opening she drew a folded paper, brown with age.

She held it out to Kamakura. He took it and opened it. It cracked into four pieces. He laid it out on her colorful quilt, like a jigsaw puzzle. TA stepped forward and looked down at the map. The drawing on the paper showed a road, a pile of rocks with distinctive shapes, trees, three canyons splitting off from the road, with small circles, perhaps denoting caves, placed along the edges of the canyons. One circle had an X drawn on it.

Eliza and Mrs. Gabaldon conversed for a moment. "She says that's the old road to Los Alamos, the front one. There's another road now, to the left, that hadn't been built then. That's all she knows." She drew herself up and with a cold voice she continued forcefully, "Please leave, you have your information and your behavior has upset me. Do not return."

Kamakura gathered up the pieces of the jigsaw map, bowed deeply, "Thank you," he said, and turned to leave the room.

As TA started to follow she heard the front door open. A man called out, "Anybody home?"

Eliza went rigid, her eyes widening. She spun toward them. "Go out the side door at the end of the hall! It's my father!" she hissed. She pointed down the hall away from the living room.

Kamakura marched down the hall, refusing to run. TA, clutching the silk bundle of maps, heart pounding, back cringing, crowded his heels. Just as he opened the door she heard an enraged bellow, sheer violent anger, no words, the words came later.

"Yee-ahhhh! You invited that damn Jap here!" The rest was incomprehensible, in Spanish, words run together in such anger that TA could feel them clawing her skin.

She was out the door, leaping off the porch, running to the car. She yanked open the driver's door and throwing in the maps and case, to hell with their value, she fell behind the wheel, digging for the key in her purse. Finding it, she thrust it in the ignition, twisting it, throwing the car in gear, hearing the rear door open and thump shut; she slapped the door lock shut with one hand as she reversed into the street; slamming the car into forward before it came to a complete stop, it screamed and bucked but started forward.

Bang! Something hit the back of the car. Looking in the rear-view mirror she saw the leather trunk, the poor trunk, lying broken in the road, its contents spilled around it in shimmering heaps, a gray-haired man, dancing an enraged maniacal jig among the silk kimonos.

They turned the corner and he was gone.

CHAPTER 10

NORTHERN NEW MEXICO

SATURDAY PM, OCTOBER 28, 2000

She drove to the edge of town and then pulled over on the side of the road. Turning, she faced back so she could see Kamakura as they talked.

"Do you want to go back to Santa Fe?"

"No, we have all afternoon. We will go look for the cave."

He consulted the road map. "We need to go back through town and take another road. I will direct you. Turn around and go back the way we came."

They retraced part of their path and then cut over and picked up another well-traveled road that led them past a road sign directing them to Santa Clara Pueblo and Los Alamos. On their left was the Rio Grande with its golden cottonwoods and buildings made of adobe glowing warmly in the sun. The homes had long ristas of drying red chili hanging down along their walls. Beyond the river was a giant butte, flat-topped, dark and ominous, a leftover volcanic core from a less benign geologic time. A road sign pointed toward it and informed her it was Black Mesa.

They came to a highway. A sign pointed left to Pojoaque and right to Los Alamos. She turned right. Kamakura took over, reading signs, guiding her right, past a Y in the road with signs pointing left to White Rock and Bandelier National Monument and right to Los Alamos.

She could hear him fitting the brittle pieces of the 56-year-old map together. "Here, turn here." He was leaning over the back of the seat pointing toward a dirt road. She turned and began driving slowly under pine trees that cast blue shadows across the dust. They rattled across a cattle guard, broken and twisted barbwire scrabbling away from it on either side.

"Park here," he said, indicating a pull off that had been used for picnics. To her left she could see a cliff pitted with natural holes and caves dug by Indians many hundreds of years before.

She got out of the car and paused, hands on her hips, remembering her anthropology classes. She was looking at a talus slope of eroded rock at the base of a south facing cliff. The cliff was volcanic in origin, a creamy pink. It was pitted and pocked with tiny indentations and large holes made by air bubbles when the volcanic flow was oozing across the earth. Along the base of the cliff face at the top of the slope were manmade caves, dug and scraped by Native Americans long ago. These caves had been lived in by tribes forever gone, their descendants scattered and entwined with other tribes who were settled today up and down the Rio Grande Valley. Some of the caves had been used for storage and some had been used as a kind of back room with a house of rocks built in front of the cave. The houses had been roofed with logs set into the cliff and the holes were still there above the cave entrances.

Kamakura got out of the car and looked around, holding the pieces of map in his hand. He studied the cliff. She tried to look over his shoulder but he shrugged her away.

"Yes, climb up there and look." He indicated one group of caves, set apart from the rest.

She wished she had packed sturdier clothing. She glanced down at her slacks, they weren't new but they still looked nice. I have a feeling you've had it, slacks, she thought. Oh well, she'd bill him if they got ruined. At least she had on walking shoes and not heels.

The weather was brisk, even in the sun. As she climbed the slope at the base of the cliff she could feel the warmth of reflected sunlight radiating from the pinkish cream rocks. The caves had been hollowed out on the south face of the cliff so they would receive the sun's warmth all winter.

Large chunks of the cliff had fallen in the past. Did any fall while the cliff village was occupied? Surely some had fallen in the several generations of occupancy. Was anybody flattened or did the inhabitants have warning? Did rocks creak and groan before they gave way? She looked nervously up toward the top of the cliff, looking for ominous cracks. There were plenty.

Some of the cliff had tumbled down the face, breaking into bits and pieces and with the help of nature a slope had been created. There were huge bergs of rock leaning at angles against the cliff face, deep shadows hiding ancient secrets.

A jay screamed in a tall pine growing from the detritus near one of the cave entrances. She looked up and saw him hopping along a branch. He was a deep iridescent blue with a black crested head. He cocked his head and gave her a flirty look. She stopped climbing to admire him, wishing she had a crust or cookie. She felt around in the bottom of her pockets and came up with a cinnamon Tic Tac. He hopped nearer.

"Here birdie, chip, chip." She held up her hand with the Tic Tac on her outstretched palm. He stretched out his neck and peered at her, looking intently at her face and then at her hand.

"Come here, come on guy. See, a nice Tic Tac. It'll give you a good cinnamon breath, the girls will love you."

The bird screamed and flew up from the tree. She laughed, "I think you just flipped me off you nasty old bird." She watched him fly up the cliff face and disappear over the edge.

She tossed the Tic Tac into her mouth. Lunch, she thought.

A squirrel chattered from the same tree, sitting tall with his tail feathered in the sunlight.

She glanced down at Kamakura. He was marching around the car in short steps, stopping to look up at her, and then at the sky and the trees they were parked under. His body language indicated impatience with her slowness but at times unwillingly interrupted by appreciation of the landscape.

She climbed higher and entered the shade of the cliff. The temperature dropped ten degrees. With her eyes shaded, she could see a narrow opening in the shadows, blending perfectly with the cracks and depressions in the rock face. It was the entrance to a long-deserted-home. Peeking in, she could see where countless fires had blackened the ceiling and walls, the smoke streaming up to a small opening chipped in the outer wall and venting into the open. The floor of the cave was circular, perhaps seven feet across.

She turned sideways and, crouching, worked her way into the cave. Once inside it was noticeably cooler. She stood, her knees flexed, her height probably a good six inches taller than the former occupants. The cave smelled dusty and sooty, even after hundreds of years. Her eyes gradually adjusted to the dim light and she could see that the rock floor of the cave was covered in dirt, fine dust, dried leaves and mouse droppings. Across from the entrance were three empty Coors beer cans.

If Douglas and Hana had left the map case lying exposed in the cave it would have long since either been found or covered by sand and dirt. The chances of them leaving it in an obvious place were scant. They had probably buried it, perhaps in a storage area scooped out long ago by the original inhabitants. She knelt and using her bare hands, she scraped some of the sand away. Under the loose dust and sand was hard packed dirt and below that was rock. She rose and stepped out to search for a knife-shaped rock, then returned to the cave with her tool and dug through the dirt to the cave floor. Even with proper tools this was going to be difficult.

She rocked back on her heels and assessed the cave. She'd work only at the back of the caves as they wouldn't have left it near the front. Maybe she'd get lucky and figure out right away in which cave they had hidden the map. She stood, narrowly missing braining herself on the roof and crouching awkwardly, she worked her way out of the cave.

Once outside, she looked down at Kamakura. He was sitting halfway in the car, one foot resting on the ground. He was smoking a cigarette. As she looked down, he looked up. She waved and turned to the next cave entrance.

This cave was larger than the last, a good ten feet across. The roof was also higher and the doorway taller. There were a couple of squashed pop cans and some burnt wood from a fire. Graffiti on the walls consisted mostly of love notes, but buried under all these was an old peace symbol from the Viet Nam war era. She wondered if under those, were messages about Korea, or Kilroy from WW II. Perhaps there had been Indian cliff dweller graffiti under that. All was covered now.

She exited the cave and walked along the cliff base, entering every cave that she came to. All showed indications of recent occupancy. One of these caves might have been used by Douglas and Hana but if they had hidden anything here, it had probably long since been found. The light was fading and it was becoming impossible to see anything in the caves.

When she walked out of the last cave the sun was disappearing behind the cliffs across the canyon. Kamakura was again pacing. She climbed slowly down, hampered by the lack of light, but ran the last bit where there weren't many rocks to trip her.

"Nothing. This could take quite a lot of time. There are probably more caves back up the canyon. Don't you want to hire a few more people? I'm going to have to dig grids in the floors of likely caves and we'll probably need permits to do that."

"I don't want anyone to know we are looking. If people find out, they will look too and I might lose the map. You are getting paid well to keep looking." He walked around the car and climbed in the back seat.

"OK, it's your money, but I'm stopping to buy tools when we get to town. I won't do full scale grids so perhaps we won't need permits." TA got into the driver's seat and they pulled away.

Entering Santa Fe she detoured to a shopping center with a Wal-Mart. Kamakura sat in the car while she went in. She went first to the clothing department and selected a pair of sturdy jeans, a heavy sweatshirt, tee shirts and a denim jacket. As she passed the men's department she noticed stocking caps and tossed one into her basket. She found tennis shoes and socks next. Then she circled over into hardware and tools and found a trowel, a hand rake, rock pick, flashlight and batteries, whisk broom, work gloves and knee pads. As she was turning to leave she saw packages of painters' masks and added them to her cart. She paid for it with her Discover card and saved the receipt. She would claim it as a business expense.

As she crossed the parking lot she noticed a large store that promised engineering supplies and maps. She dumped her purchases in the trunk and then cut back across the lot to the store. It was closed but there was a man working behind the counter. She knocked and held her hands up in a begging gesture. He came over to the door. "We're closed. We'll open again on Monday."

"Please, please, please," she begged. "I have to go out in the morning on a search and I need a contour map."

"Oh, all right. But be quick. I'm due at a dinner party and my wife'll kill me if I'm late." He opened the door.

She went quickly to the map cases at the back of the store. She consulted the New Mexico map on the wall and picked the contour map showing detailed elevations of the area where she had been searching. Each canyon and cliff was defined.

She paid and thanked the man profusely as he pushed her out the door.

She found Kamakura sitting as silently and patiently as a Buddha. He came alive when she showed him the map and instantly confiscated it for his own use. She silently cursed not having had the forethought to buy two.

When they pulled into the car park by the La Fonda Kamakura exited and started walking back toward the hotel. Just as he entered the hotel he turned and called, "I will meet you at the car at seven am, tomorrow."

That was the last she saw of him that night.

She sorted through the Wal-Mart bags for her new clothes and grabbed the sack and the silk bundle which held Hana's maps. Arms loaded, she went to her room where she put Hana's maps on the desk and headed to the bathroom for a shower.

In her fairly clean nightgown and drying her hair she called room service and ordered a cheeseburger, fries and a chocolate shake.

While she was waiting for the food she called Ezekiel. He reported all was quiet in San Francisco and wanted to hear a complete description of both maps. She promised to get back to him on the descriptions, pleading exhaustion. He reluctantly agreed to wait.

She scarfed down her meal, called the desk for a wakeup call, set her travel alarm just to be doubly sure she would be on time, and fell into bed.

CHAPTER 11

NORTHERN NEW MEXICO

SUNDAY, OCTOBER 29, 2000

The chirping of her travel alarm woke TA. She reached out, turned it off, and held it for a moment, admiring it. It had been a present from her grandmother on her sixteenth birthday, a little flat silver box bound by a gold ribbon. Inside was a clock face on one side and a small oval cutout for a photograph on the other. This one had a family portrait of TA and her grandmother. The photograph had been taken when TA was ten, soon after she had gone to live in Colorado.

She remembered her grandmother's comment when she opened her gift. "You're going to go far, TA. I can tell that by your interest in maps. This is to be sure you wake up in time to get to your destination."

TA had laughed, enjoying the double meaning of going far and maps, and acknowledging her teen love of sleeping late, unless something interesting was happening.

She lay there a moment enjoying memories until her wakeup call interrupted. She thanked the automatic machine, and leaped up to pull on her new clothes. She hurried down to the car.

Kamakura was waiting, standing impatiently by the back door. She wondered why he wasn't already seated in the back and then remembered she had the only set of keys. Ah, the power had suddenly shifted.

She smiled cheerily at him. "Good morning, Mr. Kamakura. I hope you haven't been waiting long." She checked her watch. She was right on time.

He bowed to her but remained silent. She bowed back and then quickly unlocked the driver's door and reaching in she threw the switch that unlocked all the doors. He opened his door and got in.

She slid behind the wheel and said, "We need to stop at the grocery store to get some water and food. I saw one on the way out of town." He nodded.

She drove to the store and parked. "Would you like me to pick up anything for you?" she asked.

"Yes, some water, thank you," he answered.

She got out and entered the large store. She grabbed a cart and started wandering the aisles. She was hungry and wanted something for breakfast plus a lunch.

She found milk, orange juice and added fruit, and a handful of string cheese and jerky sticks. Next she found bottled water and added a six pack of quart size bottles. At the checkout counter she saw a stack of boxed donuts and threw one into the cart.

Back at the car she dumped the sack of groceries on the front seat and grabbed a bottle of water to hand to Kamakura. Opening the carton of milk she started drinking it as they drove out of the parking lot.

Less hour later she turned in onto the track and brought the car to a gentle stop. She turned in the seat, "Do you want me to drive to the same spot as yesterday?"

He studied the maps he held in his hand, both the old hand-drawn one and the topo map. "No, I have compared both maps. I think we need to go on beyond where we were yesterday. Go cautiously, I will tell you when to stop.

As they passed the spot where they had parked previously he suddenly called, "Stop!"

She stomped on the brake. "Go back, I want you to go up and smooth over where you dug yesterday. I don't want anyone to know we've been searching."

She backed the car up and parked under one of the tall trees. She got out, mumbling to herself, "Why didn't he tell me yesterday? I'd have gotten a rake at the store." It didn't help any to see him sitting back comfortably, calmly peeling one of her bananas. She popped the trunk and pulled out the garden hand rake. It should do nicely; too bad it didn't have a long handle so she wouldn't have to squat.

She ran up the incline to the first cave and entered. She paused to let her eyes adjust to the light. There were the holes she had dug with her improvised rock tool. They could have been made by any amateur archaeologist. He was just being paranoid. She quickly raked the dirt back over the holes and scuffed dirt over the raked areas. She backed to the entrance and looked. Pretty good but there was no way she could truly erase the marks without digging up the entire floor of the cave and re-smoothing it. "Oh well," she muttered, using a tone that was reminiscent of her youth. What it really meant was 'tough shit.'

She left the first cave and heard the pulse of wings and a raucous scream. She looked up, the jay from yesterday, at least his attitude was familiar, was just settling on a branch of a nearby Ponderosa. He extended his body, tipping his tail up in the air and stretching his neck and head down at her. He cocked his eye and called again. His body glowed a brilliant deep sapphire blue, his head and crest as black as obsidian. Light glinted off his feathers.

"So sorry, Mr. Jay. Nothing now. Hey, I have doughnuts or perhaps you would like some string cheese but they're in the car. Very good stuff, low fat cheese and high fat doughnuts! Come by for lunch."

She laughed and entered the next cave. Again she raked and scuffed. That was the best she could do. On to the third she went and quickly finished. She ran down the hill to the car. Mr. Kamakura was sitting where she had left him, studying the map. A banana was gone and two of the doughnuts.

She got into the car and started the engine. "OK, where to next?" she asked.

"Continue down the track and I will tell you where to stop."

They drove down the track, the tires rolling up a dust cloud that hung in the sunshine filled air behind them. They came to a cattle guard and clunked across it. The road circled around a spiked column of cream rock, streaked with colors of rust and spotted with gray-green lichen. A gray-green bush, its color matching the lichen perfectly, nestled at the column's base. The road straightened and continued for another sixty feet and then ended in a turnaround.

"Yes, park here."

She turned off the engine and they got out of the car. He stood, shielding the map from her, looking up along the cliff face.

There was a scree of detritus and large rocks that had cleaved down over the centuries. The cliff, glowing in the sun, rose above the residue of its past. It towered over them, tall ponderosa pines waving from its upper edge.

The sun shone down on the cliff, the tall dark, dusty pines, the soft dirt under her feet and on her face. She could hear insects humming, flitting through trees that would soon be bowed under winter's snow. TA shut her eyes and faced the sun. It baked her face softly. She drew a deep breath of the thin high mountain air, pungent with spicy baking plant odors and eons of pollens

"There. That is where you dig today," the voice of Kamakura broke in on her thoughts.

"OK," she said. "All three in that group?"

71

He nodded.

She turned to the car and stripped down to her tee shirt and jeans. She turned the sweatshirt into a bag to carry her tools and lunch and started climbing.

At the first cave, she dropped her load turned to wave at Kamakura. He saluted her with the map. She chose the larger middle one to excavate first.

The going was easier than yesterday, the knee pads and the pick, trowel, and rake making the digging more comfortable and rapid. The face mask took some getting used too but when she removed it she found it was covered with fine dust particles so she replaced it.

Instead of gridding the entire floor she made double concentric circles around the inner edge of the cave, skipping the area in front of the door. Assuming the map was hidden in an existing storage compartment used for grain or ceremonial equipment it would be near the wall, out of the way of normal traffic. Nobody was going to hide something in the middle of a cave floor.

She was pleased to find that the packed earth and dust layers were thinner at the back of the cave away from the entrance. It was going to be easier than she thought to dig to the rock floor.

She had almost completed the first cave when she heard a noise outside the door. She paused, kneeling and looked up. A shadow covered the entrance and then Kamakura stood in the doorway. Watching her. He turned and disappeared. She could hear him walking along the top of the scree toward another group of caves.

TA finished the first curve in the second cave and then broke for lunch. Face mask hanging around her neck, gloves shucked, she sat in front of the cliff face on a flat rock. It was one of two that had sheared from the cliff face as one piece and separated on impact into two, forming a comfortable table-bench with a slanting back. She sat soaking up the fall sun, warming herself after being in the cool caves all morning. She opened a stick of string

72

cheese with her teeth sipped water between alternating bites of cheese and apple.

Wind murmured softly in the trees, insect sounds and intermittent bird calls. Her jay friend hadn't shown up for lunch.

She could hear an occasional car off in the distance on the main road; one seemed to be coming nearer. The sound grew louder and then a dusty pickup with a group of teens appeared. It clunked across the cattle guard. Interesting, she thought, she saw them entirely cross the iron bars of the guard before the sound of their crossing carried up to her. She tried to remember the speed of sound but couldn't.

The kids seemed full of cheer, probably because they had skipped going to church with their families. They waved merrily to Kamakura, standing by the car and to her, sitting against the cliff, as they circled the parking area and disappeared back the way they had come.

She finished the second cave with no results, not even a bead. Her back was tired, her shoulders ached, her knees hurt even with the pads she was wearing. She stood and went outside. As she stretched something caught her eye. A blue tailed lizard was whisking across a sunlit rock. He paused to peer at her from the shade of another, his throat pulsating in terror. Then, as she stood quietly, he disappeared into some crack hidden by the shadows.

She raised her face to the sun. Revitalized, she turned to the last cave.

As she worked her mind went back to her own teen years. She had loved to read about all the voyages of the great explorers and conquerors and had traced their routes around the world, dreaming that she too would someday explore and create new routes and see new sights never before seen by man. She had learned about latitudes, longitudes, minutes, seconds and degrees. She traced the travels of Alexander, Genghis Kahn, Saladin, Pliny, Odysseus, Eric the Red, Leif Erickson, Lewis and Clark, Byrd, Peary, on and on. She learned about hardships and triumphs. Romance novels had never interested her, but the romance of exploration and adventure had.

She straightened up, reminisces put aside, as she found three small turquoise heishi beads up against the back wall. That was her entire treasure for the whole day. She carefully wrapped them in a used string cheese package and tucked them into the watch pocket of her jeans.

It was still quite light so she walked along the cliff face, peeking in other likely caves. None seemed to fulfill the requirements she had listed in her mind. The cave should be a trysting place for young lovers, lovers in an era that frowned on premarital affairs. It had to be romantic and secretive and preferably, slightly domestic-looking.

She returned to pick up her tools then climbed down to the car. She turned to look up at the cliff; glowing pink in the setting sun, the caves had almost disappeared with the light shining directly into them and with no shadows to make them stand out. The sun dipped further and the cliff was striped in two colors, bright above, and half way down there was a demarcation line and the lower part turned blue with evening shadows. She turned back to the car.

Kamakura was sitting in the back seat studying the map. She loaded her things and getting behind the wheel, she turned to him. "I looked in all the caves to the right, and didn't see any that looked as if they might be the ones. Did you find any likely ones?"

He lowered the top of the map and peered at her. "I think to the left, around the corner. There are five caves there. The map Douglas made indicated five caves. I thought there were just three but the fold and tear in the paper disguised two marks."

TA wondered when he'd had this revelation. She looked at him for a moment, stretching it out meaningfully. He returned to the contour map, ignoring her.

She sighed and turned to face forward, reaching into the grocery sack for a snack. All the cheese sticks were gone and half the donuts. She grabbed a donut and drove them back to Santa Fe.

When she parked at the hotel, he exited the car and turned, "Tomorrow at 6." Then he was off across the parking lot.

She got out, joints aching, dusty and sticky. When she returned to her room she took a long shower and then, rather than going out, she called down to room service again. It's his penny, she thought. She ordered a club sandwich, fries, hot tea and a slice of double chocolate cake that the voice at the other end of the line assured her 'was to die for.'

She ate lying on her back in bed, watching TV. The cake lived up to its promise but she was asleep before the last mouthful. She woke in the night to the sound of the TV, the plate still balanced on her chest. She turned off the TV and set the alarm. Flipping off the light she fell asleep almost before she had pulled up the covers.

CHAPTER 12

NORTHERN NEW MEXICO

MONDAY, OCTOBER 30, 2000

TA woke to her alarm clock's chirping. She sat on the side of the bed, holding the tiny clock, when it occurred to her; there had to be two layers to the cliff. The first layer was on the bottom, where she had been working. The second, newer layer, on top but set back a bit from the lower layer.

She jumped up and dashed into the bathroom. She grabbed the toothbrush and was brushing her teeth while she trying to climb into her clothes one handed. This was the day, she knew it. She had cracked the map. She could hardly wait to get downstairs and tell Kamakura. She was out the door in five minutes.

She galloped down the fire stairs and out the side door of the hotel. He wasn't in the parking lot. She unlocked the car and got behind the steering wheel before she thought to look at her watch. It was 5:42. She was due at the car at 6:00, of course he wasn't here yet. She forced herself to lean back and try to relax. It didn't work.

She remembered her yoga exercises. She sat breathing in and out, concentrating on her inner being. That didn't work. She shut her eyes shut, breathing, peeking out through fluttering lids, concentrating for a millisecond before flitting a glance back at the hotel.

76

The side door opened, it was him. He came across the lot at a deliberate pace. He paused momentarily when he saw her already behind the wheel and then he opened the back door and slid in.

She started the car even before the back door slammed shut. "I think I have the answer," she exclaimed. She could feel him lean forward.

"I think there are two layers to the cliff. The second layer, the upper one, isn't visible where it breaks. I think that's where the second set of five caves is, just set back enough so they aren't visible from the parking lot below."

"Ahhhh," she could hear him exhale as he leaned back. "Yes, that might be it." He was quiet, thinking.

She drove to the grocery and they both got out. She felt herself resenting the time it took to get food but knew if she didn't eat she wouldn't be able to keep digging for any length of time.

Kamakura was already checking out and by the time she paid he was leaning on the car waiting for her. She hurried out and unlocked the door.

As she was leaving the parking lot she heard their tires squeal. She forced herself to take a deep breath and slow down to the speed limit. All they needed was a ticket.

In what seemed like hours, they finally turned down the dirt road, passed the free standing rock with its lichen, and parked in the turnaround.

She forced herself to take a yogurt and spoon from the bag and climbed out. They leaned against the side of the car and looked up at the cliff. It stood, gray early morning shadows covering it, silent, secret, a puzzle to be solved. The sun was just touching the tips of the trees. Where to begin the climb? If her theory was correct, the Indians had climbed it constantly, and Hana and Douglas Fairbanks had climbed it too.

She peeled the foil from the top of the yogurt and started spooning it up. Still she looked. She could see no visible crack where they had climbed; surely she would have noticed one before now, when the light was better. She began to doubt her theory. Maybe they had used a ladder. Nuts, double nuts. If they had, she was up a creek without a paddle. No, she snickered, down a cliff without a ladder.

"Well, I'm going to haul my stuff up there and start looking. I think there has to be reasonably simple access or they wouldn't have used the upper level."

She caught his look. "I'm sure my theory is correct," she defended herself. "Well, working on the lower level hasn't panned out and I'm sure there's an upper level."

She gathered up her food, drink and tools, wedged them down her sweatshirt front after tucking the band of the shirt into her belt. It made a good pouch. She started climbing.

When she got to the top of the scree she dumped her load on what she had started calling *her* rock and began wandering along the face of the cliff. She went left, past where she had worked the day before. No luck.

She turned and climbed back the other way. As she came back toward the rock seat where she had left her supplies, she saw a visitor. The jay was back. He was sitting on the orange. She laughed; it looked as if he had laid a bright orange egg almost as big as himself.

As her laugh bubbled out in the early morning stillness he gave a leap of surprise and flew straight up about two thirds of the way along the right side of the slab and with a flutter of feathers, he disappeared behind it, seemingly into the cliff face itself.

She stood in amazement, looking up at the spot where he had disappeared. Could it be? Had the slab of rock broken off and slid down over the ancient stairs. She walked around to the other side of *her* bench. The back of the bench was slightly tilted, leaning back against the cliff. She put her face against the crack and tried to see behind it. Nothing. Too much shadow. She tried reaching behind it. At shoulder level she couldn't extend her arm more than a foot or so.

She backed off and tried to peer behind. No dice. She went back to the slit and squatted down, trying to see in. It was leaning perhaps sixteen inches away from the cliff wall at the base. She bent her head down almost to the ground but again she drew a blank.

What if there was a snake back there? Not a friendly bull snake but a rattlesnake, a rattlesnake with attitude?

Nothing ventured, nothing gained popped into her head. It was another quotation from her grandmother. Gee, was Grandma's whole conversation full of trite quotations? No, it was just that sometimes, these old quotes were apt. She sighed and lay down on the ground and started wiggling into the crack.

She lay facing the cliff and extended her left hand in as far as she could reach. All she could feel was a rough wall. She scooted her left shoulder in and then her head, still feeling nothing but wall. Wait, her finger tips weren't touching anything! She pushed herself further and felt around. She was feeling a smooth step, hollowed in the center by countless feet. She pushed further. Her head and shoulders were in. She had nothing to pull herself forward with, no protrusions to grab. She scrabbled with her feet, pushing herself onward. Oh God, don't let me get stuck. Her arm and head were resting on a step. Luckily it was a broad step. These old ruins had very narrow stairs, just a slot or sometimes just toeholds. They were easier to make and much easier to defend. She had read about one where if you didn't start climbing with the correct foot you ended high up on a cliff with nowhere to go. She pushed with her toes and she was in. She pulled herself sideways, still unable to turn on her back, and then her hips and feet were free. She turned and looked up.

She was inside what had once been a cave. The front part of it had split, probably sometime after Hana and Douglas Fairbanks had last visited, considering the difficulty of access. The part that had broken off was the long slab that she had been calling bench and bench back. The back curve of the cave, blackened with soot from long ago fires, was still there. She was sitting at the side of it where stairs ascended to the cliff above. She looked at the stairs, light was reflecting down from where the early morning sun hit the cliff. She heard a screech and the beating of wings echoing in the stairwell. The jay had left.

The stairs varied from one foot to 18 inches in width, each step about eight or ten inches above the last. They were blocked from the outside view by another whole hunk of cliff that had cleaved long ago, before even the ancient Indians' had inhabited the area. The Indians had carved the steps up an existing crevice. The slab protected their access to the upper level from the eyes of wandering enemies who wouldn't have been able to see the stairs or the upper caves.

TA pulled herself upright and started ascending the steps. She ran her hands along both walls as she climbed. They were smooth, polished by countless stroking of long dead-fingers.

Her eyes came level with the upper tier of caves and she climbed up onto a narrow walkway, hidden from the valley floor by more slabbed and broken rock. There, behind the wall of sheared cliff was a path, dirt-covered now but smoothed by ancient feet. It was as narrow as two feet in places and as wide as six feet in others.

There were a series of caves on her left. The stairs had emptied onto the path at one end. The path continued around the edge of the cliff and she followed it, counting caves. There were five caves before the path ended at a drainage chute eroded into the cliff below her feet. Perhaps this was an easier way down? It was split all the way to the base of the cliff and partially filled with broken rocks carried by the drainage water. The rocks, small and large, were tumbled and wedged in the crevice with a dead tumbleweed caught part way down. She could just make out the scree that started at the base of the lower cliff. She studied it thinking it would be possible to descend this way if she braced her back against the side and prayed a lot as she climbed down. At least she wouldn't get caught behind that big slab. Yeah, but she could break into a zillion pieces if she misjudged where she was going and the rocks let go. A premature burial. At least it would be a free burial. "Here lies stupid" would say the sign over it. She'd go back the way she came in.

Turning back she inspected the entrances to the caves. All the openings were low, easier to defend and probably left low so they would be less visible from below. Douglas Fairbanks had marked the middle cave on his map as being the one where the map was hidden but like a little kid that wanted to wait for the best part, she found herself looking in the entrance of the end cave, the one nearest. It was small, perhaps six feet across. The curved ceiling and walls were sooty and unchanged from hundreds of years before when it had been abandoned. There was a matate rock leaning against the inner wall. The broad slightly concave rock had been used long ago by an Indian wife as the base for grinding corn. She would spread the corn on the center and with two hands she held a large rounded oblong rock called a mano and ground back and forth until she had a coarse flour. The matate had been left behind when they moved – much too heavy to take with them. Who knew what had become of the mano.

Looking through the entrance to the next cave, she could see another matate left behind. This cave was slightly larger but empty, except for the metate.

TA walked back to the first cave and looked in. It was very small, evidently used for storage. There were several old pots lined up along the back wall, a treasure trove to any archaeologist or pot collector. She didn't go in.

Cave number two was completely empty, perhaps eight feet across, soot blackened, cold, silent. Backing out she turned to the middle cave, the one marked with an X on Douglas Fairbanks' map.

Leaning down she looked in. Yes, this was the cave. There was a fire laid. It had been waiting for over fifty years. Near it was a folded blanket, dust covered, mouse-shredded, but waiting too. She crawled in and as she did, a movement caught her eye. She stopped, heart pounding, until she realized that she was looking at her reflection in a dusty mirror leaning up from a shelf along the side wall. It was one of the cheap mirrors that were available from the 5 and 10 Cent Store, the predecessor of Walmart. The mirror was about 6 x 8 inches, framed in black painted wood, dusty now, age spotted, but still faithful to its purpose, catching her reflection as she entered. They had probably used it for combing their hair before returning to Espanola and the real world, away from their private sanctuary. She walked over to it; the actual cave was approximately six feet high, contrary to the door, which was less than three feet. There was a cheap comb lying on the shelf in front of the mirror.

She turned and inspected the cave. Her eye was caught by something inscribed on the back wall of the cave. TA walked toward it and looked. It was a heart with their initials. Her toe felt an indentation in the floor just below the heart. Was this where they had hidden the map?

Kneeling, she dug with her hands. Her fingers immediately felt stiff cloth. She scraped back the dirt and there it was. It was a bundle wrapped in cracked oilcloth. The cloth was covered with a design of red roses and little old-fashioned blue teapots, the kind of cloth people used to buy by the yard in five and dimes to cover their kitchen tables.

The bundle was heavy! It must weigh ten pounds or more. She laid it on the cave floor and carefully opened it. Inside was a simple cylinder approximately two feet long, made of reeds and bound in the middle by a gold band about two inches deep, leather thongs twisted around the entire length of the cylinder. Each end of the cylinder was capped by gold, glowing softly in the muted light. The ends were inscribed but she wouldn't be able to tell what the design was until she got it out in the daylight.

Rewrapping the cylinder and cradling it in both arms she crawled out through the cave opening. Once in the sun she couldn't resist squatting there and stripping off the oil cloth. The reeds that made up the outer cylinder looked like any pond reed; it would take a botanist to say what type of plant they came from. The leather straps were old and cracked, with animal hairs still sticking out of it here and there. Whoever had tanned it had left the fur on but the years had worn it away. The caps, each extended approximately two inches down on the cylinder ends, and the center band, were indeed gold. They were inscribed with etchings of little animals. She looked closely. One cap showed miniature hoofed animals: deer, elk, big horn sheep, pronghorn, and buffalo. Each was exquisitely small and beautifully detailed, all with their heads up on alert, ears flicking, and eyes wide. Their flanks had tiny lines of etched hair. The elk had his head thrown back, rack resting on his shoulders, nose sampling the air. The buffalo alone had his head down, one tiny hoof pawing the ground. There was a 3-dimensional soaring eagle on top, his claws clutching wisps of silk thread, all that was left after so many years, of the original tassel.

Turning the cylinder over, she studied the gold cap on the other end. It had smaller animals, rodents busy with their day, a prairie dog was digging out his burrow, tiny rump in the air, tail flipped over his back. A beaver sat upright, munching a tiny twig, and a raccoon paused in his fishing, sitting up in tiny watery swirls, peering at the artist; two squirrels flitted among a spray of leaves and a chipmunk sat on a rock with a mouse nearby.

The center band too, was etched, this one with predators. There was a mountain lion bounding, tail swinging, feet extended; a coyote stood alertly, ears up, watching a bear who was fishing, a tiny salmon being batted through the air. A wolf trotted along, followed by two tumbling cubs.

TA stopped and raised her head, wasn't this supposed to be a Japanese map? A map brought from Japan to the United States just before the Second World War? These animals were North American. They were found nowhere else, except in zoos. Kamakura had said it was fourteenth or fifteenth century. Could it be? A map of

83

North America before Columbus? Had the Japanese explored the West Coast hundreds of years ago?

Bending over the case, she tried to get her nails under the edge of one of the caps. She paused, her mind's eye seeing a picture from a storybook of long ago. It was of Pandora opening the dreadful box.

TA shook her head, erasing the picture, and tried to pry loose the cap. It wouldn't release. She bent over to study it and noticed for the first time that there was an inscription etched around the top edge of the cap. She tilted the cylinder to the light. It was in Japanese script. No, it didn't look Japanese. Whatever, she couldn't read it.

Twisting the cap didn't work. She flipped the cylinder over to the other end and studied that cap. Again she tried twisting it. The cap sat as if welded. She squatted there at the edge of the oilcloth studying the case. There was nothing to do but to call Kamakura and let him know she had it. Maybe she would get to see what was in it when she took it down to him. Her hopes of writing a paper on her find were fading. He'd never let her study it; it was too rare, too fine, for anyone but an established scholar.

Picking up the map case she stood and walked to the edge of the path. The rocks protecting the path were about waist high and made it invisible to those below. Some of the rocks were dislodged and she stepped up on one to see over the edge to where Kamakura waited. She raised the map case above her head in triumph, planning to call down to him, holding high the prize.

Balanced on the rock, cylinder high above her head, she looked down and froze. There were two cars parked below, not one. Another car had joined theirs. As she watched, arms aloft, she saw Kamakura get out of the back seat of their car and advance to meet two men who had gotten out of the other car. They met between the two cars and stood talking for a moment. One of the men took something out of his pocket and pointed it at Kamakura. Kamakura jerked and in slow motion he half turned away and started to fall. It was only then that she heard the shot. The man had shot Kamakura! The sound echoed and re-echoed off the cliffs surrounding the valley. Slowly Kamakura sank to the ground. It was like watching an underwater pirouette -- slow, graceful.

Jerking back, she crouched behind the rocks. Too late and wrong move. The motion had alerted the two men. As she knelt she could hear the sound of their voices. They were discussing something; probably her imminent demise! Silence for a moment, then crunching of feet on the loose rock at the cliff base. They were climbing to the cliff face.

She felt an adrenalin rush. Her mind took on an almost crystalline clarity. She had to make a choice. She could stay where she was and hope they couldn't get to her, but if they did, she knew they'd kill her. They had to be after the map, the map she held. And she had witnessed the murder.

Or she could go down the way she had come. But it emptied right out above where they were climbing. Her lunch was spread out on the rock below like a signpost announcing where she was.

A third choice was to go to the end of the path and descend through the cleft. It was around the corner of the cliff from where they were climbing. It would give her some time, perhaps enough to get out to the road or at least to hide.

She was halfway along the walkway to the cleft before she made a conscious decision to climb down that way. She jammed the case down through her sweatshirt neck and into the waistband of her jeans. She stuffed the sweatshirt bottom into the waist securing the cylinder as best she could. She'd need her hands free when she started down.

Hitting the cleft running, she let her eyes and reflexes take over, started down, bracing her back, trying not to dislodge any rocks. Down she inched through the first part, back to one wall, shoes against the other and then she came to a wedge of rocks that she had

85

to climb around. Feet were groping for steps, hands bracing on the side walls. Trying not to pull any rocks down. She scrabbled, around the first group of rocks, crunching into the dry tumbleweed. The noise was like firecrackers! She could hear her panting breath, sounding like a St. Bernard. She forced herself to breath slowly and quietly.

She came to another chute that was just wide enough to put her feet on either side, and inched down spread-eagled, hands and feet out, vulnerable. What if they came around the corner right now? The words from an old song popped into her head, *all of me, take all of me.* She giggled. Oh God, take my sense of humor and dump it. Please help me get out of here!

She was down. She began running along the upper edge of the scree. At a group of tumbled large rocks she dropped to all fours crawled behind them. Her thudding heart was deafening. Trying to slow her heart she cocked her head to listen for the men. They must have found the entrance to the stairs. She could hear one of them yelling from above. She heard a snapping, rustling sound. He'd found the old oilcloth and was saying something as he waved it. The other answered. Why hadn't she taken Japanese in college? Her heart and breathing slowed.

She heard a closer noise, just a ruffle of air. She lifted her head and peered over the edge of the rocks just as a yellow and white butterfly rose on a thermal current and paused, hovering in front of her sweaty face. They eyed each other, poised. She was reminded of the movies where a helicopter comes up over the edge of a cliff. She blew gently at it and it planed away, slanting down toward the valley below.

She heard another shout from above, they were nearer. Rocks falling. A scream. She risked a look. The whole slide of rocks rolled down the hill. The man had evidently tried to come down the cleft and dislodged them.

The rocks stopped rolling and the dust cloud started to dissipate. There was silence for a moment and then more discussion. It hadn't killed the one that fell. A peal of laughter rang out. Good grief! Here they were killing people, trying to kill her, climbing around mountains, falling down cliffs and they were laughing! Didn't these guys have any class? If they were killers shouldn't they act like killers, like on TV. You didn't kill someone and then start joking; everybody knew that.

She risked raising her head to look over the rocks. They had just come around the curve of the cliff. One of them saw her and let out a shout. As she jumped up and started running she had the satisfaction of seeing one of them was scraped, dust covered and limping.

She tried to run diagonally down the hill and immediately discovered it was a bad move. She was slipping sideways, starting to fall. She heard a shot that galvanized her into a sideways turning leap that sent her aiming directly downward. She ran like she had never run before. She hurdled boulders, tried to clear a bush that seemed to suddenly spring up in front of her, she crashed through the top part and kept going, rocks, grass tufts, bushes, she could see them in her lower peripheral vision as she hurled downward, faster and faster.

She hit the flat and almost collided with a huge pine tree. As she dodged around it bark suddenly sprayed outward. Two bullets had hit just where her head had been.

She ran through the trees, footsteps deadened by dust and long dead pine needles. The sun slanted down through the trees, illuminating each dust mote that she kicked up. It was as if her eyes could see more clearly than they had ever seen before. Each clump of grass was made up of clearly defined blades. As she flung herself across a dried creek bed there wasn't just generic gravel underfoot, it was as if each little pebble had a character of its own.

Was this how people saw, people whose lives were about to end? Seeing vividly, each minute item of their surroundings? Surroundings that they are going to leave forever? Even as she ran she could feel the skin on her back flinching.

She ran parallel with the cliff and saw a break in its face just ahead. She angled toward the break, climbing a hill of eroded tuff. Even in her panic she defined it in her mind as the bubbled volcanic ash that was often lighter than water. Her mind was working on several planes, one turned back toward the two men, one turned forward looking for escape and still another defining and evaluating what she was seeing.

She crested the hill and ran through the cut in the cliffs; she was on a level perhaps 50 feet higher than the valley she had exited. She ran up a dry stream bed that periodic rain water had cut through the cliff from the upper level and had then exited to the valley floor below. She continued across the tuff and at the narrowest part of the cut, cliffs jutting up on both sides, she came to a mass of old gray tumbleweed, too wide to vault, she plowed through and suddenly fell, feet first, six feet straight down.

.

CHAPTER 13

NORTHERN NEW MEXICO

MONDAY, OCTOBER 30, 2000

The tumbleweeds broke her fall. She found herself sitting up to her shoulders in the prickly stuff, breathing in gasps, crouched on a crackly mattress of plant razor wire, blood trickling from various slashes. Carved walls, dug long ago, surrounded her. She looked higher; gray jagged tumbleweed was silhouetted against the turquoise sky.

She knew from Anthropology classes she had taken that she was in a deer pit. The Indians had carved the pits in narrow bottlenecks of canyons and then driven panicked deer up the canyon and into the pit. She had been driven by the same panic, chased by men who meant her harm, driven to her frightened self-destruction.

She couldn't get out, at least not easily. Survive! Hide the map case! She pulled it out of her shirt front and slid it as far down as she could along the edge of the pit's wall, nestling it near one corner and pulling tumbleweeds over it; then she scooped herself a hole right down to bedrock. Lying down flat and reaching around her she scooped as many undamaged tumbleweeds as possible and fluffed them up around and over her. She lay still, listening and trying not

89

to sneeze. She was covered in pollen, dust, probably mouse droppings, and doodoo from gazillions of bugs and beasts.

Quiet, she told herself. Listen. Her heart sounded loud enough to be heard a half mile away. She concentrated on inner peace. Dump that thought. Meditation? Forget it. She couldn't hear anything except her inner mechanisms; even her stomach added a gurgle. The walls of the trap were blocking outside sounds.

There was a scratching above her head – feet scuffing across the rock. She held her breath. Her blood was rushing in her ears. Her eyes were clenched so tight she could see stars behind her lids. She slowly exhaled and opened her eyes. There was a large red ant crawling up the tumbleweed branch that was about three inches in front of her eyes. He paused and they looked at each other. She blew at him, trying to get him out of her face, her space. He tumbled back but hung on with two legs, feelers waving frantically. With great effort he swung until he could get purchase with his other four legs and, she could swear, gave her a reproachful look as he continued up the branch and out of sight.

More of the scuffing scraping sounds, and then voices. Men's voices, discussing the pit, discussing it in English? Why were they speaking English when just a few moments ago they were chasing her and shouting in Japanese?

Oh God! Oh please God! Please don't let them see me! She prayed, repeating her plea over and over in her mind.

"Come out! I have a gun."

TA froze, mind and body.

"Come out! We've got you covered."

Her mind kicked into gear. They're going to kill me! What a place to die – the bottom of a deer pit! They'll probably bury me under this pile of tumbleweeds. I'll molder away, oozing back into the soil. No, I'm on rock, I'll be a puddle! Ugh! I'll dry up and I'll become a people pancake, lumpy with bones. Ish!

"I said come out now. I can see you"

She felt her muscles contracting involuntarily as her reflexes took over. Legs flexed, her body rolled over and was already rising when the soles of her feet came in contact with the pit floor. She pushed off, launching herself upward, the muscles in her legs strong, shooting up like the frightened deer for which the pit had been made.

A man stood at the edge of the pit, leaning down, holding a gun and pointing it at her.

Oh God, I'm going to be shot! In a blur her upward movement was violent enough to bring her arms and shoulders to the lip of the pit. She braced her left arm on the edge, then reached up and caught his trouser cuff with her right hand. Scrabbling up his leg and then his body; her weight pulled him forward and in an effort at balance he leaned back and threw his hands upward; his gun went flying through the air. In her panic TA continued to claw upward, her weight shifted his balance back even more and then they both crashed back, his head hit the rocks and TA, sailing past his shoulder, splatted, face forward, onto more rocks.

Blinding light. Blackness.

CHAPTER 14

NORTHERN NEW MEXICO

MONDAY, OCTOBER 30, 2000

TA woke feeling sick, dizzy and very uncomfortable. It took a moment for her to realize she was being carried and with realization came panic and then pain as she was suddenly thrown through the air and her aching head came in contact with a hard object. She heard grunting and felt herself jostled as her legs were pushed up toward her chest. "Rape!" she mumbled.

"Give me a break, lady!" A man's voice puffed.

She peered down her body and saw a hot sweaty red face. The man was evidently attempting to stuff her into something. She looked around, trying to keep her head still; she had the grandmother of all headaches. She was being shoved into the back seat of some kind of jeep. She grabbed the back of the seat and pulled herself upright, panic flooding her body, getting ready to go into attack mode.

Now she could see him only from his neck down and he seemed to be wearing a uniform. There was another man sitting in the front seat slumped against the side window. He had what looked like a bloody tee shirt wrapped around his head and from what she could see, he too, wore a uniform.

The first man grabbed her legs, which were dangling outside the door, and started cramming them in.

"Stop, I can do it," she croaked. She pulled her legs inside the jeep and he slammed the door.

He then walked around the vehicle and slid in behind the wheel. Rather than starting the vehicle he swung around in the seat and studied her as he caught his breath. He looked hot, sweaty, decidedly dusty and very annoyed. He leaned forward and, reaching into his pocket, he pulled out a red and white handkerchief and tossed it to her. "Here, you need this for your forehead." She caught it and applied it to her throbbing head.

"Who the hell are you and what're you doing here? This is a restricted area. Didn't you see the signs? What were you doing in that fuckin' hole? Gawd, I didn't think I'd ever get Henry back here."

"My name is Titania McGovern. I was running away and I fell in, so I was hiding."

"Hiding? Running away? From what?" he asked.

"I was running away from the murderers. They were chasing me." She tried to sit up straight but her head hurt.

"Murderers? How do you know they were murderers? Where were you running from?" he asked.

"Because I saw them shoot Mr. Kamakura, that's why. Quick, let's drive through there," she motioned back through the cut beyond the deer pit. "You can catch them before they get away."

"Me? Catch them?" He gasped. "I'm a security guard. I'm not a cop. I'm paid to keep trespassers out of restricted areas. I'm not paid to catch murderers. We're going up to the hospital in Los Alamos to get you and Henry stitched up, then I'll notify the police and the FBI." He faced forward in the seat, put the jeep in gear and started the engine.

"FBI?" she asked. "How come the FBI?"

"Most of this area is still under the FBI, along with the local and state police, that's how come. There're still lots of government projects going on around here."

"Don't you have a radio? You could call the police so they can catch the murderers. This is really important, you know. Mr. Kamakura's lying dead back there."

"The radio doesn't work down here," he answered. "I'll put in a call when we get up to the top of the mesa."

"But what if they leave before the cops come?"

"So they leave, at least they won't leave three more corpses behind. Besides, if the guy's dead he won't mind waiting," returned the man.

He started the jeep and drove up a narrow rutted road.

"How did you know I was hiding there?" asked TA.

"We saw you from up above. Ever vigilant, that's us."

"Ha," croaked Henry, speaking for the first time. "George stopped to take a leak. He likes to see how far he can shoot off the cliffs. Ever vigilant, a rat's ass, ever peeing, that's George."

The back of George's neck turned red.

"Well, at least I saw her," he said.

They were driving up a road that wound around some tall pointed pink stalagmite shaped rocks sticking up from the canyon floor. Each point had a rounded rock balanced on top. Strange, thought TA, wondering how a volcano and erosion had managed such a curious anomaly.

The jeep turned up a steep road carved into the side of a cliff and at last they emerged on top of the mesa. George pulled out a microphone that had been hanging on the dash and began talking. TA strained to hear but he kept his voice lowered and she could only catch a few words.

He tossed the mic back in its holder as the dirt road joined a paved road with normal traffic. They drove into town and turned into the emergency entrance of a hospital.

As they pulled up and parked George turned to her, "The cops and FBI will be here soon and they'll take your statement."

He got out of the car and went around to help Henry out, draping one of the injured man's arms around his neck to hold him upright. TA sat, not sure if he was going to handcuff her or open her door to escort her in. He bent down supporting Henry with his arm and peered through the window at her, "Come on, lady. I can't carry you both." She opened the door and joined them.

He half carried Henry, who seemed to be woozier by the moment, and together they walked through the entrance. The receptionist looked up and hit a button behind the desk, calling for someone to come help. An orderly came out and Henry was shoved down into a wheelchair and pushed off through swinging doors behind the receptionist.

TA then received the undivided attention of the woman who went into officious high gear, "Name, date-of-birth, address, Social Security Number, insurance carrier." TA leaned against the counter as she answered. George had stationed himself by the swinging door where he could keep an eye on her and still watch through the door's window to see what was happening to Henry. Evidently not much, as he soon joined her at the receptionist's desk.

"Card please," asked the receptionist.

"Card?" asked TA.

"Yes, insurance card please."

"I haven't got my card. I haven't any ID with me."

The receptionist gave her an icy stare. "No card? You said you have insurance so you must have a card. How can I process your forms without a card?" She glared at TA. TA shrugged. The receptionist gave an exaggerated sigh, picked up the phone, and punched buttons. "We have a woman here who wants to be seen. She *says* she has insurance but she doesn't have a card." The receptionist sat listening to a screeching voice on the line, meanwhile tapping her long red nails on the counter and glaring at TA through narrow, slitted eyes. "Yes, she *seems* to be bleeding but you know how blood always makes it look worse than it really is." She listened some more and then dropped the phone back into its cradle.

"Fill out and sign these forms," she shoved the papers, attached to a clip board with a pen swinging from a chain, at TA. "Someone will be out to get you, have a seat over there." She nodded at a line of chairs.

TA sighed and slunk over to a seat, thankful the bleeding seemed to have stopped. They'd probably kick her out if she bled on the hospital floor. She filled out the papers, mostly promising to pay anything not covered by her insurance and returned the papers, clipboard and pen to the desk.

George was leaning wearily against the wall still watching her and the emergency room window. After a long wait, an orderly came out and beckoned to her. No solicitous wheelchair for her. The word must have gone out – indigent, no proven insurance.

She was shown to a gurney in a cubical and told to sit. A nurse would be in shortly. The privacy curtain was drawn, shutting her off from the world. She sat on the edge of the gurney, swinging her legs, head aching, exhausted. The curtain was pulled back and a nurse walked in carrying a tray covered by a towel.

"Well now, had a little accident, did we?" She set the tray down and looked closely at TA. "Wow, are you a mess!" She exclaimed, turning into a human. "What happened?"

"I fell in a hole down in the canyon." She reached up to her temple and felt it gently. "Is it bad?"

"No, probably not, but you'll need stitches and probably X-rays. You look pretty scratched up on your hands and face; I'll be cleaning them, too. After you're tidy the doctor'll stitch you closed."

She filled in a form with an edited version of how TA had received her injury and then she set to work mopping and scrubbing. To TA's horror she then plugged in an electric clipper.

"What are you doing?" TA gasped. She put up a restraining hand.

96

"Now, don't worry." the nurse laughed gaily. It wasn't her hair. She revved up the clippers like the start of a NASCAR race.

TA gritted her teeth and braced herself. She could feel the razor pulling at her temple hair.

The nurse turned off the clippers and put them down on the tray, laughing. "Now that wasn't so bad, just a little patch and when it grows back no one will ever see the scar. You wait here and I'll call the doctor." She left, pulling the curtain shut behind her.

Soon the curtain was again opened (why didn't they just leave it?) and the doctor came in followed by the nurse. He read the chart, took a flashlight and looked into TA's eyes and ears and then pulled on rubber gloves and after giving her a few shots of lidocaine to numb the area, stitched her up. "Only four stitches, hardly a scratch. You won't look like Frankenstein, only a zombie, ha, ha. You had a pretty hard knock so we'd better take X-rays. When we're through you have some people waiting to talk to you." The doctor and nurse left shutting the curtains behind them.

It was immediately pulled open and the same orderly that had brought her came in with a wheelchair and down the hall they went to X-ray. Half an hour and three X-rays later she was wheeled back to a new cubical and left alone. Curtain closed. She waited.

The curtain was opened and the doctor and two policemen entered. Did they always come in pairs? "The X-rays look fine." The doctor said. "You can go now. These gentlemen would like to speak with you." He left, leaving the curtain open.

TA looked at the policemen. They stood considering her. The older man finally spoke. "Let's find a little privacy before we begin." They were soon being escorted down the hall to an empty conference room with a round table and six chairs positioned around the table. There were no windows but it did have a nice poster advertising the beauties of New Mexico hanging on the wall. She was parked under the poster facing out into the room.

The men did not sit down but stood between her and the door, observing her. Finally, the younger one pulled out a notebook and pen and the older man hooking his fingers in his belt, rocking back and forth in his cowboy boots, cocked an eyebrow at her and began, "We hear you had a little trouble. George says you saw a murder. I'm Detective Chavez and this is Smith. Where and when did this murder happen? Do you know the victim's name? Just take your time and start from the beginning." He stood rocking, rocking, looking at her expectantly. Smith stood one pace behind him, pen poised over the notebook.

TA drew a deep breath, marshaling her thoughts. She started at the beginning when Mr. Kamakura came to the shop and finished up with being found in the bottom of the deer pit. When she finally paused she could tell that they were skeptical. She again gave them Lt. Samson's name, just to prove to them, what? That she wasn't lying? As she studied their faces she felt a sense of frustration.

"Okay, Ms. McGovern. We'll check this out." The notebook snapped shut. "In the meantime we have somebody else who wants to talk to you. He should be along pretty soon. Please wait here." They started out but Chavez turned as they were going through the door. "Don't leave the state until we clear this up." Since the state was over 120,000 square miles TA felt that gave her quite a bit of latitude. He turned back to her one more time, "Don't leave this room until after the FBI sees you." He pulled the door shut behind him.

TA sat and waited. She could hear people in the hall but no one knocked and no one entered. How dare they! How double dog dare they! She was the injured party. She was the one that reported the murder. But who was being detained? The murderers? Nooooo! The innocent wounded helpful person. The person who needed to go to the bathroom. The person who needed lunch. The person who was thirsty. She snorted as she suddenly realized that she was indignantly spluttering in her mind.

The snort turned to laughter. It was all so stupid and governmental for her to be detained when there was a body lying down in the canyon. For all she knew there might be bodies all over that cliff. Tucked in cave holes like so many acorns preserved by some demented super squirrel spawned by nuclear waste that had been strewn fecklessly across the landscape by unwise Los Alamos geniuses. The cops might come back and pin lots of murders on her, what did they care if she were innocent?

Suddenly she heard voices, laughter, the doorknob turned and the door half opened. A man stood holding the knob as he talked to somebody in the hall. He was tall, six plus feet and dressed conservatively in a navy-blue suit, dressed FBI, but the awesome thing about him was his hair, the color of an Irish setter, deep dark red. He swung around and they looked at each other. He stood perfectly still, inspecting her. She felt a visceral jolt. God, she thought, this is it. I never thought I would see him, the man of my dreams. He is so gorgeous! Oh God, keep me from making a fool of myself! She tried to look away but she couldn't. She sat and stared.

He gave a little shake, as if coming to task, and came into the room, shutting the door behind him. He walked forward and stood three feet in front of her. She couldn't take her eyes off him.

"Hello, I'm John Doe, FBI." He reached into his pocket and pulled out a case which he flipped open to show her his badge. He pulled out one of the chairs from the table and sat. Reaching into his pocket he removed a small tape recorder and turning it on he recorded the date and time and his name.

He set the recorder on the table and turned to her, "I have some questions. Your name, please?"

"Wait. Did you say your name was John Doe?"

"Yeah. My parents had a terrible sense of humor...and your name is?"

"TA McGovern."

"Tah?"

99

"No, the initials T and A. It stands for Titania Ariel. My mother named me." Oh God, make me shut up, I'm babbling.

"Where are you from?"

"I'm from Colorado, no I was born in New Mexico. I mean, I'm living in San Francisco." She paused a moment to collect herself. Idiot, she thought, he'll think I'm an idiot!

She drew a deep breath. "Let me start again. I got hit on the head." She lightly touched her temple and as she dropped her hand she looked at it. It was filthy even though the nurse had scrubbed it. She looked down at herself. Now, when she wanted to make an everlasting impression she looked like a dirty burglar. She was wearing dusty jeans, a filthy sweatshirt and she still had her painters mask hanging around her neck. She reached up and pulled it off over her head and tried to crumple it to fit in her pocket.

He leaned back in his chair and pulled out a notebook and pen (are they born with them?) "Why don't you begin at the beginning. How did all this start?"

"Please," she found herself saying. "I need to go to the bathroom and I need a drink of water and maybe something to eat?" Her request had turned into a plea.

He laughed. "Sorry. I can't let you go by yourself but I'll wheel you to the bathroom and then we'll find you a drink and some food."

A half hour later they were back in the meeting room and she began her story. She started with the shop in San Francisco and the first meeting with Kamakura. She progressed to the dead bodies and Lt. Samson, then on to Kamakura's return and flying to New Mexico. She told him about Eliza and about the detention camps, about following Douglas Fairbanks' map and looking for the cave and finally cracking the puzzle of the map. She described the pinion jay and how he had showed her the opening and how she had crawled behind the rocks and climbed the stairs. And then she stopped.

100

He was leaning forward, enthralled. "Did you? Did you find it?"

She equivocated. "I looked over the edge and saw a second car. Two men got out and Kamakura met them and they talked. They shot him. Then they saw me and came up the scree. My lunch was spread out like a sign post. I ran to the other end of the shelf and went down through a crack in the cliff." She paused, remembering the panic.

"One climbed up the stairs," she continued, "He found where I had gone down and tried to follow. He fell but I guess he wasn't hurt too badly because they laughed." She paused a moment and drew a deep breath. "They came around the curve of the cliff and saw me so I ran. They shot at me and I ran through the trees and up through a cut in the cliff and then I fell in the pit. The deer pit." He didn't question the pit, he must have taken Anthro 101, too. "Then, when the guards came, I thought they were the murderers and I guess I panicked." She stopped.

How could I lie to him about the map? Oh well, I'll turn it in later, after I've had a chance to study it. Besides, it isn't lying, it's omitting.

She sat back and looked at him. Oh my, he is such a hunk, she thought. He was studying his notes.

He looked up, "Is that it?" he asked, pen poised.

"Yes," she croaked. Did lying mute you? She cleared her throat, "Yes, all I can remember now."

"Okay," he snapped the notebook shut and slipped it in his pocket. He stood, adding the tape recorder to another pocket. "Come on, let's go."

She looked up at him aghast. Was she going to jail so fast?

"Oh," he said solicitously, bending over her. "Are you able to walk? I'd like to take you back down to the canyon. Can you make it?"

She felt him, his essence, and for a moment she couldn't breathe. He touched her shoulder and she looked up at him.

Their eyes met, locked. He feels it too she thought. She made an effort to overcome her weakness, her twitterpatedness, shades of grandmother again, and launched herself up off the wheelchair.

Unfortunately, as she shot upward, he leaned over and the top of her head connected with his nose.

She fell back into the chair, clutching her aching head and he reeled back holding his nose, blood squirting through his fingers.

"Shit," he exclaimed, leaning over to avoid getting blood on his suit and at the same time groping for a handkerchief to stem the flow.

He stood, handkerchief to nose and she sat holding both hands to the top of her head. They looked at each other and burst into laughter.

"Sorry," they said simultaneously and again burst into laughter.

She decided to be frank. Hell, why not? "It's you," she said.

"Me?" he asked. "Because I'm the FBI?"

"No, because ever since you walked in I've been twitterpated." Now he'll really think me a fool she thought, wishing her head felt well enough to beat it on a wall. Oh God, make me drop dead right now!

"Twitterpated as in Bambi?" he asked, starting to grin under his handkerchief.

His eyes crinkle when he smiles, she noticed delightedly.

He kept grinning and looking at her as he backed to the door. He opened it and glanced out.

He's running away, she thought.

He called something to someone and came back into the room. "I ordered a couple of ice packs for us," he said.

Say something, anything, dunce! She sat, mute, watching him, feeling like a dolt.

"Now, about Bambi," he said, standing, looking at her, "If I remember correctly twitterpated is another term for being very attracted to a person of the opposite sex." He paused, looking at her with a raised eyebrow, a tiny smile just at the corners of his very kissable mouth. He was still holding his nose with his bloodstained hand and despite that he made her middle feel like warm cottage cheese, all curdled and soft.

She squirmed in her chair and was infuriated to feel a blush rising, spreading. Die, she thought, die right here at his feet and turn to dust like one of those old vampires that get hit with a ray of sunlight. Just dissolve like a shape-changer from Star Trek Deep Space Nine and flow away through a crack. Anything to get away from this embarrassment!

"I was just thinking the same thing," he continued speaking. "Not quite so graphically but nevertheless, very, yes, twitterpated. Oh, not you," he continued. "Me, yes, twitterpated is a very good word, describes it completely." He paused and gazed at her, beaming.

"You are…" he continued, but broke off when a knock sounded at the door. He backed to it, still looking at her, opened it and glanced over his shoulder to see who was there.

"Oh, thanks," he said, receiving a wet towel and two ice packs. He shut the door and brought her an ice pack. He mopped his face with the towel and then looked at her inquiringly.

"You missed a bit on your left cheek," she said, pointing. He mopped again.

"Here," she said, rising, one hand holding the ice pack to her head. She took the towel and wiped his cheek gently, breathless to be so close. It was turning into a caress. She gave a shaky laugh and backed away.

"There, you look fine, just a little swollen," she said.

He applied the ice pack to his nose and stood looking at her over the top of it.

She giggled. He looked ridiculous and so cute standing there holding the blue ice pack to his nose and peering at her over the top.

His eyes crinkled. "Oh," he said, "First you ruin my face and then you laugh at me. By the way, my nickname is Buck, since we seem to have gotten to a first name place in our relationship."

She grinned back, feeling in control for the first time. "I like it," she said, and then dramatically fanned herself with her hands. "Things are getting too hot around here. Let's go. I think we both need some fresh air."

"Good idea," he said. "Come on, the car is parked out by the side door."

He led her down a hall and out to a dark blue BMW convertible.

"Wow," she exclaimed. "Cool car. Is this what they give FBI agents to drive? Do the tax payers know?"

"I wish," he laughed. "No, the company car is at the shop. This is mine. I wanted a Viper but this is nice." He smiled proudly and ran his hand possessively over the trunk as he walked around to open the passenger door for her.

CHAPTER 15

NORTHERN NEW MEXICO

MONDAY, OCTOBER 30, 2000

Through town they went and swooped down toward the murder site with cliffs towering on their right and a canyon on their left. As they leveled out TA directed him toward the dirt road and Buck slowed to turn in. There were several fresh tracks in the dirt. They drove along the cliff and soon came to the parking area which was now filled with official cars. State police, city police, and sheriff were all there--but the rental car was missing.

The meaning of the missing car hit TA like a blow to her solar plexus. Missing car meant missing purse, missing ID, missing credit cards, missing money, missing room key card. She felt as if her head, already throbbing, would explode. Panic was starting to take over. She reached out and grabbed Bucks arm. "The car is gone!" she squeaked.

"Yeah, the killers probably took it."

"But my purse was in the trunk. My ID." She tried to take deep breaths.

"Don't worry, we can cancel the credit cards," he reassured her as he swung into one of the few spaces left to park.

105

"You don't understand, all my ID. My driver's license, my credit cards, my hotel room, my, my...oh yeah, my medical card." She snorted, and with that laugh she felt in control again. If the FBI can't help, nobody can. Relax, she told herself. Don't panic yet. She sat back and eyed the scene.

There were uniformed officers everywhere; looking in the forested area inspecting trees and the ground under them, climbing the scree and checking out the cliff dwellings, and photographing everything in sight. A police dog and its handler were standing in the shade of a tree. The whole area looked like someone had kicked an ant hill of cops. TA noticed some were picking up things, too far away to tell what, around the rock she had been calling her bench-table. Probably bagging her lunch for evidence if the murderers hadn't already eaten it.

Buck walked over and started a discussion with the man who seemed to be directing the operation. She leaned against the car, waiting for him. They were pointing, laughing and discussing. He finally came back toward her and she pushed herself off the fender and walked to meet him in the middle of the parking lot. "Well, they found a lot of blood that wasn't hidden very well."

He gestured toward the cliff. "Explain the layout to me."

She pointed at the table rock. "There are two layers to this cliff. The bottom area is obvious. It's composed of tuff," she heard herself go into lecture mode. "The bottom layer was laid down by the volcano and then at a later date the second layer was laid down on top of the earlier layer. Early Indians dug out the caves that you see.

"I set my lunch on that rock where you see the troops picking up stuff. Behind the bench that held my lunch is a large slanted rock leaning up against the cliff." She paused for him to look. When he nodded, she continued. "That slab is tilted slightly and I crawled behind the bench rock and the slab and found a cave opening."

She stopped when he turned to look at her with a raised eyebrow. "I wasn't nuts, a jay showed me an opening back there. He'd

106

been sitting on my orange and got spooked when I came up on him. He flew up and around the upper part of the leaning slab and he didn't come out. Anyway, it's narrow but doable if you aren't built like a linebacker."

He laughed and she continued, "There is another residential cave behind that slab and at the front side of it is a staircase that goes up to the second, newer layer of tuff. There are five caves up there, two are for storage, one with some beautiful pots in it, and the others were for living. Douglas and Hana had set up housekeeping in the middle cave. There's a walkway in front of the caves and at the far end is a slot in the lower cliff that had rocks and tumbleweed lodged in it. I initially went up the staircase and when the murderers started chasing me I went down through the slot to the scree and around the base of the cliff." She gestured to the cliff in the direction she had run.

"Where's the deer pit?" he asked.

"This cliff face ends, probably cut by erosion. I didn't have time to study it." She laughed. "Anyway, a cut in the cliff wall opens to higher ground and beyond the cut the cliff continues. The deer pit is between the two end cliff faces."

"Okay," he said. "We'll check the pit area out tomorrow. Let me go talk to Chief Lujan and then we'll go to Santa Fe and get you back to your hotel."

He walked over to talk to the man directing the troops. They had a long talk with much laughter and then he returned to her still chuckling. "I told him what you told me. He's leaving a guard on duty for the night. He says he's going to pick the fattest and oldest people for guard duty. That way, nobody is going to be tempted. Anyway, he wants you to show him how to get to the upper level. Are you feeling well enough to crawl around in there?"

"Sure, but not just anyone can go in there, you know."

"Okay. Let's go have a skinny contest," he said.

Again they crossed the parking area and met with Chief Lujan. They explained the problem again and he turned and called out several names. Some men and women broke off what they were doing and came toward them. The Chief explained what they needed. One officer, looking pale, raised his hand. "Can I bow out? I don't do well in constricted spaces." He was excused.

TA looked over the remaining group and picked two young women. Both were slender but loaded down with gear. TA gestured toward their heavy belts. "Take off all that stuff. Do you have cameras? If they're bulky we could lower a rope from the upper ledge."

The women broke away and went to their cars to leave all gear behind. One of the deputies got a length of rope that he brought back and gave to TA.

As they climbed to the cliff base they introduced themselves– Pilar and Angela. TA explained the procedure to the women. The rope posed a problem until Pilar suggested she hang it over her foot and pull it in after her.

TA lay on the ground and demonstrated the entry mode. She was soon in the hidden cave and Angela and Pilar had joined her. They climbed the stairs and walked out on the upper level. Pilar went to the edge of the pathway and dropped the end of the rope over after securing it around her middle. She hauled up a mesh bag filled with camera equipment a flashlight and a radio.

They set the bag aside and TA gave them a tour of the site. Angela stuck her head in the storage cave and gave a whistle. "Wow," she said, "treasure." She keyed the radio and reached Chief Lujan. "If you haven't done it already, you need to get someone from the Indian Museum in Santa Fe or the anthro department at UNM in Albuquerque. These pots are wonderful."

"On my list," he replied.

They moved down the walkway, visiting each cave in turn and when they got to the slot that TA had climbed down both women turned to her with looks of admiration. TA made a deprecating gesture and said, "You don't know what you're capable of until people are trying to kill you."

They nodded. TA got the feeling that it was a 'been there, done that," kind of nod.

Everything was photographed, then the equipment lowered back down and the rope coiled and left in the center cave. They returned down the stairs and wiggled their way out, feet first.

TA climbed back down to the parking area and joined Buck. "Now?" she asked. "Now can I go get a shower?"

He made a production of looking her up and down. "Yes, I think that would be a very good idea. In fact, let me dust you off before you get into my wonderful car. Here, give me your sweatshirt." He took the shirt and snapped it a few times while dust swirled in a big cloud. Next he had her turn around and he flapped it against her jeans. When the dust clouds started to abate he gave her the okay to get in the car.

Laughing, TA entered.

On the way back to Santa Fe Buck explained that between them they had decided that Chief Lujan would get in touch with the governors of the two nearest pueblos, Santa Clara and San Ildefonso. The forensic team would be handling Indian artifacts in the form of the matates and the old storage pots. He was also going to contact the anthropology department at the University of New Mexico, the Indian museum in Santa Fe and the people at Bandelier National Monument as they would all want to send an observer over. They would want to get involved in any new artifacts from the area. All in all, it was going to be a busy day with lots and lots of people.

"Nuts," he said, "I better call the Chief and ask him if he's thought of port-o-potties, drinking water and trash cans. I sure hope people bring their own food and don't expect the government to feed them."

CHAPTER 16

SANTA FE

MONDAY, OCTOBER 30, 2000

It was late afternoon when they drove into Santa Fe. By the time they entered the La Fonda parking lot TA was practically bouncing in anticipation of taking a hot shower. To be clean, a wonderful thought. They entered the lobby and walked to the desk. TA presented her most winning smile to the hotel clerk. It was not returned.

The desk clerk moved back a step from the desk with a look of distaste on his face and through stiff lips, enunciating carefully, he asked, "May I help you madam?"

TA had an uneasy feeling about the whole situation. "Yes, I'm a guest here and I've been in an accident. I've lost my purse and my room key card was in it. Would you please make me up another card? My name is TA McGovern, from San Francisco." She looked at him expectantly.

The clerk turned to the computer and gave it a few taps. He sighed deeply. "I am sorry madam, you are not registered here, nor have you ever been registered here. Perhaps you are confused and were staying at another hotel?" He sneered quietly at her. The message was that she wasn't going to pull any tricks with him. He was on to her and would she please leave his immaculate lobby and continue her scam down the street at a lesser hotel.

TA sneered back. "The room was booked by Norio Kamakura. He was my employer. Perhaps the room is under his name."

The clerk returned to his screen pecking. "Kamakura with a K?" he asked.

"Yes," said TA, leaning against the counter with relief. Yes! They had Kamakura registered and it would now be easy to get back into her room.

"He checked out this afternoon. He didn't mention you," announced the clerk triumphantly. It seemed to have become an 'I knew you were trying to cheat us,' situation.

"How about my room, that Mr. Kamakura booked?"

"He checked out the second room, too."

"Well my things are in that room and I want them."

"I believe both those rooms have been cleaned, just a moment while I check with housekeeping." He picked up the phone and turned away from her while he spoke quietly to someone at the other end of the line. He hung up and turned back to her. "Both rooms have been cleaned. There was nothing left in either room."

At this point Buck stepped forward and flipped out his ID. "FBI" he said. "Get your manager out here. I want to see both rooms. Also, print out a hard copy of all transactions to the rooms. Are there any security cameras covering the halls to the rooms, and is there one here at the desk? I want the tapes from those, too."

The clerk came to attention.

Soon, accompanied by the Assistant Manager, they were on their way to her room. The manager keyed the door and opened it. He stepped back to allow them to enter. It had indeed been cleaned. Nothing of TA's was left.

Buck turned to the manager. "Seal this room, no one is to enter. We'll have a team go over it. I'll let you know when it's available again. Now, I'd like to see the other room."

111

Down the hall they trooped and into another, larger, nicer, suite of rooms. Typical, thought TA. These rooms, too, had been emptied and thoroughly cleaned. Buck, "Okay, seal the room." The manager nodded and together they walked back to the desk.

The desk clerk, now oozing helpfulness, had a large manila envelope waiting, bulky with security tapes and copies of room receipts. Buck gathered them up and pulling out his cell, he walked to the middle of the lobby and began punching numbers. After an extended conversation, he signed off and turned to TA who, sunk into a lovely, deep and squishy couch, was dozing off. "Wake up, wake up. We're going to eat!" he exclaimed. She shot upright and saluted him. "All right! At your service!" she exclaimed.

They drove to a Blake's Lotaburger, a New Mexico fast food restaurant known for its large hamburgers loaded with green chili. After scarfing down a burger, fries and coke, TA felt her energy return. During dinner they discussed the plan for the next day, including TA taking Buck to the deer pit. She still hadn't told him about the map case and, feeling more guilty by the minute, couldn't figure out how to tell him without coming across as a criminal, a thief and someone he wouldn't want to have any more to do with.

She put her guilt on the back burner as they walked out and got in the car. "Walmart okay for some clothes for you?" asked Buck.

"Yes, but I'll have to owe you. I'm temporarily short of cash, ha, ha." she replied. She started making a list in her mind of everything she was going to need.

When they got to the store, they grabbed a cart and headed for the women's clothes section. TA started filling the cart with a new sweatshirt, a pair of jeans, three tees, underwear, socks and a medium weight jacket. Next she headed for the toiletries section and picked up the basics. Turning to Buck she asked "Toothpaste and shampoo?"

"Have those," he replied. "Crest and Suave."

"What flavor Suave?" she asked. TA was picky on her shampoo scent.

"Wild Cherry Blossom," was the reply.

"Right on," she said. Her favorite too.

Buck paid for the purchases and they dumped them in the trunk of the car. When they got in the car he turned to her. "TA, I'd like you to stay at my apartment where I can keep an eye on you. I'm just not comfortable with you being in a motel by yourself. Until this gets cleared up, I'd like to keep you close. It's a small apartment but you can have my room and I'll sleep in my study, there's a futon in there I can use. By the way, the apartment has a washer dryer unit and you can wash those new clothes without having to go out."

TA, looking out through the window, nodded. She was finding it more and more difficult living with her guilty secret. "The apartment's fine, but I don't mind sleeping on the futon." At least she could let him have his bed.

"No, you take the bed. After everything you've been through you need some rest." He started the car and soon they pulled into a modest apartment complex.

They both gathered the bags from the trunk and Buck escorted her into his apartment. It was on the second floor and rather small but immaculately clean.

She threw the dark clothes in the washer and pulling out a pair of clean panties from their package she headed into the bathroom. Stripping, she tossed her dirty clothes out through the door to be added to the wash. As Buck gathered up the soiled laundry she peeked around the door and announced, "I forgot to get a nighty or robe. Do you have anything I could use?"

"How about one of my tees?" he asked.

"Thanks, that should work," she replied. "Just hang it on the door knob, please."

113

CHAPTER 17

SANTA FE

MONDAY, OCTOBER 30, 2000

TA, wearing Buck's tee shirt which came almost to her knees and toweling her hair dry, walked barefoot into the living room. "Well hello," said a strange male voice. She braked so hard her feet slid on the wood floor.

Holding the towel like a bullfighter's cape across her body, ready for a charge, she looked up. Buck was nowhere to be seen but two strange men were lounging on the couch, feet and open pizza box on the coffee table, Bud Lites in their hands, looking at her admiringly. The testosterone in the room was so thick you could cut it with a saber; one of which was leaning casually in the corner of the room.

Pulling her wits together, TA decided to be cool. "How do you do?" she said, at her most coolness. "I'm TA, Titantia Ariel McGovern, Buck's witness houseguest. Who are you two gentlemen?"

They both leapt to their feet and bowed. It was like watching a Tweetle Dee, Tweetle Dum couple from Through the Looking Glass, only these guys were a heck of a lot better looking.

They bowed to her and went into an obviously well-rehearsed spiel: "How do you do? We're the dirty dogs from ARF." They were

114

both over six feet. The slender one indicated his partner, "May I present Demetrius Bean. Call him Tige, but he does not live in a shoe."

With that ambiguous statement he nodded to his friend to continue. The other giant looked like an escaped dark iceberg. He gestured to his buddy and said, "Meet Nathan Hale Murillo, also known as Rin Tin Tin, just call him Rinty." He beamed at her.

Both came around the coffee table and offered their hands. "How do you do Tige and Rinty?" TA responded. She put her hand in the giant hand of Tige. He kissed it with the grace and class of a fifteenth century courtier. Her hand was passed to Rinty, slender and pony-tailed, who bowed deeply and pressed his lips gently to her palm. It tickled.

She backed up and sat in a chair near the door to the bedroom, draping the damp towel modestly over her legs. "OK," she said. "Explain ARF and I know who Rin Tin Tin was but who was Tige and what's with the shoe?"

"ARF" said Tige, "is short for Artifact Recovery Force. It's privately funded but quasi-governmental and set up to recover lost and/or stolen artifacts around the world. We look for any country's artifacts, not just United States. Since the acronym is ARF it stood to reason that the worker bees code names would be the names' of famous dogs. You know Rin Tin Tin but Tige was the name of a dog that was used in advertising Buster Brown shoes back in the 40's. To quote 'I'm Buster Brown, I live in a shoe; this is my dog Tige, he lives there too.' There was a picture of them in the shoe. I kid you not. I picked the name because I liked it. Not many dogs are named after a tiger."

TA digested this information and then got right to the point, "Where's Buck?" she asked.

"He had to go back to the La Fonda to sign some papers and hand off the tapes and stuff to the forensic team. He'll be right back. Want some pizza and a Bud?"

"Sure," she said and added "What's with the saber?" She indicated the sword leaning in the corner.

Rinty got up and retrieved a Bud and a paper towel sheet from the kitchen. He pulled a stool over beside her chair, and added a slice of pizza to her makeshift table. "The saber is a present. Buck collects swords; he's an excellent fencer, by the way. We found it over in Spain when we were there–little bar in Andorra had it hanging above the fireplace. They were redecorating so we bought it. We're trying to bribe him."

TA raised an eyebrow in enquiry.

"We want him to leave the FBI and join us. He'd be a natural and he wouldn't even have to change his nickname."

TA took a bite of pizza and studied them as she chewed. She was totally impressed. She seemed to have fallen into a time warp where all men were large and gorgeous. She swallowed. "What are you doing here, besides trying to bribe Buck?"

Rinty took over the speaking while Tige ate another piece of pizza. "We were in this area and after hearing about the missing maps it seemed like we might be needed. Buck reported to his superiors that you had found two maps at the Gabaldon house and that they were in your La Fonda Hotel room that was cleaned out. He also said that there was another map that you were searching for when Kamakura was shot. Anyway, our boss was notified and so here we are."

TA took another bite of pizza while she thought this over, guilt flooding her entire being. She could hardly swallow the pizza. Boy, do lies and omissions come back to haunt you, she thought. She was choking over this thought when a key was inserted in the door lock and Buck entered.

Buck beamed at her. She had trouble meeting his eye. He turned to Tige and Rinty, "I see you've met," he said.

"Yeah," said Rinty, "we've been explaining that since the dirty dogs from ARF have arrived, she has nothing to fear. We'll sniff out the maps and all will soon be found." He smiled smugly.

116

Tige saluted him with his half-eaten-pizza slice and swallowing, he asked, "Want a beer?"

Buck was opening his mouth to answer when his cell phone rang. He raised a hand in a 'minute' gesture and grabbed the phone. "Doe here." He said and listened. The caller had quite a bit to say before Buck answered with "OK, be there as soon as we can." He hung up.

He turned to all of them and announced, "That was Chief Lujan. The car has been found in somebody's back forty over in La Cienega. That's an artists' colony off I-25 just south of Santa Fe. I guess they thought the country was pretty empty there and no one would notice. The land owner's dogs noticed and he called the police. They're waiting for us before they open it but they think the body is in the trunk, at least the dogs think it is."

TA jumped up. "It'll only take a minute for me to get dressed." She turned toward the bedroom door.

"Wait," said Buck. "You stay here and get some rest. You have a concussion remember. You don't need to go running around. We'll go check it out and look for the two maps you found and maybe the other map you were looking for. Anyway, we'll be back soon enough. I promise you won't be missing anything except maybe a dead body. Get some rest and in the morning you might be needed to identify Kamakura."

"Wouldn't it be more efficient for me to go identify him right away," suggested TA.

"Probably," he replied, "but it's not going to happen. Get some sleep and we'll be back soon." He thought for a minute and turned to Tige and Rinty. "Let's take your car, it's bigger and I want to leave TA with transportation just in case something comes up." He turned back to TA. "Here are the car keys," he put them on the counter. "And twenty dollars just-in-case. The car is filled. You're not supposed to take it unless some emergency happens." The men trooped out the door leaving TA standing there with several unspoken but spicy words trembling on her lips.

TA stamped into the bedroom and seeing her clean clothes piled in a basket she sorted and folded and laid some out for the next day. By the time she was through with that chore she had calmed down enough to consider going to bed. She returned to the living room and picked up the unused beer and the empty pizza box and took them to the kitchen. She checked the front door lock, leaving the safety chain swinging free so Buck and his buddies could get back in, she was heading into the bedroom when the saber caught her eye. The loose security chain made her nervous enough to grab the sword for protection. She switched off the lights and retreated to the bedroom. Leaning the sword up against the wall at the head of the bed she climbed in, sure she wouldn't sleep. She switched off the bedside light and tried to relax.

She woke several hours later when she heard a noise at the front door. Leaping up, she pulled on her jeans with one hand and grabbing her bra and tee shirt with the other as she started across the room, finishing dressing as she went.

She paused inside the bedroom door, listening intently. It didn't sound right. That wasn't a key sound; the lock was being jimmied. The door opened but the lights didn't come on. She quietly drifted back to the bed and grabbing the sword she returned to the doorway. Peeking around the door frame she could see just enough from the outside ambient light. There was a dark figure moving across the room and through a streak of light that filtered in from the slightly opened curtain. He was dressed entirely in black and wore a black hood. Oh God, she thought. It's a ninja. I swear it's a ninja.

A tiny beam of light was suddenly switched on in the living room. The ninja had a flashlight. He was sweeping around the apartment looking for something. The map, she thought. They know I have it because they saw it when I was running. They're looking for the map.

Okay she thought. SCREAM! She did.

The ninja reacted by leaping across the floor. Unfortunately he went toward her, not away. She moved back into the middle of the bedroom. "Get out!" she screamed. He didn't. She crouched, as he came into the room, and extending the sword she spun in a half circle. All her body motion was in the sword as it struck his thigh and sank into the bone. He let out a howl and threw himself back; ricocheting off the bedroom doorframe he hobbled across the living room, out the front door and was gone.

She vaulted across the room hitting the light switch with one hand and shoving the door closed with the other. She latched the safety chain and then pulled a kitchen chair across the room and jammed it under the knob.

Her feet felt sticky and looking down discovered she was walking in a blood puddle. Yich! She half hopped using one dry foot and her clean heel on the other foot and made it into the kitchen. She leaned up against the sink while she washed off her bloody foot.

While scrubbing, her mind was spinning through options, she had to get that map and she didn't think she had time to wait for Buck to get back. She'd call Buck and tell him to get back here. Wait. No phone. Shit! Okay. She'd take the car and retrieve the map and then come back here to the apartment. She'd leave a note telling him where she had gone and maybe they could hook up along the way.

She went to his computer printer and slid a sheet of paper out. Sitting at his desk she wrote him a note:

A ninja broke into the apartment. I hit him in the leg with the sword and he left. I didn't tell you everything when we talked. I had the map in its case with me when Kamakura got killed. It's in the deer pit. I'm going to go get the map and I'll bring it here. I wasn't going to keep the map but I wanted to see it and I thought if I told you or the police that you'd take the map away before I could see it. Sorry. Dumb move, but I really, really wanted to see it. TA.

She took the note into the living room and put it on the coffee table with a can of unopened soup from the cupboard to hold it down. She pulled the coffee table into the middle of the room so the table and note would be the first thing that would be seen when the men entered.

She pulled on shoes and jacket and discovered she had overlooked buying a purse. She tucked Buck's money and keys in her pocket and then found a paring knife. She wrapping it in pizza cardboard she stuck it in her pocket. The saber was too noticeable to take.

Going out the door, she threw the lock and pulled it closed. It wouldn't latch. After experimenting, she ended by tying the inside door handle with string, and fastening it to a kitchen chair wedged under the outside door handle. The door stayed shut.

In the car, seatbelt on, she turned the key and inspected dials and levers. Impressive! Backing out carefully, she put the car in forward and shot into the road.

CHAPTER 18

NORTHERN NEW MEXICO

TUESDAY, OCTOBER 31, 2000

The car was a charmer, lovely to handle and if asked, TA would have said it was eager to please. She was through Santa Fe and on the now familiar road headed toward Los Alamos.

The sun was just beginning to appear over the mountains as she came to the last stretch of road before the turnoff. To avoid awkward questions by the police guarding the caves, she'd have to park out by the road and cut across through the woods. There was a narrow pull off, small, but with enough room to accept the car and hide its front end in behind a squatty pinion tree. She got out of the car and set off through the trees in what she hoped was the correct direction to the deer pit

The sun was just tipping over the horizon and it was still dark enough to be rough going, even with the flashlight. Stumbling along through the forest, tripping and catching herself as she kicked rocks and rebounded off trees, she finally came out into a clear area. She saw the cut between the cliffs over to her right. "Thank you God," she said aloud.

She crossed the clearing, climbed over the swirls of flattened rock and walked through the cut. There it was. She could see the tumbleweeds ahead.

She approached carefully and was soon standing on the edge of the pit. Off to the side she spied tumbled scree at the base of one of the cliffs and walked over to inspect it. Ahh, a bunch of squarish rocks that weren't so large she couldn't handle them; a case of Goldilocks, not too big, not too small, but just right.

She selected the rocks she needed and carried them to the pit and pitched them in. The sun was well up and lighting her work area by the time she was ready to descend. This was probably the scariest part of the whole operation. If she fell, she would be in serious trouble. Nobody knew she was here except Buck--if he had received her note.

Oh, well, nothing ventured, nothing gained. She sat and swung her legs over the side and paused. It isn't going to work. She pulled herself back from the edge and peered down. It was about a five foot drop to the bottom of the pit.

Okay, time to rethink. She sat looking around the edges of the pit. The far side was lower. Walking over to it she sat, rolled to her stomach and carefully lowered herself over the edge. Her feet dangled free. She let go and fell. It was only a short drop to the bottom. She was standing in tumbleweeds and if she stood on her tippy toes she could see over pit's edge.

She turned and plowed over to the spot where she had left the map case. Yes, it's there. She gave it a hug before reaching up and setting it on the ground outside the pit. She set to work moving her flat rocks into a balanced pile

She stepped to the top of her rock pile and tried pulling herself up over the edge. Not easy. She stepped down and clearing a path to the far wall. Turning, she ran as fast as she could in the limited

122

space, mounted the rocks and threw her upper body over the edge of the pit. It worked. She ate dust but most of her body was lying outside the pit. She scrabbled the rest of the way and stood up.

Grabbing the case she headed back to the car.

CHAPTER 19

NORTHERN NEW MEXICO

TUESDAY, OCTOBER 31, 2000

At the car, she placed the case carefully on the passenger seat, belted it in, gave it a pat, and turned the key. As she looked back over her shoulder, preparing to back out on the highway and turn around, she saw a black car coming up on her. She ducked. After it passed she backed and turned around.

In her rear view mirror she was horrified to see the car that had just passed her turned also. She accelerated but it was right on her bumper. She couldn't see who was driving but she was sure of one thing. This wasn't good. The ninja had a buddy--and here he was.

She headed toward the Rio Grande Bridge, crossed it, came to a straight stretch of road and pressed the accelerator to the floorboard. Mistake! The car sped up so rapidly that it fish-tailed. She got it under control and took a fast glance in the rearview mirror. The car behind her had dropped back slightly, probably from a sense of self-preservation. But he was still there. She kept her speed up and tried to keep her eyes on the road and not look in the rearview mirror. She was going much faster than felt comfortable. She needed all her attention on the road.

124

What to do? Where to go? Where was safe? Her mind raced as she tried to think, the landscape zipping back in her peripheral vision. She needed to find Buck. Anyone else would want an explanation and that would take too long. She'd probably be dead long before the whole explanation was out and the person she was telling it to would be dead also.

Buck was on the other side of Santa Fe and surely she would remember the name of the settlement when she saw the road sign. She came to Pojoaque and turned right onto I-25 South, back toward Santa Fe. There was more traffic on the freeway and she reduced her speed to accommodate the driving conditions. Looking in the mirror she saw the black ninja car-- as she thought of it--take up a position behind her. Weaving through traffic, eye out for police, she soon came to the by-pass road that circled the side of Santa Fe. It was fairly straight and she could see traffic conditions well enough to speed up. The ninja car stayed with her.

Just past Santa Fe the by-pass rejoined the main highway and glancing back she discovered the following car had been joined by two others.

Her pursuer stayed behind her, practically sitting on her rear bumper, while a white one pulled up beside her on the inside lane and the third, tan, came up beside her on her right. A road sign flashing by that read "La Cienega." That was the town that Buck said they were going to, but there was no way to turn in. She was blocked.

On they went, the cluster of cars creating a traffic hazard for other cars. She tried slowing down but they matched her speed and maintained their positions.

A large semi came up from behind and loomed over all of them. The blocking cars didn't budge. It blasted its air horn. The car on the inside accelerated and slipped into the lane in front of her. The truck passed and she pulled in behind, riding in the truck's slipstream.

Her mind worked feverishly trying to make an escape plan. If she exited and got into a town they would have to fall back but there were no towns. The only turnoffs were to Pueblos that were a distance from the highway leaving plenty of space for them to force her off the road. She had passed a casino on the other side of the highway but the exit cut under the freeway and emptied into a gas station and parking lot. She could envision herself careening off parked cars. She'd have an accident and the ninjas in the chase cars, the enemy, would be on her in an instant.

She saw a large sign announcing the towns of Bernalillo and Placitas. Bernalillo was to the right and Placitas back across to the left. Bernalillo it was. She'd pull off at the last moment and drive into downtown Bernalillo.

She tried not to give any indication of her plan. As they approached she accelerated, cut in front of the car on her right and dove down the off ramp. They remained with her and the car on her right pulled up close enough to block her right turn. She looked at the driver as he executed the smooth move. He was Asian, his face expressionless.

She had just a moment to react. She spun the steering wheel to the left and was suddenly on her way to an invisible town called Placitas. She accelerated and went shooting up a hill and onto a narrow two-lane road.

She drove along the tight road, pines and shrubs hanging over the edge, houses scattered off each side. When she arrived in Placitas she discovered it was just a patch of buildings, some deserted, a bar and then she was at the end of the town and in open country. A road sign informed her she was on the way to Sandia Crest.

The Crest flashed into her mind. Top of the Sandia Mountains, overlooked Albuquerque and there was a restaurant and a tram that operated year round. In the winter it carried skiers and in the fall and summer it took tourists and hikers up and down the mountain. The tram was a glass-sided box that could hold quite a few standing people that ohhed and ahhed over the magnificent scenery and wildlife. The only other thing she could remember about it from when she was a teen were the fossil sea shells on the top of the 10,000 foot mountain that had risen from sea level over hundreds of millions of years.

Well, the Crest it is. She checked the rearview mirror and saw that her contingent was still following. She didn't know cars very well but it seemed that her BMW was going to be better at getting around mountain curves than the other cars.

She flashed past a picnic area and then another. As she rose in altitude, the pines became interspersed with yellowing aspens. Occasionally she caught a glimpse through the trees of the valley below. There were no cars descending. The road was empty except for the cars following. The drivers behind must have noticed the absence of witnesses also because she heard a ping and realized the passive chasers had become aggressive. They were shooting at her.

A road sign denoted curves ahead. She sped up; whirled around a sharp turn and into another and saw a third still ahead.

The road continued to climb, the trailing cars sped up also and as she entered a switch back she saw one stop and the door opening. The Beamer whirled through the curve and came back out into view of one car lower down. It had stopped and there was someone leaning against it supporting a rifle that was aimed at her. Her passenger side window shattered and the bullet exited through the canvas roof.

Bump, bump. She had run out of pavement and was on a bulldozed road. Well, the Beamer could take curves but she sure hoped the bulldozer had cleared off any major rocks bigger than an egg!

She spun through another sharp curve and noticed there were no more guardrails. No pavement, no guardrails. She accelerated a bit more and was delighted to hear a distant squeal of brakes and a loud crash. One down, two to go.

Suddenly there was a pickup coming down the road toward her; innocently descending into a fire fight. Then it passed and she strained to hear if one her followers fired a shot. She couldn't hear anything but the Beamer's motor and the slipstream from the broken window.

The road widened and became paved. Suddenly there was a stop sign pointing right to the Crest and left to I-40 and Albuquerque. Unfortunately left was miles longer. Right, the Crest, was considerably nearer and there would be people. She chose the Crest as the remaining two chase cars came into view.

She pulled away from the stop sign, her tenacious entourage following, and headed upward to the top of the mountain. Paved road, lots of switchbacks and soon she was driving through extended parking lots with a few scattered parked cars.

TA could see the Crest Restaurant and the tram-loading platform above her. People that wanted to use either of them or to take in the magnificent view had to park in the car lot and walk up. At the end of the lot was a service road, blocked by a wide metal swinging gate secured by a chain. There was a man unlocking the chain for a garbage truck waiting to exit.

She floored the accelerator as the gate swung open and drove through. She squeaked around the side of the waiting truck and rushed up the remaining road to the tram platform.

As she parked and prepared to get out, she heard gunshots. Squatting between the open door and the car side she peeked around the end of the car. The gunman in the lead chase car had shot the gatekeeper. Both cars proceeded through the gate and the lead car drove around the truck. The truck driver went into action and pulled forward into the second car.

She had thought that if she managed to get to people she would be safe. Obviously not. She leaned into the car and gathered up the map case. The darn thing was so heavy. She jammed it down through the neck of her sweat shirt and into the top of her jeans and then squatted by the far side of the car. As the remaining chase car pulled up, she leapt up and started running toward the crest.

CHAPTER 20

SANDIA MOUNTAINS

TUESDAY, OCTOBER 31, 2000

There was a group of people gathered at the edge of the escarpment, setting up hang-gliders. This might be her answer. She knew how to hang-glide. It had been a few years but she had learned as a teen and loved it. She ran toward them, conscious of heavy breathing coming up behind her; suddenly the sound stopped.

She risked a glance over her shoulder. The man chasing her had stopped and was leaning forward with his hands on his knees. The gun was still in his hand but he was puffing so heavily it was doubtful he would have been able to aim it accurately. The high altitude had caught up with him.

She merged with the hang-glider crowd. There was a pile of equipment stacked in the middle of the group. Evidently she had entered a club of hang-glider enthusiasts. She helped herself to a helmet and simple harness and slid into the equipment as she sidled up to the front of the line. A hang-glider had just been readied for a rider. It was perched at the edge of the cliff like some brightly colored triangular moth, nose pointing to earth, straps hanging down from its belly, the back edge pointing up toward the sky. As she reached for it she heard a shot and then two more. The people

129

around her threw themselves to the ground, shouting. She didn't hear any screams of agony, so she guessed no one had been hit.

She squatted and slid under the glider. Pulling the Velcro straps on the harness she was wearing, she frantically tried to tighten them. It was loose enough for her to turn and hook the carabiner clip to the glider straps; not a good thing to be so loose. All the harness straps should be tight. She felt a bullet whiz by her head and saw a tiny hole appear in the glider fabric.

No time to tighten straps. She stood and balancing the glider, she took two running steps and was off the escarpment and heading down toward the tall pine trees below.

Her memories and reflexes took over and she managed to aim in a more level trajectory. Following the mountain's contours, down she swooped toward the plains below, and as she glided she felt the map case slide out of her sweatshirt, past her cheek and it was gone, shooting like a missile down into the Ponderosa pines that clustered below.

She felt the glider jerk slightly and, looking up she saw a guideline flapping loose and another bullet hole in the wing. She couldn't see behind her. Glancing sideways she saw the tram rising toward her from the terminal at the foot of the mountains. If she could follow the tram lines down it might be possible to land at the terminal and she'd call the FBI. The police were probably already on their way.

Again she tried to look back. There should be a sister tram sliding down from the restaurant on the Crest. They traveled, one from the top and one from the bottom on two separate sets of lines, passing on either side of each of the two towers.

She maneuvered the lines and bar and was pleased to see the nose of the glider responding to her directions. Some of her skills were still there and the detached line hadn't caused too much damage. As she was congratulating herself she suddenly saw one of the tram towers right in her path. Maneuvering the nose of the glider up in a steep ascent she found herself slipping from the loose harness. Her feet dangling, almost standing in air, she was carried toward the tall tower. The glider moved more slowly because of the braking power of its almost upright position. She crashed into the cross arm near the top of the tower and frantically transferred her arms and upper body to the tower's arm, constricted fingers releasing the loose harness which slid off and hung limply as the glider hit the edge of the pole, teetered for a moment and then sliding along the side of the tower it pulled free and floated gracefully down on the tram's guide wires.

TA, hung on for dear life, arms and legs embracing the towers giant arm. She watched the glider slide majestically along the wires, looking like a paper airplane made of brightly colored wrapping paper. For a moment she thought it would collide with the rising tram, but as it came to the bottom of the wire's curve it slowed, paused, and then slowly tilted to the right, hanging for one breathless moment before it fell, spinning gently, colors flashing, and disappeared into a tree-filled ravine.

She lay lengthwise along the tall cross arm, legs and arms frantically pressing tightly against the metal, balancing precariously above the rocks many feet below.

She glanced up, the first gondola car of the day was ascending from the tram station and proceeding in stately indifference toward the Crest. The cable on which it rode was directly below her feet.

Holding on tightly, she turned slightly and twisted her head just enough to see the descending gondola coming down from the crest. She couldn't believe what she was seeing and she didn't want to. There was a man standing upright on the roof of the descending gondola. He was actually dressed in black, like a TV ninja including the face mask. This was impossible. She had definitely disabled the ninja that was at the apartment. Two? America was invaded. He must have been in one of the cars that had followed her.

Clutching her perch, she watched in horror as he raised his arm and threw something at her. It glistened in the sunlight as it rotated toward her. She had nowhere to go, nowhere to hide as it flashed past her cringing nose and hit the top of the tower crosspiece she was hugging.

The ascending gondola was approaching. As it passed under her, she released her hold and slid with a whining scream, down onto the roof passing beneath. Her feet hit the roof and she threw herself forward, grabbing for protrusions frantically as she started to slide. She was stopped by something sticking up from the slick surface and she grabbed it. She lay motionless, spread-eagled, trying to become one with the roof. Her cheek was resting on the gondola's metal sheaving, her white-knuckled hands locked to the edge of a trap door that led into the car below.

Not thinking, just acting, she worked her right hand over to the latch and popped it up. The door lifted slightly, and she flipped it up, nearly sliding off as she raised it, pinching her left hand where it was holding on at the hinge. "Sheesh!"

She reached forward and hooked her hands on the edge, pulling herself along until she was looking down into the gondola. There were three openmouthed tourists peering up at her.

"Hi!" she said as she pulled her legs up and awkwardly started to descend. Legs dangling, hands holding the edge of the door, she glanced back and saw the ninja throw another disc. It seemed to spin in slow motion as it sparkled in the sunlight, looking like a shining pirana aiming right at her.

She released her grip on the sides of the door and crashed to the floor of the gondola. Lying there she looked up and saw the disc sticking in the edge of the trap door. Jumping up, she ran to the window of the car and threw a finger at him.

He was standing on the other gondola and when he saw her gesture he threw his arms above his head in frustration. Like Rumplestiltskin, he stamped his feet and like Rumplestiltskin, it was his undoing. His foot hit the edge of the roof and over he went, plummeting down, splayed and whirling as if practicing some macabre kung fu exercise. He hit the trees, landing on the tip of one giant pine. It bent sharply under his weight and then sprang upright, catapulting his body upward again, over and over, arms and legs bending independently, and then down, growing tinier as her gondola continued its steady ascent up the mountain face. He disappeared from her view.

CHAPTER 21

ALBUQUERQUE, SANDIA TRAIL

TUESDAY, OCTOBER 31, 2000

Herbie Quintana, 17, AWOL from the Albuquerque Academy, was sitting by La Luz Trail, just below Sandia Crest. A Slim Jim hung rakishly from the side of his mouth as he rummaged in the depths of his backpack, looking for an errant apple, when he heard a crack and a rustle coming from the top of the Ponderosa pine that he was leaning against. Looking up through the branches he could just make out the shape of a dark cylinder twisting its way down through the branches. With a last snap it dropped onto the backpack in his lap.

Herbie was the crowning glory of his large extended family of high achievers, straight A's, quarterback, captain of the debate team. He had been fast tracking on a predetermined path to law and politics but at twelve Herbie had mapped out his own chosen path. He had loved fossils since he was three and was taken to the Natural History Museum in Albuquerque's Old Town. He spent his summer at digs in various parts of New Mexico, Wyoming, and Utah.

"It builds up the old muscles, and introduces him to grass roots areas of our country," said his parents. Seeing politics in his future, they always made sure he had some political and legal textbooks to take with him. Herbie always dutifully read the books, knowing he would be quizzed on their contents when he returned, bronzed and muscled, to his home. He also borrowed the leader's reference books and memorized them too.

This Tuesday morning Herbie had packed a lunch, put a few things in the back of his Mustang, and kissed his folks goodbye, but instead of heading to school he drove to the Crest with plans to prospect for fossils along the hiking trail. He also planned to do some heavy thinking about how to break the news of his choice of schools; dumping Harvard and law and embracing Virginia Tech and paleontology.

With the landing thump, schools and fossils flew out of his mind. "Holy Shit!" He looked up through the tree but saw only blue sky. He had heard nothing before it hit the tree.

The cylinder was beautiful; a cap with a tiny soaring eagle. There was an etched design around the sides of the cap and looking closely he saw that the central band and the bottom cap had etchings too. It wasn't light enough, under the trees to see exactly what was incised. He tilted it over to a streak of sunshine and gasped. Animals, there were tiny animals etched into gold. He tried to open it. The ends were tightly stuck. He gathered up snacks and stuffed them back in his pack, hooked the rock pick to his belt loop and, cradling the cylinder in his arm, as he climbed back up the trail.

He wondered what to do with this beautiful thing that had dropped in his lap. He knew he couldn't keep it, but thought he could take it home and check it out. Maybe he could get it open and see what was inside. He wondered who to call to report finding it; police, UNM, or the Park Service, since this is Park land?

The rest of the climb was taken up with rationalizing why it couldn't be returned to the "proper authorities" immediately.

As he approached the parking area he saw lights flashing through the trees. His path led him into the open where official cars were parked everywhere. Uniformed men, State Police and Park Department personnel were moving busily around intermingling with men in dark suits, clothing not usually seen on the mountain top.

Identifying the suited men as FBI, Herbie withdrew into the trees and watched as a covered body was brought up over the cliff edge on a stretcher by more official people, this time dressed in the uniforms of rescue personnel.

Instead of making Herbie's choice of which authority to notify easier, it had suddenly become much more difficult. First and foremost was his overwhelming desire to inspect the tube more closely. Considering all ramifications of just walking into the midst of all this activity was dizzying and picking out which law enforcement group to approach was more so. He felt as if he might be sacrificing himself to a feeding frenzy of competing arms of the law. That the cylinder was part of all this activity was obvious but his desire to keep it was overwhelming.

He decided to take it home until things calmed down and the authorities had enough time to appreciate it; justifying to himself that he would call the FBI by 9:00 pm that evening. He picked the FBI because they obviously were at the top of the heap.

Decision made, he stripped off his jacket and wrapped the cylinder in it. He casually held it under one arm and strolled into the parking lot. He paused for a moment and looked about with innocent interest, making sure he was noticed by a few police; just a kid coming back from a hike.

He walked to his car, threading in and out of official and tourist vehicles and walking on the periphery of the activity. Once he got to the car he opened the trunk and took out his picnic blanket. He wrapped the jacket covered cylinder lovingly in the blanket and tucked it at the back of the trunk. Closing the trunk, he stood for a moment and surveyed the parking lot; just a kid interested in what was going on.

Herbie opened the driver's door and paused to pose and peer. Satisfied that he had been noticed and dismissed, he got in and drove back to Albuquerque.

CHAPTER 22

THE QUINTANA HOME

TUESDAY, OCTOBER 31, 2000

A frustrated Herbie was sitting on his bed, the cylinder in his lap. He had tried opening it by twisting and turning, pulling and pushing. Nothing worked. Nine o'clock, his self-imposed deadline for calling the FBI and confessing, was approaching and he had nothing to show for his efforts. He had had visions of calling the FBI and casually asking if someone had lost a beautiful antique cylinder that had a wonderful – fill in the blank – inside. The vision was disappearing and a new one was beginning to materialize that involved handcuffs and being arrested for interfering with an ongoing murder investigation. It was a murder case, he had decided, because one, there was a body and two this case, cylinder, tube, whatever, was so fucking gorgeous that it was obviously worth killing over.

His bedroom door flew open and his sister, Ruthy, walked in. She was carrying a basketball and tossing it from one hand to the other. Ten years old, obnoxious, bossy, cute and self-assured, the apple of everyone's eye, she had come to check on Herbie before getting ready for bed.

"Whatcha doin', Herbie-berbie?" she asked. "Want to shoot a few hoops before bedtime?" She punctuated her request by throwing the ball at his head. Instead of catching it, as he usually did, he dove sideways, clutching the cylinder in protective arms. The ball bounced off the wall behind him and ricocheted down, hitting the cylinder square on the cap. The cylinder flew from his arms and hit the carpet, the ball continuing on, ricocheting off his desk lamp and knocking it to the floor. Herbie rolled the rest of the way off the mattress and reached for the cylinder. As he gathered it up, the cap fell off and rolled under the bed.

He sat, legs spread, arms wrapped around the cylinder, thinking, oh wow, oh wow. Ruthy sprang across the room, "Sorry, sorry, sorry!" she said. "I thought you'd catch it. Are you all right? Did I hurt that thing?" She indicated the cylinder as she hovered over him.

"What is that, anyway? Where did you get it? Let me see." She knelt beside him and then crawled forward, under the bed and came out with the cap in her hands. "Criminy, this is pretty. What is it? Let me see the rest. Where did you get it?"

"Quiet," said Herbie in a whisper. "The folks will hear you." He laid the cylinder across his lap and peered inside. It was easy to see in because his desk lamp was lying on its side by his leg and it was shining directly down the tube.

"Holy Moley, wow." He was looking at gold. A roll of gold. He reached in and pulled on it gently. It was loose but his fingers were too large to get a good grip. He tilted it with the open end down and shook carefully. It didn't fall out. "Here, Ruthy," he said in a whisper, breathless with excitement. "Be very careful. Try to work it free. Gently, gently. Don't let it bend." He laid it out along the edge of the bed with the open end pointing at her.

Holding her breath, Ruthy bent forward and slid her fingers into the tube and pulled on the roll of gold. About three inches slid out and then it caught. She twisted it slightly and it slid easily out onto the rumpled spread.

"Oh," she said. For once, Ruthy was speechless. They knelt at the side of the bed looking at a roll of gold that was almost as thin as paper. It was approximately as long as the cylinder that it had been in and seemed to be several layers thick.

Herbie pushed the cylinder across the bed out of the way and turning the roll of gold he gingerly tried to unroll it. It didn't want to unroll. He sat back on his heels, frustrated. "Wait," said Ruthy. She rose and rushed from the room.

He heard her running down the hall and in a moment she returned carrying two long knitting needles. She knelt beside him and inserted the long plastic needles just under the edge of the roll, one from either side and slowly lifted them. The end edge of the roll lifted.

"Now," she said, "straighten the bedspread as tight as you can and then put on some gloves. You aren't supposed to touch artifacts with bare hands. Try unrolling the tube away from the needles while I hold the edge down." He looked at her in amazement. His little sister never ceased to astound him. He went over to his desk and dug around in the chemicals he used when working on fossils and found a box of rubber gloves.

Pulling on the gloves, he carefully unrolled the tube. Soon it was lying spread across his mattress close to the side of his bed. He picked up two pillows and used them to hold down the two end edges of the gold. He and Ruthy were looking at a sheet of gold as thin as a heavy sheet of paper and perhaps two feet wide and over a yard long. His bedside lamp was on, as was the room's top light and with their illumination he could at last see what had been in the cylinder,

A map. A beautiful, detailed map. It looked like it was of the California coast and then inward stretching past the Grand Canyon, showing the Colorado and Rio Grande Rivers. The map pictured as far east as the great lakes and as far north as lower Canada. There was a lot of writing along the edges and in empty places in the corners. The writing was in Chinese, ancient Chinese.

Ruthy was bent over the writing and haltingly translating. He leaned down beside her and together they manage to decipher the first few words. "The Most Exalted and far seeing General Zheng He, under orders from Zhu Di Emperor of the Great Dynasty of the Ming, ordered five ships to sail West past the…"

They stopped reading and turned toward each other. Herbie spoke first, "We never should have unrolled this, we might have damaged it. I need to call the FBI and turn it in and we need to get hold of Professor Chan so he can read it. And then," he paused and looked at Ruthy, "we need to tell Mom and Dad."

Ruthy gave him a sisterly look, "What do you mean; *we* need to tell Mom and Dad? I never saw this thing until half an hour ago." She paused and took on the poor little child look she had been working on for nine of her ten years, and continued. "I just helped you unroll the map. "

Herbie gave a brotherly sigh that he had been working on for nine of his sister's ten years. He turned to the phone and picking it up he dialed information and soon had the local FBI office on the line.

"You have reached the Federal Bureau of Investigation, how may I direct your call, came an automated voice."

"Huh," suddenly tongue-tied and brain dead, he paused. Regaining speech, "I was up on the Crest today and I found an old cylinder." He gave his name and home phone number. Hanging up he sat watching the phone, waiting for it to ring. It remained silent.

He turned to Ruthy who was also watching the phone intently. "Go brush your teeth and get ready for bed. I promise to call you if the phone rings." She gave him a disgusted look and reluctantly got up and left the room.

He decided to follow his own advice and, leaving the map spread across the bed he went into his bathroom and grabbed his toothbrush. He was just applying toothpaste when the phone rang.

141

"Ruthy," he called as he dove across the room and grabbed his phone. She came thundering down the hall, foaming at the mouth, toothbrush forgotten in her hand.

"Hello," he said, as he picked up the phone. To his horror, he could hear his father on the phone in the kitchen, also answering.

"Is this the Herbie Quintana residence? a male voice asked.

"Among others," replied his father in a frosty tone. He didn't believe in late evening callers.

"This is agent John Doe, Federal Bureau of Investigation; may I please speak to Herbie Quintana?"

There was a pause, and in a voice that had ice cycles hanging from every letter, his father replied, "This is Frank Quintana, Herbie Quintana's father, may I ask why you wish to speak to my son?"

A pause from the other end of the line and then the agent spoke in an equally ice laden voice. "Yes, he called in relation to an ongoing investigation. It is in regard to an incident that happened on Sandia Crest today."

Herbie's father, quick-thinking attorney, didn't miss a beat. "Is this about the murder that was reported on TV this evening? Just a moment, I will consult with my son."

At this point, Herbie spoke. "Dad, Mr. Doe, I'm here. Mr. Doe, my dad doesn't know anything about what I called you about. He thought I was in school. Dad, I skipped classes today and went up to the Crest. I have information for Mr. Doe. Mr. Doe, a cylinder fell out of the sky and landed in my lap. I brought it home. I know I should have tried to turn it in earlier but it was so beautiful, and I wanted to see what was inside. Anyway, it's all right and I have it here at the house. I could bring it by tomorrow or you could come and get it and the map now."

"How do you know it has a map in it?" asked Buck.

"It's a beautiful map of the California coast and east to the Great Lakes," replied Herbie. "And," he added, "it's gold."

"What?" You opened it? Is it damaged?" The anger in Buck's voice was enough to make Herbie's father step in.

"My son is very responsible. Before you start making threats I suggest you get over here and inspect this map and cylinder, map case, whatever the item is." He gave explicit directions on how to get to the house and then, without waiting for a reply, he hung up. It would have been a more decisive gesture if Herbie hadn't been listening in from another phone thus leaving the line open between Buck and Herbie.

"I'm really sorry, sir, it all sort of "just happened." I don't think anything is damaged."

"We'll be right there," replied Buck. "But before I hang up, what did you mean the map is gold?"

"Someone took gold and rolled it into a thin sheet and used it to write on, well, they incised it, would probably be correct. I guess they didn't have paper. There is a lot of writing on it describing who ordered the trip. It was from the time of the Great Dynasty of the Ming and Emperor Zhu Di and Admiral Zheng He were calling the shots."

"What? It's Japanese, they sound Chinese. How do you know, anyway? Surely you must be mistaken."

"No, what made you think it was Japanese? It's written in ancient Chinese – well from around 1400, I think. At least that's when Admiral Zheng He and Emperor Zhu Di were around. Anyway, to answer your question, we study Chinese from Professor Chan-- my sister and I, that is. I plan to go to Mongolia and China and it seemed best to find a Chinese tutor.

"Look," he continued. "This is a school night and I need to get to bed. We can talk when you get here. Besides, the map's spread across my bed and I think it would be best if you re-rolled it. Anyway, please get over here now. Thanks," he finished, remembering his manners.

Herbie hung up the phone and noticed Ruthy plucking at his arm, her back to him. She was facing the bedroom door. He turned around. Both his parents were standing in the doorway and the looks he was receiving were definitely not friendly.

Following the principle that "one picture is worth a thousand words" he gestured toward his bed. "Look," he said. Their eyes followed his gesture and both took a involuntary step toward the bed. The map, glinting softly in the ceiling light, was stunning.

"My God, Herbie. Where did you get this?" his father said. Both Herbie's parents moved reverently forward.

"It's like I told that FBI agent. I was sitting under a tree up near the Crest and it fell down through the tree branches and landed in my lap. Luckily I was holding my backpack in my lap or I might be talking to you in a soprano. It landed with quite a clunk. "

Herbie's mother interrupted him, "Are you all right?"

"Yes."

She continued speaking, "Then would you be so good as to explain to us what you were doing up on the mountain when you were supposed to be in school?"

"Uhhh, I needed to think. I guess now isn't the time to talk about it, but I wanted to sort out what I really want to do with my life. Maybe we could talk about it? Now doesn't seem like a good time--with the FBI coming over is the time."

Frank Quintana gave Herbie the "exasperated parent" look, "Herbie, you know you can talk to us anytime, but" his humor coming to the fore, "the announcement that you need to talk could have come at a better time."

Naomi broke in, "Ruthy, you look like you have rabies, go finish your teeth and get a robe. Yes, you may stay up." She turned to Herbie. "Get your teeth brushed while you're waiting." She turned to her husband, "I'm going to make coffee and put out some cookies." She left the room.

144

Ruthy left to rinse, Herbie to brush and Frank stood, hands behind his back in the "don't touch" stance of a five-year-old, leaning over the map.

The doorbell rang. The FBI must have broken every traffic law in the book.

CHAPTER 23

THE QUINTANA HOME

TUESDAY, OCTOBER 31, 2000

The whole household, Frank, Naomi, Herbie, and Ruthy arrived at the front door simultaneously. When the door was opened they were greeted by a group of tall people.

First in the door was a slender young woman, who shook each of their hands enthusiastically and murmured her name, which sounded to Frank's astounded ears like TA McGovern.

Next each of the men introduced themselves and also shook hands. However the man named Nathan Hale Murillo, instead of shaking hand with Naomi and Ruthy, bowed and kissed their hands. Ruthy giggled.

Herbie led the whole group back to his room. His parents stayed in the hall within earshot but the rest of them crowded into the bedroom where the map glowed across the bed.

Everyone froze. It was a magnificent sight. The whole room seemed to shimmer in the warm color. TA gave a gasp and approached slowly. She reached in her purse and pulled out gloves and a magnifying glass and then, dropping the purse to the floor, she bent over the bed.

"Ohhhh, it's so beautiful. Look, here's Morrow Bay and there's San Pablo Bay and San Francisco Bay. How accurate. Here are the Sierra Nevada Mountains."

She moved on across the map, naming landmarks and exclaiming in wonder as she went. She pointed out Sequoia trees, Joshua trees and tiny herds of animals incised on the plains and when she came to the area of what is now eastern California and southern Utah, she stopped in amazement.

"There's the Colorado River." Her finger traced eastward. "And the Grand Canyon. Over here is the Rio Grande and it runs right through the area where the map was found. It shows pueblos!" She looked up and laughed in delight. "This is amazing."

Frank cleared his throat and spoke, "It's very late and this is exciting but we have two children that need to go to bed, so perhaps we could continue this tomorrow at your offices?"

"Oh, sorry," TA apologized, "I completely forgot where we are. I'll get this map rolled up and put away and we can give you back your house." She turned to the map and carefully removed the two pillows that were holding the ends down. With a bit of urging it rolled up in a loose roll, much too large to fit back in the map case.

TA turned to Naomi, "Do you have a box or something that we could transport this in? I don't want to try to roll it back to its original shape. I'll return anything we use."

"I think I have the perfect thing," Naomi said. "I'll be right back." She turned and disappeared down the hall and returned in a few moments carrying a large turkey roaster complete with lid. Several dish towels were draped over her arm.

She set the roaster on the end of the bed, removed the rack, and lined the pan with a large clean terry dish towel. TA deposited the map in the pan. It fit beautifully. They placed rolled towels on each end and side of the map and then gently draped a towel over the top, tucking the map in by pushing the edges down along the sides of the pan. The lid was fitted and the map was in a perfect container, with handles at both ends to carry it.

Demetrius retrieved the map case and lid and Herbie ran to the linen closet to find a large fluffy towel to wrap it in.

After making arrangements for the children to come downtown the next day and give statements they all shook hands. The front door shut and they walked to the car.

Herbie and Ruthy were sent to bed with the promise they could sleep as long as possible but also with assurances that they would be going to school tomorrow where they could share all their adventures with their friends.

Frank had a case in court the following day, so Naomi called her office and left a message that she would be late and would be leaving early.

The house was soon dark, but it took a long time for everyone to fall asleep.

CHAPTER 24

ALBUQUERQUE

TUESDAY NIGHT, OCTOBER 31, 2000

They rode back to the FBI offices through almost empty streets; TA cradled the turkey roaster on her lap. She found herself humming under her breath. This is all so unbelievable. It's gorgeous! The gold, the incising, neat, neat, neat! "The animals, did you see the animals?" she exclaimed out loud.

The quiet was broken and they all started speaking at once. Demetrious: "Did you see that case? Damn! Do you realize how long and what skill that took?"

Nathan: "Do you realize how accurate the mapping was? It was all done at ground level! And what about Chinese, not Japanese? Those kids were amazing."

Buck: "Did you see how much writing there was? I can hardly wait to get it translated. As soon as we get back to the office I'll get on line and find a translator. We could use the kid's Professor Chan but we need to find a second person, one that can read ancient Chinese accurately. Perhaps we can get them to work together. Did you guys see how good those kids were at translating? My God! That little Ruthy is really something. What a responsibility it would be to be raising two kids like that!"

Nathan broke in, "Hey, this's what ARF is all about. It's riddled with hidden resources no other agency has. We should be able to get an expert here by tomorrow. When we tell them what we have, they'll be renting private jets to get to us."

Buck pulled the car into the parking garage. "Do you want me to carry that for you, TA?" he asked, not expecting a yes but it seemed the gentlemanly thing to offer.

"Ha, you're out of your mind," snorted TA. "Mine, all mine. At least until we get to the office." She clutched the roaster to her chest as she walked toward the elevator.

Once in the office, they went to a large conference room and TA placed the roaster on the long table that ran down the middle of the room.

She turned back to the men. "I've been thinking. We need to find translators and we need sleep. The map shouldn't be laid out and rolled up more often than necessary. As much as I hate to say it I think it should be locked up in a safe until tomorrow. I need to find a length of wool felt to put under it and some weighted rods for either end. Demetrius, the map case needs to be locked up, too. That case alone is priceless.

"By the way," she continued. "You all do know that this belongs to the Chinese government, not the Japanese, don't you? It's pretty obvious to me that this was done by a Chinese exploration expedition." She laughed, "Say that ten times fast.

"Anyway," she finished, "I imagine the Japanese government will be involved because it was once owned by a Japanese citizen. Although, after being around Mr. Kamakura, I think a lot of things are not as they seem."

Buck called the duty officer to open the vault. They carefully placed the roaster and towel-wrapped case on an empty shelf and swung the door shut.

Nathan and Demetrious found empty desks and started searching for an expert translator.

Buck checked with the people on duty and they soon had rooms in a nearby hotel.

On an emotional high, and finding it almost impossible to rest, TA finally settled into a nearby desk chair and called Ezekiel. He had been getting ready for bed but was soon in his office, pulling down reference books, the phone tucked under his chin. She was suddenly aware that the three men were hovering over her. "Got to go, Ezekiel. I'll call tomorrow afternoon when I know more."

"We have an Ellen Foster flying in tomorrow. She's a professor at Stanford and should be arriving by noon," reported Nathan.

"I took a chance that it wasn't too late and contacted Professor Chan. He'll be here at noon also. When he heard that Herbie and Ruthy had translated a few lines, he was thrilled. He wanted to talk genius children but I told him he'd be seeing them tomorrow." Demetrius chuckled.

"The hotel rooms are booked so let's get going," said Buck. "He looked at TA and grinned. "I have a surprise for you," he said. He went over to a corner of the room and picked up a suitcase.

TA let out a whoop. "My suitcase! Where was it?"

"In the wrecked car up at the Crest, your purse was there, too. It's in the suitcase. And guess what? We found the other maps in their hotel room, they'll be here tomorrow."

"Are they all right? Were they damaged?"

"They're fine. Our people looked at them and said no bending or rips. They're still wrapped in the silk. They didn't try to put them back in the case; afraid of damaging them.

"Come on, let's get going. I don't know about the rest of you but I think if I don't get some sleep I might fall on my face." He tried to look wilted but wasn't too successful.

"Okay." TA gave in. "Let's get going." She was suddenly exhausted.

They were soon checked in at the hotel and in their rooms. TA prepared for bed and was asleep before she turned out the light. It was still on when she woke the next morning to a pounding on her door.

CHAPTER 25

ALBUQUERQUE

WEDNESDAY, NOVEMBER 1, 2000

TA started to unlock the door but stopped suddenly, remembering all the unpleasant surprises in the last few days. Peeking through the door security window she was relieved to see Buck trying to peek back.

She unlocked the door. As he slid in he gave her a lascivious grin and inspected her nightshirt. She looked down and saw she was wearing her B. Kliban tee; the one with the cat sitting on a stool playing a guitar and singing:

Love to eat them mousies,
Mousies what I love to eat;
Bite they little heads off,
Nibble on they tiny feet.

His grin turned into a genuine laugh as he read his way through the tee. "Love it" he exclaimed.

She grinned back and then asked, "So, why knocketh thou?"

"I wanted to be sure you were awake. Meet us downstairs for breakfast in about half an hour?"

"For breakfast, I'll be there in twenty minutes. Out, out." Twenty minutes later, wearing a navy suit and a dash of lipstick, she was pressing the down button at the elevator.

When the elevator opened she saw the three men standing there looking out at her. "Hola, amigos!" she exclaimed. They answered her with enthusiastic holas.

After eating, they pushed their dishes away and planned their morning over a last cup of coffee. TA needed to find heavy felt and weights to hold the map down; the men needed to file updated reports to their bosses. They decided she would drop them at the FBI office and then go out for supplies.

She checked the yellow pages in the lobby phone book and made a list of stores. Fifteen minutes later they pulled up in front of the FBI office and she waved goodbye to the men.

First on her list were the weights. She hit it lucky in the first office supply place. She came away with several sets of catalpa sticks, heavy, beautifully finished and felted on one side, each a foot long. They were meant to hold down curling architectural plans and would do well on curling gold.

Her next stop was the upholsterer's. They had felt meant for pool tables and she bought a yard of dark green knowing the gold map would look beautiful resting on it.

It took a bit to talk her way back into the restricted parking garage but was finally okayed by the FBI office.

When she entered she was greeted by everyone coming out to say hello and wanting to help spread the felt on the conference table. There was soon standing room only. She retrieved the roaster and dramatically set it in the middle of the table. "A drum roll please," she said. Several people obliged by beating pencils on the back of the conference chairs. TA lifted the lid, removed the covering towel and set the rolled map carefully on the felt.

There was a collective gasp of astonishment. "Oh's, ahs, wows" filled the room. She used a ruler padded with a clean dusting cloth,

154

to gently start unrolling the map. As soon as she had a few inches of map flat on the table she set the first weight on the edge and then continued unrolling, using the weights to hold the edges down. Finally she reached the other end and set the last weighted stick on the end of the map.

"Okay everyone. Look, but don't touch; hands behind your backs, just like you tell kids at stores." They laughed and obeyed. They formed a line around the table; everyone wanted to call attention to particular details that caught their eye.

Magnifying glasses were handed out.

Knowing it would be awhile before she could sit and admire the map, Ta went into the room where the men had been working, She saw only Nathan. "Have the other maps gotten here from Santa Fe?" she asked

"No, the person bringing them got held up. We don't have a new delivery time yet. Sorry, I know you want to see them again. Heck, I want to see them. If I hear anything I'll let you know."

She sat down at a vacant desk and called Ezekiel. "Hi, Ezekiel. I thought I'd get to inspect the other maps but there's a delay in transferring them. How are things at your end?"

"Until we get a time frame, it's impossible to do much research. Call me as soon as your translators know anything. You did say Ming Dynasty, didn't you? How accurate do you think the children were in their translating?" he asked.

"I'd say they were probably pretty accurate. These kids are simply amazing. It's almost noon so the translators should be arriving pretty soon. I'll let you know as soon as they come up with an approximate date and then you can start looking. I'd certainly start at Ming, for sure."

"Okay," answered Ezekiel. "About the other maps; I'll check out Admiral Perry's expedition and try to find out if they worked with any Japanese cartographers."

Nathan stuck his head around the door frame and announced, "Professor Chan is here and Buck just picked up Professor Foster at the airport." He disappeared.

"Got to go, Ezekiel; the translators are arriving. I'll call soon."

CHAPTER 26

ALBUQUERQUE

WEDNESDAY, NOVEMBER 1, 2000

TA walked toward the front of the office and saw an older Asian man. He was nothing like the elderly semi-retired professor she was expecting. Not the stereotype of the Chinese sage with a partially bald head, long mustache and benign expression. This man was in his fifties and over six feet tall, full head of thick white hair, pencil mustache, debonair. In fact, he looked a little like Errol Flynn, the movie star from the thirties, who had been known for his dash and pizazz. He wore jeans, navy turtleneck with a Harris Tweed sport coat and dark brown half boots. No glasses. No serene expression for this guy; he was a take charge, twinkle in the eye, sexy, hip and noticeable man. Demetrius and he were in an enthusiastic discussion about the translation; she joined them.

After an introduction, she led the way to the conference room where the map was displayed. A half a dozen people hung over the table, debating what types of trees were depicted in the area that was now known as northern California. They stepped back when Demetrius, TA, and Professor Chan entered the room.

Chan drew a sharp breath when he had a clear view of the map. Stepping forward, he gazed at it for almost a whole minute and then gave a small shake, as if coming awake. He picked up one of the magnifying glasses and leaned forward, looking closely at the lines of characters around the outer edge of the map. The words circled the map like a frame, several columns across, running in defined groupings all around the edges. In some cases, there were groups near the drawings of landmarks that were easily recognized by twenty-first century eyes.

He straightened and turned to Demetrius and TA. "Definitely Chinese--late fourteenth or early fifteenth century. May I please have a tablet and a tape recorder?" Without waiting for a reply he turned back to the map.

One of the FBI left the room and returned with a stack of yellow legal tablets and a tape recorder. He gave a tablet and recorder to Chan and placed the rest on one end of the table along with an assortment of sharpened pencils and ball point pens.

There were voices coming from the front and TA went out to find Buck coming in with a middle-aged Chinese lady. Diminutive, plump, steel gray hair cut in a disorderly bob, she was wearing black slacks and the slickest green-gold metallic tennis shoes TA had ever seen. L L Bean jacket with a neck scarf in bright turquoises, reds and yellows completed her outfit. Glasses rested on top of her head. She was laughing at something Buck had said. All in all, she was delightful and looked like just the kind of professor TA would have bonded with when she was in school.

She spied TA coming from the back and stepped forward with her hand held out. "I bet you're TA," she said. "I'm Ellen Foster, Buck told me all about your adventures. What fun! You're a survivor." She shook TA's hand enthusiastically. TA upped her wish that she could have had such a professor.

"Really nice to meet you. Professor Chan is in the conference room with the map. Come see!"

As they entered the conference room, Professor Chan straightened up and turned to greet them. He froze and then let out a shout,

"Moon Child! At last, we meet again!" He stepped forward and embraced tiny Professor Foster in an enthusiastic hug. "I thought I'd never see you again! I looked everywhere for you, but I didn't know your name. Oh my dear, dear Moon Child." He cradled her in his arms and rocked them both gently back and forth.

"Fredo, you big Hobbit. It's been so long. Lots of water under the bridge. How long has it been? 1967, '68? My God, 32 years and you still live in New Mexico?" She leaned back and beamed at him. They stood facing each other, oblivious to the people watching.

TA turned to Buck and raised an enquiring eyebrow. He shrugged. I don't know anything, he mouthed at her. They turned to Demetrius and he shrugged too.

TA cleared her throat. Professor Foster turned to her. "We were together in Haight-Asbury and then a commune up in Taos, way back when. Hippie era, my dear, no one knew anyone's real name. Family names were for the establishment. We chose the name we wanted to be known by; lots of fun and lots of games." She laughed and turned back to Chan. "My dear, darling Hobbit, I loved you so."

He stood looking at her, a smile on his face. "And here we are at last and working together, too. Oh, Moon Child, we have so much catching up to do."

Professor Foster smiled up at him and then reached out, took his hand, and guided him to the table. "Tell me what you know about this amazing map."

Chan visibly pulled himself back to the business at hand and began talking. "Ming Dynasty, Emperor Zhu Di and Admiral Zheng He are mentioned. I'm just starting through the credits so it will be a bit before we get to the good stuff like exploring and their trip to North America." He turned to TA, "I understand you found this map in a cave near Los Alamos? What else can you tell us about its history?"

159

TA explained about Kamakura hiring her to find a map that had been in his family for generations. She touched on the relocation camps, Hana and Douglas Fairbanks and their secret cave, their deaths, the Bataan Death March and Mrs. Gabaldon writing her letter.

"I'm not sure Kamakura was telling the truth. It could be he isn't related at all. We might never know, since he's dead. But somebody sure wants the map. There are even ninjas involved."

"Ninjas?" exclaimed both Fredo and Ellen Moon Child. They turned to each other. "Are they still around?" he asked.

"I guess they've become popular again. Not sure for all the right reasons. I understand some of the Yakuzas have members that are practicing Ninja-ites," said Ellen with a smile.

"Yakuza?" asked TA. "Aren't they like organized street gangs?"

"No," said Buck. "Yakuza are an international crime grouping composed of several 'families'," he made quote signs with his hands. "They have members in several countries and are highly organized; mostly based on Kyushu. They're brutal."

Chan spoke up. "Let's go into these histories later. I'd like to hear more. Moon Child, you're probably the most knowledgeable because you're still working in the field. Why don't we get back to transcribing and could we please have a sandwich? I'm starving. We can eat and work and then take a break when the kids get here and talk. Oh, when you order sandwiches, get a couple extra for the kids. They'll be starving; they're always starving," he added.

Buck ordered the lunches and after eating, he, Demetrius and Nathan grabbed tablets and disappeared into the office that held several desks with computers.

TA opted to stay with Chan and Foster and became their secretary. They would translate a word or phrase, compare notes, discuss meanings and then dictate their consensus to TA.

She was astonished that they were able to translate as well as they could and finally asked: "In old European languages, so many of the letters and words and especially the spelling is so different from what is written today. Isn't that the case with Chinese?"

The professors welcomed the break and sat back in their chairs to teach. Foster started off, "Evolution of the written word is generally the same in all languages and the words usually evolve into a more complicated form. In Chinese the word *house* changed from a simple box-like shape to what it has become today."

"Of course," added Chan, "with all the technical terms we have now and all the words we add daily, language is changing rapidly. Americans use root words from all the main language groups around the world. Way back, when men started living in groups, it was subsistence speaking – north, south, east, west, kill, eat, come, go, sleep, fire, hot, cold, mammoth, saber tooth, and later horse, cow, I.O.U., etc. and then mankind started really communicating! The words maintained their roots and that's what we're translating."

"Remember," Foster continued, "by the 1400's when this map was etched, the run of the mill average educated Chinese men and women were way more knowledgeable than the average educated European. Anyway, what we're doing here is looking for the root symbols and surmising the word in context with the phrase. Many of the words are surprisingly close to what they are today."

Chan explained, "Of course, this is rough translating and by the time this map is stuck in a glass case in some museum, it will have been retranslated many times. There are people out there that specialize in nothing but ancient languages and we don't have anywhere near the knowledge that they have. I can't wait until they get to retranslating. On the other hand, we don't want to be embarrassed, so we'll do the best we can."

They all turned back to the map and set to work. Time flew and suddenly they heard young voices coming from the front office. The children had arrived and everybody was glad to take a break.

As the adults joined the children in the office, Herbie gave up trying to contain Ruthy. He turned to Demetrius with enthusiasm.

They had met in the hall and he had been trying to talk and keeps an eye on her while discussing the ARF organization and some of their cases that had popped up in his computer search.

Ruthy whirled toward Professor Chan and happily launched herself onto him with a mighty hug, exclaiming, "Have you seen it? Isn't it super cool? Have you figured it all out? How did they get the gold so flat? Dad says they used a stylus to write on it. They had to walk all those distances didn't they? Horses hadn't arrived. Isn't this exciting?" He stood beaming down at her.

She suddenly let go of him and spun toward Professor Foster. "How do you do? I'm Ruth Quintana." She drew herself up straight and extended her hand. "I'm a friend of Professor Chan. Are you the person who came to help translate the map?"

Professor Foster smiled and gently shook her hand. "Yes, I'm Ellen Foster. You must call me Ellen. Professor Chan and I are working on translating the map and we're hoping you and Herbie can help. It's spread out in the room over there. Want to see?"

They all walked into the room that held the map. Ruthy and Herbie stood admiring it and then grabbed magnifying glasses and began a close examination. They exclaimed over each small picture. Finally, having worked their way all along both sides of the table, Herbie raised his head and noticed the sandwiches. "Are those for us?" He was assured they were and both he and Ruthy took one to eat as they again surveyed the map.

A full mouth didn't stop Ruthy's questions. "Do you know the date they traveled? Is it hard to scratch the lines in gold? How far have you gotten?"

Professor Chan answered patiently, "Around 1400, 600 years ago. If they used a metal stylus, it would be like writing with a pen, only they would have to press harder. Gold is pretty soft. We've barely begun the translation."

Food consumed, the children were ready to begin working. At first, Ellen had had reservations about how much help they would be but was soon enthusiastically answering questions and debating word meanings.

They settled in different areas of the map and the room became quiet, with pens scratching across yellow tablets, with occasional comments or questions.

TA marveled at the amount of work that was being done. Contrary to her earlier reservations, the children were actually a big help. She thought Professor Chan must be a fantastic teacher and these kids a joy to work with. Time flew.

Restless, she excused herself and wandered into the office where Buck, Nathan, and Demetrius leaned back in their chairs, feet on the desks, talking. She heard the word Yakuza mentioned.

"Have you found out any more on the Yakuza? Was Kamakura a member? What have you found out about him?" She felt like Ruthy, full of questions.

"Well," answered Buck, "we just have an initial report; their profiles will be coming in this evening, sometime. However, we do have some basic information and it's really interesting." He turned to Demetrius and Nathan, "Which of you two guys had Kamakura?"

"Me," stated Nathan, "Kamakura was a distant relative. That wasn't his real name. He was a smalltime criminal who specialized in white collar crimes. He was probably picked because he could speak English and looked respectable. He wasn't alone; he had his small gang of thugs. His ninja-wannabees all showed up in our system; small time enforcers with aspirations of climbing higher in the ranks. They belonged to a gym together and played at being ninjas. I guess, far from home, they thought they could indulge in their fantasies and they didn't need Kamakura anymore."

"Yeah," chimed in Buck. "The man that was driving the last car, the one who shot at you and went over the cliff, was the ninja in the apartment. He must have been one tough cookie because you really did a number on his leg. I'm surprised he could walk. The forensic people said you cut his upper thigh to the bone. It looked like he lost close to two pints of blood. His red count was so low that as he drove up toward the Crest at higher and higher altitudes he would have gotten weaker and his thinking fuzzy. The binding looked homemade so he hadn't had any professional help."

Demetrius continued. "The guy that was driving the car that got taken out by the dump truck is alive. He's not talking and has asked for a lawyer. He got bruised and scuffed up by the air bag but otherwise he's fine. He's in isolation at the jail here in Albuquerque."

"How about the flying ninja?" asked TA. "He seemed super tough, just like a Jackie Chan movie."

The men laughed. Buck picked up the narration, "Yeah, he was one tough dude. He specialized in the shuriken, the flying star. In his spare time away from being a criminal he entered competitions and won quite a few. He also excelled at kick boxing. It's surprising he missed when he was throwing the shuriken at you. The information noted that he had quite a temper. I guess that was his undoing. Never have a temper tantrum standing on a tram roof."

"Hey," said TA, "give me credit. I'm a real good ducker. It landed just where my head had been a second before."

Professor Chan stuck his head in the office. "Naomi, Mrs. Quintana, is here to pick up the kids. It's after five."

They all got up and went to greet Mrs. Quintana. She was in the conference room admiring the map and asking questions. She soon gathered up her children, who went reluctantly, and was out the door. Promises were made that they could come back tomorrow after school and they could stay longer.

After the turmoil of departure, the adults looked at each other. Ellen broke the quiet, "Let's go back to our hotel and tidy up and then go out to eat at some quiet restaurant. I want to know more about your research. Also, I want to know what Fredo has been up to all these years. I'm sure he feels the same way about me."

Fredo, a name they had all adopted, spoke up. "Since all of you are in hotels and I have a house why don't we eat at my place? I'll stop on my way home and pick up dinner. Italian? Mexican? What's your preference?"

They chose Mexican. "After all," said TA, "this is the land of red or green." Only Nathan had to have that statement explained. "Around here all waiters at Mexican restaurants always want to know 'red or green', explained TA. They're asking if you want red or green chili." She looked at Fredo, "don't forget to get sopapillas. Do you have honey?"

"Yep, a big bottle and it's local." He turned to all of them, "the works? Tamales, enchiladas, re-fried beans, etc. etc.?"

"Yes," they all shouted together.

Buck added, "We'll bring the beer. Any requests?" Several brands were suggested and noted and they all returned to the conference room to wrap the map and transfer it to the walk-in safe.

TA decided that re-rolling the map would unnecessarily stress the metal so the felt was just flipped over the map surface and it was held rigidly straight as it was carried into the back of the safe and laid carefully on the floor. She tore three sheets from a tablet and using a wide marker she wrote STAY OFF and CAREFUL on all of them and laid them on top of the wrapped map.

They signed out at the front desk and went to the garage where they separated with Dr. Chan driving off in his vintage MGA and the rest of them crowded into one of the FBI fleet cars.

CHAPTER 27

PROFESSOR CHAN'S HOME

WEDNESDAY, NOVEMBER 1, 2000

They pulled into Fredo's driveway an hour later. In a quiet older part of the city, its welcoming windows spilled light across lawn and hedges. The house had an enclosed patio with a metal gate shaped in circles and bars in the Frank Lloyd Wright style. As they unlatched it they could hear chimes in the distance and the front door was thrown wide by a welcoming Fredo. A tiled hall led into the great room; oriental and Navajo rugs were scattered about. The furniture was New Mexico mission style, carved wood with cushions. A fire-place with dancing flames, fronted by a well-used leather recliner, filled one corner of the room. It was lovely and peaceful, filled book-cases along two walls and full length windows along another.

"Welcome, welcome," said Fredo. "Would you like to sit and have a drink or would you rather come to the table and eat?"

Everybody opted for eating and drinking and they were soon gathered around a long rustic wooden table set with four Mexican candlesticks holding flickering candles, colorful woven placemats, heavy old silver and large bright plates.

The scent of baking meat, melting cheese and green chili wafted out of the warming oven. Corn tortillas, warmed in the microwave

166

added their own distinctive aroma. Everyone helped carry the food to the table. Fredo dumped chips in large Mexican bowls glazed in flowers and birds. TA and Nathan reached in the fridge and brought salsa, guacamole and assorted beers.

Eager eaters passed the food with exclamations over the variety, beauty and wonderful smells. Demetrius and Nathan were unfamiliar with some of the dishes. New Mexican food is unique and different from the universal Mexican food offered elsewhere.

Sopapillas with honey made up the dessert. TA demonstrated the proper eating technique. She bit off one corner of the triangular puff, poured honey in through the hole, and rocked it to spread the honey. Leaning over her plate she bit off a large bite and rolled her eyes in enjoyment. Her audience applauded, and they all reached for their own treat.

Fredo put on a pot of coffee. As it perked they loaded the dishwasher and washed their honey coated hands.

Back at the table with coffee in front of each they started sharing information. Buck easily slid into the mode of facilitator and turned to Fredo and Ellen. "I know it's early yet but what have you found out?"

Fredo took over. "Definitely early 1400's. It's written in Mandarin." He paused and pulled some folded papers from his pocket and began reading aloud. "In the time of the Great Dynasty of the Ming, during the reign of The Yongle Emperor, Zhu Di, exalted by the Gods, Infinite in wisdom, appointed the eunuch Zheng He, giant among men in both stature and knowledge, to be grand Commander of all the ships of the country." Fredo refolded the paper.

"That's not precise and there are a lot of words complimenting both men that we haven't been able to translate, just surmise."

Ellen spoke up, "One interesting thing we've noticed is that the narrative that runs around the map was written by three people; two were Chinese, the first was highly educated, the second much less so, probably an apprentice or minor official along on the trip;

167

the last writer was Japanese and the information's in Japanese. We started at the beginning of the story, but if you like we could 'read the end of the book' first? It's up to all of you."

"If you choose the end first we'll have to get someone else in. Neither of us is conversant in Japanese. I have a colleague at Stanford or perhaps ARF has someone closer that could help," added Ellen.

"Let's start from the beginning," said Buck. The others nodded. "Tell us something about the Ming Dynasty and what you know about the Emperor and Zheng He?"

Ellen started, "Well, the Empire of the Great Ming was 'one of the longest eras of orderly government and social stability in human history' as one of our esteemed colleagues wrote. It lasted 276 years from 1368 to 1644. The Yongle Emperor Zhu Di was emperor from 1402-1424. He built Beijing. He had wood block printings made to spread information about Chinese culture to all the outlying provinces. Made everyone more cohesive."

Fredo gave a snort of laughter and commented, "He invaded and occupied Vietnam in 1406 but the Ming pulled their troops out by 1427 because of the guerrilla warfare. Sound familiar?"

"Zheng He" exclaimed Ellen, "was extremely interesting. He was born into a Muslin family and was captured when he was about 12. They castrated him and trained him for various court functions. However, he was extremely bright and because of his size, he stood out." She and Fredo laughed. "He was noticed and advanced. The reason we laugh is because he was not only a genius and quite a statesman, he was also around seven feet tall. They describe him as standing seven7 chi tall and five chi around. The Ming value of a chi was about 12 inches. Whatever, this was one *big* man. Oh, there are several portraits available if you want to see what he looked like."

Fredo took up the lesson. "He was a court administrator and then an Admiral. He built an impressive navy to take on diplomatic mission along the coast to the east and then south to open new trade routes and to find information about neighboring kingdoms. One tale says he brought back a giraffe. They made seven voyages and went as far as East Africa."

"The fleet he built is something worth reading about. It was called the treasure fleet because they carried gifts to the rulers of other nations and those rulers sent back gifts to China. Some of the ships, built to impress, were huge, the largest built until relatively recent times. In fact some of the ships were so large the scholars didn't believe their size until somebody excavated a rudderpost that corresponded with a ship over 500 feet in length." He paused to take a drink.

Demetrius leaned forward, "Alright, I'll bite, How big were they?"

Fredo looked up at the ceiling for a moment, obviously marshalling his thought, "Okay, for comparison, Columbus's Santa Maria was 62 feet long and the Mayflower was around 100. The largest ship in the treasure fleet had nine masts and was 417 feet by 171 feet. The biggest probably never went on ocean crossings but traveled in calmer coastal water, still, who knows. Anyway, the ships that size were built for commanders and deputies and probably the Emperor and his close court and, of course, everybody's families.

"Then they had horse transports, water and supply ships, troop ships, and war ships. The ships that carried horses had eight masts and were 338 feet by 138 feet. Anyway, this can all be found on the internet. I do love computers," he added enthusiastically. "The ships descended in size down to a patrol boat that used 8 oars and was 121 feet long."

"Which ships did they use for the voyage to North America?" asked TA. "Surely not that huge ship."

"I think they used the troop transports. The drawings on the map show ships with six masts and the troop ships had six masts. Those ships were 220 feet by 82 feet. They would have had to do some serious refitting because they didn't know how long they would be away from land.

Whew!" He leaned back in his chair and pretended to be exhausted by all the lecturing.

Next it was Buck's turn, to pull out notes." I looked up Yakusa. They're kind of like the mafia. They're organized crime, not just Japanese, though they started there. Now they've spread internationally. And get this," he continued, "They're strongest on the island of Kyushu.

The name yakusa comes from the words ya-ku-sa, which translates to 8-9-3 and is a losing hand in a popular game called Oichu-Kabu, a form of Baccarat – shades of James Bond!

Buck turned to Demetrius and bowed to him, "Your turn, oh learned one."

Demetrius bowed back, "Thank you, my man, and well done on your research." Taking out notes he turned to the rest of them; "short and sweet. Douglas Fairbanks joined the 10th Mountain Division, which was activated in 1943.

When the war started, the National Ski Patrol suggested to Roosevelt that the army needed men who could ski. The President agreed and asked them to start recruiting. They went all over the country signing qualified people up.

"Anyway, the 87th Infantry Regiment in Ft. Lewis, Washington took over the training. They used Mt. Rainier, which is over 13,000 feet high. Then they moved to Colorado to Camp Hale, at 9,200 feet. In 1942, they settled at Camp Carson, near Colorado Springs.

"10th Light Division (Alpine) became official in July, 1943 at Camp Hale under Brigadier General Lloyd E. Jones. They trained in mountain climbing, skiing and they developed special winter clothing and white camouflage and even had special skis. They practiced their rock climbing on Seneca Rocks in West Virginia. That's one tough climb, trust me, I didn't think I'd make it.

Back to the 10th. They had major battles in Northern Italy in the Apennines Mountains and the Po Valley and lost quite a few men. That's where Douglas Fairbanks died."

Demetrius folded his notes and tucked them back in his pocket and then turned to Nathen and nodded.

Nathen raised his hands in mock resignation "I bow to you gentlemen. I have nothing to add. It's getting late but before we go I'd like to turn the floor over to Fredo and Moon Child," he said, bowing to Ellen. "Please enlighten us as to your other lives."

Fredo and Ellen turned to each other and smiled. Turning back to the breathless group Ellen spoke. "I was seventeen when I finished high school. My folks wanted me to go directly to college, do not pass go and do not get caught up in the hippie movement that was sweeping the nation. But what does a seventeen- year-old do? We were living in San Francisco and there was Haight-Asbury, 1966, going strong, and I hit it running. I became a poster child for the flower children of that era. I hung around the neighborhood weaving flower wreaths, singing songs, toking with the best... and the worst. I met Fredo on Christmas Day 1966. We were in a sit-in against something or other. I couldn't believe my eyes--over six feet tall and gorgeous, his hair must have been down to his waist. God, he was magnificent! The fact he was Asian was a real bonus. I prided myself on being color-blind but my genes gravitated to him.

"I remember," she turned and smiled up at him, "You had a copy of *The Hobbit* sticking up out of your pocket. When I heard your name was Alfredo it just seemed right to call you Fredo because the hero of the Hobbit was Frodo.

"Most of us had made up names for ourselves. Our birth names were so 'establishment' and, God-Forbid we'd give out our last name. Most of us had parents trying to track us down so we pretty much had to create AKAs. I picked Moon Child for my name because I was reading a lot of Chinese literature at the time and the moon is mentioned in much of it."

She turned to Fredo, "You take over for a while."

Fredo grinned. "I was 21. From a family of artichoke farmers. I won awards and scholarships all through school. Most of the kids that were winning were from educated homes with indoor plumbing and fathers who never got their hands dirty. Both my parents were getting up in the dark and working all day in the fields. They never stopped working. They'd come in from the fields and my mother would cook. Dad would want a complete blow by blow account of all my classes and then he'd ask questions that I'd have to research. Then he'd start questioning my little sister. Don't think they ever slept. I graduated from high school at sixteen, my masters at 18 and was finishing my doctorate by twenty-one when I walked away. Ended up in Haight-Asbury – the 'happening' place."

He paused to draw a deep breath and those at the table watched him solemnly.

"Until then I had never played. I don't think I even laughed much. Life was grim, you worked hard all your life and then you died. The Haight was a whole new experience and Moon Child was a revelation. We went to poetry readings and drank coffee so strong you could stick a spoon upright in it. Heard concerts with people like Janis Joplin and the Grateful Dead and Jefferson Airplane. They told us what to think and how to act and in between we sang Scott McKenzie's song San Francisco." He turned to Moon Child and they sang the opening verse:

If you're going to San Francisco
Be sure to wear some flowers in your hair
If you're going to San Francisco
You're gonna meet some gentle people there.

Their audience laughed and clapped.

"It was getting progressively rougher and then in October there was a 'happening' and everybody gathered for 'The Death of the

Hippie Ceremony' that told young people to stay home or go home and spread the message of freedom. Don't stay in Haight-Asbury which was overrun with drugs, homelessness, and hopelessness.

"We didn't want to go home so we jumped in a VW van painted with flowers and headed to Taos, New Mexico. Taos had been an artist colony since the late 1800's with famous artists and writers wandering through. I think they invented the term 'free love.' People like D. H. Lawrence, Georgia O'Keeffe and Ansel Adams had lived and worked there. It was the land of blue skies and freedom."

Moon Child laughed. "We lived in a commune in the mountains, in teepees. We had a two holer outhouse. No door because the view was magnificent.

"It was cold, really cold, the altitude was over 8,000 feet. We spent the winter huddled in the biggest teepee, reading out loud. We read all the coming-of-age novels and went through all the 'in' books of the time. All the Hobbit books."

Everyone at the table smiled at their own memories. Continuing: "We read 'To *Kill a Mockingbird* and *The Catcher in the Rye*, and *Marjory Morningstar*. We spent a lot of time in the library because they had heat and in-door plumbing where we could wash up. All we had at the commune was a little stream." She paused to smile enthusiastically and exclaimed, "That was the year that *Red Sky at Morning* came out. Loved it. If you haven't read it, you really should. It's by Richard Bradford and set in New Mexico."

"I've heard of it." TA broke in. "I'll get it."

"They made a movie of it, too. Read the book first but be sure to watch the movie. It's excellent; funny but so poignant," answered Ellen.

"Then it all ended. I had the urge to call home and my mother started crying and begging me to come back. She sent money and I took the bus home. I planned to come back but guilt or reality caught up." She turned to Fredo, "I did try to get in touch with you but my letters were returned from general delivery."

He reached out and patted her hand. "I wasn't there. After you left I got to worrying about my folks and called them. I reached my sister. My father was dying of cancer and I borrowed money from Frank, you remember him, he always had money, I think he was a remittance man and they paid him to stay away. I hopped the first bus heading west. When I got there I only had a few days with my father before he passed and my mother didn't live a week after that. I think she died of a broken heart. She just faded away.

"You know," he said, "when my sister and I went through the house we found over $50,000 squirreled away. We sold the house and property for over a million dollars. All that time they were living with an outhouse. Why couldn't they have had a few niceties to make their lives easier? I still feel bad about it."

He turned to her, "I did try to find you. I got the money I borrowed back to Frank and asked all around for you. I even ran ads in the San Francisco papers but you were gone."

She took his hand. "I guess we've done alright but I've always missed you. Did you marry? I did. He was a professor of English History. We had a happy life. He passed a few years ago. It was cancer but it was fast. We had two girls and I have two grandchildren, a boy and a girl. How about you?"

"I married. We had a good life; did a lot of traveling. She was ill for a long time and passed a couple of years ago. We never had children, we always felt bad about that."

The table was quiet for a few moments and then TA broke the silence. "You've found each other now and you'll have a wonderful time catching up. Thank you so much for sharing such personal memories."

She stood, "I think we need to get back to the hotel. You still have days of translating and I need to see about getting a ticket back to San Francisco. I have a job and I'm sure Ezekiel needs my help." She started gathering up the coffee cups and took them to the kitchen.

Moon Child announced "Fredo will drive me to the hotel in a bit. We still have some catching up to do."

The rest of them thanked Fredo and left. TA fell asleep on the way back and managed to almost sleepwalk into the elevator. Buck saw her safely inside her room before returning to the waiting elevator.

She brushed her teeth, got into her pajamas and fell into bed without requesting a wakeup call.

CHAPTER 28

ALBUQUERQUE

THURSDAY, NOVEMBER 2, 2000

TA woke at 9:32 and stretched luxuriantly. It had been a lovely night last night. Everything was pulling together, people were getting along and all the information was fascinating. She smiled as she thought of Fredo and Moon Child and how they had found each other again. She grinned when her mind turned to Buck.

She glanced at her watch and sat up in horror. She hadn't put in for a wakeup call or set her alarm. Nobody had called her! Where was everybody? Were they all gone, over at the FBI office and working on the map?

She picked up her cell and looked at it. No calls had come in while she slept. She pressed called Buck. "Where are you?" she asked when he answered.

"I'm over at the office. We decided to let you sleep in. You've been through so much we thought you needed some down time. Take it easy today," he replied.

"Easy? But…" she paused to think of a reason that she needed to hurry. A reason she was needed at all. Maybe it was time to go home. There were no conservator duties she could perform. If the map was kept straight it wasn't going to be damaged. It wasn't as if

176

it needed repairs and besides, being gold, she didn't have the knowledge to fix anything anyway. She suddenly felt bereft.

As if he were reading her emotions, Buck spoke up. "When you get ready to come over I was wondering if you'd like to see the two maps from Hana's chest. They finally arrived from Santa Fe."

Rising to her feet, "They got here? Terrific! Should I take a taxi over or can you come get me?"

He laughed. "I'll always have time for you. When will you be ready? Have you eaten?"

"I need to get dressed and call Ezekiel. How about an hour. I'll be downstairs in the café. Thanks, see you soon."

"In an hour," he replied.

TA was just leaving the restaurant as Buck walked in the front door of the hotel. They met with a hug that was not quite romantic; but more than friendship. He leaned back and inspected her. "You certainly look a lot healthier than you did when I left you. If you aren't thoroughly awake I have something to bring you to attention." He looked at her with a grin.

"What? What!"

"I just heard that the man who was opening the gate on the Crest, the one the ninja shot, is going to be okay. And, I have the stats on those three ninja/Yakusa guys and Kamakura. Also, both maps are ready for you. And last, but not least, the translations are going really well."

She started to speak but he held up his hand. "Wait, wait. You can see everything when we get back to the office. To tell the truth, I don't know which is more interesting. After the map translation, that is. Did you get hold of Ezekiel?"

"No, he didn't answer. I left a message. I'll try again after we get to the office if I don't hear back on the way over. Let's go."

After signing in at the FBI office, TA went first to the 'map' room as she referred to it in her mind. There it was, in all its golden glory, with Fredo and Moon Child bent over it, heads together, studying a grouping of characters. They laughed suddenly and leaned back in their chairs, looking at each other in triumph. They had obviously succeeded in solving whatever puzzle they had been working on.

"How's it going?" she asked, peering down at what they had been looking at. It was a grouping of characters that looked very much like all the other groupings running around the edges of the map. Each grouping consisted of five columns of characters, perhaps three or so inches long, somewhat like a page in a book. In fact, she thought, it's a page and the next group along is another page, and so on, telling a wonderful story. The map appeared almost as if a person had taken bread dough and rolled it flat. It was generally rectangular with writing along the slightly irregular edge. In the middle were incised landmarks, the Pacific Ocean on the left and what looked like Lake Michigan on the right. The northwest coast had tiny boats and people. Scattered across the map were all sorts of identifiable animals, trees and plants. She gasped when she saw Cliff Palace, from Mesa Verde, and other groups of buildings in what was now the four corners area of New Mexico, Arizona, Utah and Colorado.

"Look," she exclaimed. "I saw this last night. They visited some pueblos This shows pueblos that were abandoned a long time ago. I'll check and see when the people left. Maybe they crossed paths. Wow! It's certainly going to be changing history books." She turned to the professors, "Have you come to anything about the pueblos yet?"

Fredo and Moon Child laughed. "Oh my dear child," Moon Child said. "You're so optimistic. We haven't even come to the actual sailing. For the most part we're translating the credits of who set up the trip."

"We did translate the script on the cylinder cap," broke in Fredo, looking pleased. "It says, 'The great land to the East is partially revealed to Admiral Zhao Huang.' He must have been the leader of the expedition."

"That's fascinating! We'll need to research his name. You know, you explained the translation process so well last night that I kind of thought you could leap along on the whole thing

"Well, I need to go check out the other maps. If you come to something really interesting, call. I'll be across the hall." She went in search of Buck.

She found him sitting at a desk with a sheaf of papers stacked in front of him. He turned to her when she entered the room. "Do you want to hear the statistics on all your playmates?" Nathan and Demetrius, sitting nearby, laughed.

She pulled up a chair by the desk and grinned. "Yes, tell me about the mysterious four."

"Okay, let's begin with Kamakura Norio. Surname is always first in Japan and China. That's a fictitious name; his real name is Nakahara Fumio. He was sixty-two, petty thief, con man, Yakusa, unmarried."

Buck pulled a second sheet of paper from the pile. "This is the guy that broke into the apartment and later shot at you. He was twenty-eight, essentially a thug and strong man. His record shows he had several drunk and disorderly arrests, petty thief and enforcer. His name was Mori Arata – Mori being the surname.

"Next," he continued as he pulled out a third sheet, "is Tanaka Hiroshi, twenty-four, in jail here and awaiting legal decisions. The Japanese government isn't particularly interested in fighting us for him. I think their attitude is good riddance to bad rubbish. He's the one the dump truck crunched. Also Yakusa, more an enforcer than anything else and was generally nasty and not too bright. He's been picked up for threatening, pilfering, and generally being annoying to the law-abiding public and he's served a few brief prison times.

The 'powers-that-be' are offering him witness protection if he cooperates. He's lawyered up and thinking about it.

And then we come to the most interesting guy in the pack." He placed the last sheet of paper in front of her. "His name was

Abe Satoshi. He specialized in shuriken -throwing stars-, loved cage fighting, worked in a circus part-time as an acrobat and demonstrating shuriken. He was also something of a cat burglar but not ever indicted. Probably the brightest of the lot but as I told you yesterday, he had a temper. That was the thing that kept him from rising in the organization."

"Okay. Would you like to know about the murdered men?" He picked up another set of papers and set them in front of her. "These are attachés number one, two and three. The first man murdered was Wang Bo. Mr. Wang, 27, master's degree from Harvard in International Studies. He was working on his law degree, nights, at Stanford. He was engaged to a young woman who works for the Chinese government, stationed in Los Angeles. They were getting married next month." Buck sighed and placed the next sheet of paper in front of her.

"This gentleman is Zhang Honghui. He was victim number two, the runner." Buck looked at her and smiled. "You never would have outrun him; by the way, he was in the Olympics in the relay and a couple of other competitions. Mr. Zhang was 32, married, father of two. His wife is a lawyer and works at the consulate in San Francisco. He had degrees in English, French and Japanese."

"The last man," he set the last paper in front of her, "was Wu Niu. Niu means ox. Appropriate, because he loved lifting weights and was very strong. The people that killed him were lucky they surprised him or he might have surprised them. He had two degrees, in botany and accounting. Interesting combination. He was 29 and quite the partier. There's a note here that says everyone they interviewed smiled when they talked about him."

"They were there to protect you, by the way. The government knew that Kamakura/ Nakahara was looking for an ancient map of Chinese origin but they decided to keep an eye on things rather than interfere. I guess the thinking was to let him do the work and then swoop in and take over. They knew you might be the key, but they also weren't keen on letting you be in danger. They were supposed to be unobtrusive but that didn't work."

They sat quietly.

She broke from her reverie. "Thanks for the background. It's sad to know the people I feared the most turned out to be the good guys." She sighed.

"May I see the other maps? Do you have a place to lay them out?"

"Yeah," Buck stood. "There's a conference room down the hall. Let's get the maps. Do you need anything else?"

"Just a yellow tablet and pen to take notes; a lighted magnifying glass and weights to hold them flat. Oh, and a cloth to clean the table."

They retrieved the silk bundle from the safe. TA could feel her anticipation growing. Buck stopped and picked up her supplies and together they entered a small conference room. She was pleased to see the table was large enough to handle one map.

She wiped down the table and then, to be doubly sure, she ran her bare hands over it, feeling for any crumb or stickiness. It passed inspection so she pulled on her cotton gloves and reached for the bundle.

Unrolling the silk she paused to admire the map case again. It was lovely and would look amazing in a display case in a museum. The maps were rolled side by side and she picked up the newer one, inserted it back in the case and placed it on a bookcase.

Turning back, she folded the silk cloth and putting it aside she unrolled the remaining map on the table. Buck, who had been standing to one side, suddenly spoke. "I have an idea, wait a second." He left the room, returning almost immediately with several boxes of staples. "I saw these in the supply room the other day. They should do just fine as weights." He set half a dozen full boxes of staples on the side of the table.

TA laughed. "I never thought of that. Perfect." She unrolled the map and placed the staple boxes along the edges. They worked admirably.

181

She studied the map for a moment and picked up her phone. "I haven't heard back from Ezekiel and I'm worried." Buck nodded and drifted from the room.

Ezekiel answered, sounding weak.

"Ezekiel, are you sick? I can try to get a flight back tonight. What's going on?"

"I'm alright, just a cold, but it's getting better. I saw the doctor. I'm treating the cough with Bailey's."

She laughed. "Gee, the best remedy in the world after chicken soup. Bailey's Irish Cream. I imagine I'll be home in the next day or two. There isn't much I can do here. I'm going over the older of the two maps that were in the trunk. It's so beautiful. It's almost topographical and there are even little fish in the ocean. I'll get pictures of all the maps before I leave. Oh, Ezekiel, I wish you were here to see it and to meet everybody that's worked on the recovery and translations. Take care of yourself. I'll be back soon." A few more words and she hung up. Worried about Ezekiel and intrigued by the map, she leaned over the table and studied it with the magnifying glass.

Later, she heard the voices of Herbie and Ruthy as they came in from school. She continued examining the maps.

She remembered seeing copies of Japanese maps dating from the mid-7th century. They had been rough topographical maps made by each province depicting their land holdings. This map was later and included the whole island. There also seemed to be a Chinese influence.

TA admired the detail of some of the coves and saw a caldera and what looked like an active volcano and the main mountains of Kyushu.

She stood and went to find Buck. "Do you have an atlas? I need a map of Kyushu. Maybe there's something on the internet?"

He spun his desk chair around and was soon pecking keys in search. "I'll see what I can find. If it looks like you can use it, I'll print it."

She went back to the map. It showed some small towns but no large cities. A mountain range ran diagonally across the island and many coves and bays were shown along its edges. The map had been made, not with a North/South perspective but to be laid on the floor with people sitting around the edges to view it.

She reminded herself to stop admiring and start assessing. Where were the problems? Grabbing the yellow tablet and a pen, she set to making notes. There was surprisingly little foxing on the map. It had been cared for, obviously and lying in a shed had not damaged it a great deal. The mulberry paper it was drawn on was certainly better than some of the papers that were used to make maps in more recent years. It didn't seem to have ever been hung on a wall, so there was little light damage and, though humidity had affected it in places, the molds had died in the dry New Mexico climate. Heat and pollution hadn't done much damage. There was evidence of coal smoke, but it was minimal. Insect damage was almost nil. This map had been cared for and cherished. She made a few notes on the tablet about areas that needed attention. She'd send her assessment along with the map--when it was ripped from her dying hands, she thought dramatically. She had already accepted the fact that she would not be the one restoring it.

Buck came in with a computer printed map of Kyushu. She made a few notes on it and slipped it into the tablet.

The map was rolled up and the newer map set out.

The maker of this map was primarily interested in Kyushu's bays, which were many, and coves, even more. There were a few towns, mostly coastal, and roads in the coastal areas. It seemed to be a mariners' map and showed the depth of water in likely harbors. It was a map to be used and there was evidence it had been. She grabbed the tablet and jotted notes on water damage and some oily substance, coal oil perhaps, maybe whale oil, had been spilled on one corner. Insect damage included silver fish and cockroach, but in a minor degree

She stretched and returned both maps to their case, and spread the silk wrap over the table, positioned the case and the notes she had made along with the computer map of Kyushu in the center. She wrapped everything in the silk and carried it to the safe.

As she was walking out, Buck met her. "Hi, I was just coming to get you. It's supper time and we let the kids choose." He laughed. "I thought they'd pick pizza but we're evidently going to a place called Tucanos Brazilian Grill. Everybody has gone ahead and if you're ready we can drive on over. It's right downtown," She was ready in a few minutes.

CHAPTER 29

ALBUQUERQUE

FRIDAY, NOVEMBER 3, 2000

Walking up to the door of Tucanos Brazilian Grill, in the cold New Mexico evening, was a welcoming experience. As they approached they could see all the happy carnivores noshing, talking, drinking and laughing. There was a large salad bar and a grilling area with racks of assorted meats turning, sizzling, spitting, dripping; scenting the air with mouthwatering smells. The room was wood paneled and had a comfortable feeling.

TA spotted their group waving at them. Platters of hors d'oeuvres sat in the center of their table. Ruthy was bent over a large bowl of salad. Herbie stood to hold a chair for her and then they were in the midst of tasting and discussing and questioning Fredo and Herbie, the only people who were familiar with this amazing restaurant. Herbie demonstrated how to raise the little red and green flags mounted on a tiny flag pole-red for doing fine and green to signal the wait staff. They raised green and ordered wine.

The menu was in Portuguese with the word's pronunciation in parentheses and the English translation following. TA was intrigued to see that center cut sirloin was alcatra (AL-KAH-tra). Besides different meats she was delighted to see they also had grilled fruits and vegetables.

Everybody ordered and promised to share. As they were being served from large slabs of meat carved at their table, Buck's phone rang. He excused himself answer it.

He returned and grinned. "Our captive ninja has rolled. He'll tell everything he knows on the condition of a reduced sentence and then witness protection here in the US. The protection part is going to be difficult because the Yakuza has long arms. If they put him into any Japanese enclave, he'll be found. If he goes anywhere else, he'll stand out. Hawaii is a possibility but the Governor isn't too thrilled with the idea. They're still working on it. The Japanese government seems pleased to dump him on us.

The meal continued, as they joyfully hardened their arteries.

Moon Child rose to leave. "I guess I'll waddle out now." TA agreed.

She and Buck drove Herbie and Ruthy home. They had to wake Ruthy to get her into the house. After shooing his sister through the door, Herbie turned to Buck and asked, "May I come back tomorrow? I don't have school tomorrow - the water will be off. May I come tomorrow? Ruthy has school. What time would be best? I'll be driving myself so I could get there any time you say." He paused and looked eager. The expression reminded her of her beloved dog, Tish, before a walk.

Buck grinned at him. "Not too early, I hope. How about between eight and nine o'clock?"

Herbie, looking very pleased, grabbed Buck's hand and shook it enthusiastically. "I'll see you then. Thanks so much for dinner. Ruthy was going to thank you but I think she's sleepwalking. See you tomorrow." He went inside and closed the door.

They could hear him through the door calling to his parents. "Mom, Dad. This was so cool and we got to eat at Tucanos too." His voice continued, but he was walking away from the door and they couldn't hear his words.

Walking back to the car, TA found herself holding Buck's hand. She leaned against him as they walked and his hand slipped from hers and his arm wrapped her close to his side. She wished that the car was parked further from the door.

He opened her car door and as she turned to get in, he gently kissed her. She was half in and half out of the car when it happened and she was so surprised that she fell back into the passenger seat. They both laughed and he shut the door and walked around and got in behind the wheel.

"You know," he said, as he drove, "We have to start getting some 'us' time together with no one around and no deadlines to make."

They arrived back at the hotel and he walked her to her door, stepped back, bowed and kissed her hand; Nathan couldn't have done it better. Looking up he whispered, "Until tomorrow, sweet princess." He grinned and walked back toward the elevator, whistling.

CHAPTER 30

ALBUQUERQUE

FRIDAY, NOVEMBER 3, 2000

The bedside phone rang at 7 am. TA, sleeping soundly, partially levitated from the bed and snatched the offending receiver from its cradle. "Yes," she croaked. A tiny voice mumbled something. She turned the receiver around and put the proper end to her ear. "Hello?"

"Hi there, rise and shine." Buck was speaking in a much too cheerful voice.

"I'm awake…now. What's the plan?"

"Meet us for breakfast in the restaurant downstairs in about 30 minutes?"

"I'll be there." She hung up.

She was out the door at 7:28.

The restaurant was practically empty. Everybody who had business in downtown Albuquerque had evidently left Friday afternoon.

The men sat at a table near the buffet happily scarfing down plates of various morning foods. She waved and went over to check out the offerings. The more she looked, the better it looked. She grabbed a plate and filled it.

"Are we good to work on the maps for the rest of the day?" she asked.

188

"No more phone calls from headquarters, so I guess we have an open agenda," said Buck.

"Herbie called me about six." Demetrius grinned. "That's one neat kid. I can see us recruiting him in a few years. He said he'd be down by 8." He laughed. "I didn't know teens voluntarily got up this early on a Saturday. He offered to come down earlier but I discouraged him by pleading adult slothfulness."

They lingered over coffee, mostly discussing the last few days and drove over to the FBI office.

As they turned on the building's street they were astounded to see several black vans and a couple of official cars parked haphazardly in front of the entrance. Lights mounted on the vehicles were flashing and several bystanders stood across the street, held back by crime scene tape. City police were standing around, most talking into mics.

Buck parked the car in front of a hydrant and they all sprang out. As they ran forward, the men pulled their badges out of their pockets and waved them at the police as they charged toward the entrance. TA hurried along behind trying to look official.

Nathan, quicker than the rest, strong-armed the door open and they bounded into the building. The office was on the second floor. They didn't wait for the elevator but surged through the lobby, waving their badges, threading their way past various official and non-official people. They hit the stairs in a dead run.

The door to the office was propped open but a large uniformed man stood in the door frame, blocking their entrance. He had been looking into the office but at their approach he spun around and held out an arresting hand, arm straight.

"Whoa there," he said.

The men held up their badges and he stepped away from the entrance. As TA tried to follow them into the room the hand shot out again. "Official ID?" he asked. Buck turned back and grabbing her arm he pulled her into the room, "She's as official as you get.

The map is hers," he said. The officer raised an eyebrow, but lowered his arm and stepped back.

People in uniforms and suits were milling around. The duty officer stood against the wall looking pissed. Herbie occupied a chair against another wall looking distressed and furious. Loud voices came from the conference room where the map had been housed before they put it away the night before.

They threaded their way through the throng and slid into the room. The map was spread out on the table. Fredo and Moon Child stood with their backs to the map, clearly in positions of defense. A tall suited man, radiating attitude, was nose to nose with Fredo, somewhat at a disadvantage because even though he was tall, Fredo was taller.

"What's going on?" barked Buck.

The man whirled. He glared at Buck. "Agent Doe?" he snapped.

"Yes."

"Get this man out of here. He has no official standing and I want him out NOW."

Who are you? What is *your* official standing?" enquired Buck in a steely voice, hands clenched, positioning himself beside Fredo and Moon Child.

"I'm special agent James P. Meacham. I'm here on direct orders from the White House."

He pulled out an envelope and removed the paper inside. Buck took it and quickly read it. His shoulders slumped.

Meacham continued, "I'm taking charge of the maps and transporting them to Washington. They'll be kept under lock and key until it's decided which country has proper jurisdiction. While ownership is being determined they'll be translated by people with the *proper* credentials, and *proper* clearance, and *proper* training to handle these things." He drew himself rigidly upright and, after puffing out his chest he tried to look down his nose at Buck, which was difficult as they were both about the same height.

Until now both Nathan and Demetrius had stood silently, poised on the balls of their feet, observing, but ready for action. Nathan stepped forward, "Nathan Hale Jones, ARF," he said, holding out his credentials. "We were called in to observe and protect this map and to see that it gets to the proper owner."

"ARF?" asked Agent Meacham, looking confused.

"Artifact Recovery Force," offered Demetrius.

With this, Agent Meacham seized on the opportunity to take command again, "What the hell is the Artifact Recovery Force and who are you?"

"Doctor Demetrius Bean, and the Artifact Recovery Force is an autonomous government agency that reports to the President, Department of the Interior, Secretary of State, Smithsonian, Library of Congress and several other cabinet offices and organizations."

"Never heard of it," sniffed Meacham dismissively.

"We perform discreetly," said Nathan.

"Huh, well it doesn't matter. I'm here to send all of you about your business and to transport the maps to Washington. I have a plane waiting, so let's get on with it."

Meacham stepped to the door of the conference room and called to someone evidently standing in the outer hall. "Bring in the case."

Tramping of feet, a few curses, and a long slender box was maneuvered into the room.

Evidently someone in Washington knew the dimensions of the map and had a box constructed especially for it. They set the box along the edge of the table and unlatched its several locks. When opened, it was obvious it was well-designed. The inside of the box looked much like a very expensive rifle carrying case, padded, foamed and felted. Meachem slid map in, covered it and the lid was shut tightly and locked.

Meacham gathered up the tablets that Fredo, Moon Child and the children had been making notes on and stuffed them in a brief case. He turned to TA, "I understand there are two more maps, a map case and a silk cover. Where are they? Did you make any notes? I'll need them, too."

TA reluctantly led him to the safe where the maps were stored.

"The maps are in their original case and the notes and case are wrapped in the silk. The case is very valuable, as are the maps, and quite fragile."

Meacham momentarily looked frustrated. "What do you suggest?"

"Let's create a box out them," she answered.

They emptied two boxes from the supply room and with quite a bit of duct tape they created a carrying case. The silk was used to protect the ancient cases.

Everything was carried out to a waiting van and then Meacham turned back for one more parting shot. "All of you who are independent contractors and volunteers are dismissed. Those of you who came in from out of town, I am authorized to pay for your plane ticket if you leave immediately. Otherwise you are on your own and the government severs all ties, with our thanks. To you people that are volunteers, the government thanks you for your service. Lastly, government employees should contact your superiors immediately for a future assignment." He gave them a stiff nod and left.

A rather unobtrusive man who had been hovering in the background now stepped forward. "My name's Frank Mankey. If you'll give me your names and destinations I'll have tickets waiting for you at the airport. Please give me your cell numbers so I can notify you of your arrangements." He pulled out a notebook and pen.

Moon Child looked over at Fredo. He shook his head. She turned back to Mankey and said, "I'll be staying for a few more days and I'll make my own travel arrangements." He nodded and turned to TA. She gave him her information and he turned to Herbie who had come into the room from the front reception area. He was looking pale as he turned to Mankey. "I live here and I want you to know that I think you're a bunch of jerks."

He turned to the rest of them and asked, "May I have your cards? Is it alright if I call or write? I just want you to know that you're all my heroes and up until now this has been the best time of my life." They gathered around him, assuring him that it had been the best time of their lives also and that they really admired him. They wished him luck and told him they expected to hear from him, gave him their cards and promised to stay in touch. He left to drive himself home.

They took the elevator down to the first floor, the cars and vans were gone, and the crowd had dissipated. Outside the building the crime scene tape that had been stretched to keep the crowd of spectators back had been removed with only a small length of tape still knotted to a no-parking sign. Their car was where they had left it, a parking ticket stuck under the wiper.

They returned to the hotel, silent. TA listlessly walked up to her room and started packing. She sat down on the still unmade bed and broke into tears. The map, the beautiful map, her beautiful glowing map was gone. She felt bereft, a deep pain in her heart, her stomach. She felt ill.

There was a knock at the door. She rose and opened it to Buck. She flung herself into his arms, deep sobs wracking her. He picked her up and carried her back into the room, kicking the door shut behind him.

Standing together, arms wrapped around each other, they rocked as she cried. Finally the tears ended in hiccups and she leaned back and looked up at him. He had tears running down his cheeks.

He stepped back and gave an embarrassed laugh. "I don't know if I'm crying for you or the map or because I'm so damn mad at the government." He pulled out a handkerchief and mopped his face.

She went into the bathroom and washed up. Her eyes were red and her cheeks flushed. She ran a comb through her hair and went back into the room. Her phone rang.

"Yes," she answered.

"This is agent Mankey. You have a flight out to San Francisco this afternoon. Continental, flight 174 at 4 pm. Check-in time is 3:00 pm. Your hotel fees have been guaranteed until noon. Thank you for your service." He hung up.

"What a jerk," she said. She turned to Buck, who was sitting in the arm chair by the window. "What now?"

He drew a deep breath. "I fly out at nine. I'll get into DC in the early morning. As soon as the regular staff is on duty, I'll go in and find out what's going on and call you with what I find out." He paused for a moment and stood, looking out the window at the mountains.

He turned to her, "I have an official debriefing scheduled for tomorrow afternoon." He started to pace. "This is unbelievable! I feel as if we've been robbed. A real slap in the face." He stopped and turned to her. "You know, by rights, that map is yours or the Gabaldons."

She stood, transfixed by the thought. It had never occurred to her that she might have a claim to the map. "But it's a national treasure. A person can't own a national treasure." She paused to think. "I guess the problem is which nation has the rights to it." She smiled. "This might become very interesting. Do you think our government would voluntarily give the map back to China? How did it end up in Japan, owned by a Japanese family? Does that mean the Japanese government has a claim, too?"

She sat in the second chair. "Do you think our government has even notified the Chinese and Japanese that there's a treasure involved?"

"If they haven't, they're idiots," said Buck. "When the Chinese consulate had three employees murdered the U.S. government sure knew something was going on. Also, the Japanese know they had a bunch of Yakusas running amuck. Yeah, they know something major is going on. They might not know quite what it is, but they'll find out soon enough. I don't think our government can exactly sweep this under the rug."

He paused and thought for a moment. "You know, this could turn into a real plus for diplomacy. Lots of news coverage, and when they finally turn the map over to whomever, that government is going to owe them big time." He thought a few more moments. "They could give the gold map to China and the other two maps to Japan. You said that one map was a treasure in its own right."

The hotel phone rang. Buck, who was standing by it, picked it up. "Hello?" He laughed. "Sorry, no such activity is going on here. Yeah, I'm the one that's sorry." He laughed again. "Okay. We'll see you in a few." He hung up.

"That was Nathan. I won't go into details. They're all packed and ready to check out. He said that Moon Child is already checked out and Fredo picked her up. We're all invited to Fredo's house for pizza and reprise. We can leave from his place when it's time for our flights."

He turned to her unmade bed with the suitcase open across it. "Is this all ready to go? Oh, no," he said, spying the tiny clock on her bedside table. He picked it up and inspected it. "This is pretty, and so small. Where do you want it? "

She rose and tucked the tiny clock in the pocket of her suitcase. She gathered up the rest of her belongings, stuffed them in, and locked the case. Her heavy coat was lying beside the now closed suitcase. They checked one last time and Buck picked it up.

As they waited for the elevator he turned to her, "I'll take this case and you down to the lobby and park you there while I run up and grab my case. I only have a few things. I really should drive back up to Santa Fe and get a few more clothes but the hell with it. They can take me as I am. "

They got on the elevator and out at the lobby. Nathan and Demetrius were lounging in a seating area in the middle of the room. Buck set her suitcase by theirs and got back on the waiting elevator.

TA went over to the desk, signed a few papers and then joined the men in the sitting area. She was at half mast, not quite standing and not quite sitting when the elevator opened again and Buck came out carrying a small overnighter.

It only took a minute for him to check out. Soon they were all getting into the official car and driving toward Fredo's house.

CHAPTER 31

ALBUQUERQUE

FRIDAY AFTERNOON,
NOVEMBER 3, 2000

On the way over to Fredo's home TA called Ezekiel. He picked up immediately. To her relief he sounded much stronger.

"I'll be home late tonight and be over to see you Saturday morning. I'll call you when I leave the apartment and bring breakfast."

"I wasn't expecting you so soon. Don't you want to stay until the map translation is farther along? If you're coming because you think I'm sick, don't. I really am much better."

"No, I'm coming because the government grabbed all the maps."

"What? Tell!" he exclaimed.

"There isn't much else to tell. Listen, we're on our way to Fredo's for lunch. I'm flying out at 4:00. I'll call you while I wait for the plane. It's a promise."

"Alright, if you promise! Soon." He hung up.

They arrived at Fredo's house which smelled deliciously of pizza. Moon Child was stretched out on the couch, a Coors Lite balanced on her stomach as she carried on a spirited conversation with someone on the phone. She was describing, in great detail, the confiscation of the map.

She saluted them with the hand holding the beer. "Have to go now, do you have it all figured out? I'll have to grab Daisy and the suitcase and take off right away. It's a two hour drive, if I'm lucky, and then I'll need to get Daisy settled. What? Oh, sorry, I thought I told you. It's a two week immersion course. I think I have eight students, but they might throw in a few more. Hank is coming down to help. Yes, he's almost done. As soon as he turns it in he'll be through. He already has a couple of job offers. I'll sure miss him. Bye Sweetie. Say hi to the kids and Asa for me. Love you lots." She hung up.

She swung her legs around and sat up. "Sorry about that. That was my daughter Emily. She lives near me and she has my dog. I'm flying in tomorrow evening and I have to grab the dog and a suitcase with fresh clothes and then I take off driving down to Monterey. I have an immersion class starting Monday morning. Ugh! I feel like I'm panting. But it's all good. Fredo is coming out when the class is over and I'll introduce him to my family and then we're going to take a road trip along the coast. Daisy's invited, so it'll be perfect. She can lie on the floor of the car or sit in my lap, the furry bozo." She paused to smile happily.

"What's an immersion class, or more to the point, what are you going to immerse in? Poor grammar, sorry. And…how big is Daisy, since you're planning on wedging her into a two-seat convertible, a very tiny convertible?"

"I teach Chinese, part of the time at Stanford and part of the time for the Navy, and all branches of the military, at the Language Institute in Monterey. The classes are intense but at the end, the participants walk away being able to at least carry on a conversation in Chinese. Hank really helps a lot, I'll miss him when he leaves. Hank's my graduate student but soon to be gone."

"And Daisy?" asked TA.

"Oh Daisy, she's my sweetheart. I found her on the street one day." She smiled lovingly.

"How big is Daisy?" repeated TA.

"She's a smallish golden retriever, kind of. Probably about 40 pounds. I don't quite know what's in Daisy. Lots of love and some poodle. Very smart and loves people and cats. She keeps finding cats and brings them in the house through her doggy door. They wander into the backyard and it's rather a problem. So far I've been able to find homes for the ones that want to stay. Daisy wants to keep them all but it's not to be. I'm not home all the time. Daisy travels well but I can't take a whole train of animals with me." She laughed and took another swallow of beer. "We all have our crosses to bear," she said. "Even Daisy."

"Come eat everyone. TA needs to leave by 2:30," called Fredo.

They gathered at the table spread with paper plates, napkins and three opened pizza boxes holding assorted types of pizza. The two things they had in common were cheese and green chili.

As they ate they discussed the maps. TA talked about the maps on mulberry paper, pointing out that most people called it rice paper but it was made from the pulp of the mulberry tree. She fielded a few questions about restoring maps. Most of the answers were technical enough to not hold much interest except in passing.

Then they got down to the subject that held everybody's interest, the gold map. Fredo and Moon Child, filling in each other's dissertation, explained that it was made in the early 1400's AD and that the Ming Dynasty was still being referred to as the Empire of the Great Ming even in the present.

Moon Child took over and went into lecture mode. "you should be aware that the Chinese people were way ahead of Europeans in so many ways. During the period of 221 AD through approximately 600 AD, Tsin and Su dynasties, they actually had books on agriculture; they were using insects to control insects, made steel weapons, accurate clocks, built water mills. They used pi in math, had a 24-point compass. The astronomers of the Tsin made lists of twenty-eight solar halos and anticipated eclipses, which the European astronomers didn't do until the 17th century."

"TA probably can tell you about P'ei Hsiu, AD 228-271. He's the father of Chinese cartography. Might have been Korean, but the Chinese claim him."

TA broke in, "He constructed a huge map of China, eighteen sheets, on the scale of 500 li to an inch. The li is equal to a third of a mile."

She suddenly noticed the clock on the wall. "Oh gosh, I have to get going, it's after two." They rose and started clearing the table. She excused herself to tidy up.

Hugs all around, everybody checking to be sure they had contact information, and full names. Hugs again. Out the door.

The drive to the airport was surprisingly short. Buck wanted to park and come in but the lot was distant. TA insisted that he drop her at her terminal.

As he pulled up, she turned and held out her hand. She wanted to throw herself into his arms. He handled it well; he took her hand and put it on his shoulder and then drew her close and gave her a kiss. If they hadn't been in such a public place, it might have grown into a great deal more. She leaned back, wide-eyed. "Oh yes, we need more of that."

He laughed. "There will be. I'll call you, you call me." He looked past her, "Oh, oh, you're being paged."

She turned and saw a sky cap leaning forward with his hand on the door handle. "Better pop the trunk." She opened the door and stepped out. "Soon."

She pointed out which suitcase was hers and as she followed the sky cap into the building she saw Buck drive off, waving to her as he went.

She checked in and found a seat at her gate. Dialing Ezekiel, she sat back to have a long conversation, bringing him up to date.

200

The plane left on time. She slept most of the way to San Francisco. She took a taxi to her apartment. Inside, she tossed her suitcase on the couch, stripped, pulled on her nightshirt, brushed her teeth and fell into bed.

CHAPTER 32

SAN FRANCISCO

SATURDAY, NOVEMBER 4, 2000

TA woke to the sound of pigeons cooing on her windowsill. She stretched, smiled, remembered Buck's parting kiss. Glancing at her clock across the room, which read one o'clock, she rose. "Nuts!" As she dashed into the bathroom, it suddenly occurred to her that the clock was a wind up and its hands weren't moving.

Back to her bedside table to check her watch, she had plenty of time to have a leisurely bath before picking up breakfast for Ezekiel and herself.

She caught the bus on the corner. At her stop, a cold wind was blowing and people hurried about their tasks.

The deli, was warm and familiar. "Hi," she exclaimed, "I'm back and I'm starving!" Her stomach growled loud enough for Donna, the clerk, to hear. They both laughed. She over-ordered and Donna packed everything into a handled carry bag for her trip across the park. Paying, she paused, "Oh, Donna, I forgot Friend. He needs a plate of lox with a dab of cream cheese, please. What do I owe you for feeding him while I was gone?"

"Nothing. We enjoy him. He's part of our family." Donna prepared a plate and TA was out the door.

On her way across the park TA couldn't see Friend anywhere. She was getting concerned when an impatient trill came from behind her. She spun around. Friend had been following her.

"Hi, Friend. Did you miss me? Let's go over by that tree and I'll give you your breakfast." The trunk of the large tree gave them shelter from the wind. Squatting, she presented Friend with his plate. He gave a roaring purr as he hunched over his breakfast. Scratching him between his shoulder blades as he gulped his meal she cautioned him, "don't gulp, there'll be something left after Ezekiel and I are through." She picked up the plate. He ambled beside her until she came to the curb opposite the shop.

She let herself into the familiar entryway, and suddenly realized how much she enjoyed working here and the whole ambiance of the place. Fresh-made coffee smells followed Ezekiel as he came wheeling in from his office, looking spry. He threw his arms wide in a welcoming gesture. Stooping, she gave him a hug and then together, they proceeded into his office. She laid their plastic tablecloth across his desk. A quick trip to the kitchenette and she returned with plates, utensils and coffee. She spread the food and as they ate she told him her story. He was full of questions and fascinated with her descriptions of the caves.

Finally, Ezekiel leaned back in his chair and with a twinkle he asked, "So, the one person you aren't telling me enough about is this FBI agent, John 'Buck' Doe. I sense there's more to this story of daring do."

TA blushed. "Oh Ezekiel, it's early times yet, but yes, there seems to be more to that part of the story." She gave a big sigh and then giggled. "I'll keep you updated as things progress." She rose and started to clear the desk.

After brunch, Ezekiel went upstairs to his apartment to take a nap. TA reluctant to go home went down to the basement to check on the drying cabinet and assess what projects needed attention. She found two books and a card with her name on it sitting on her worktable. Opening it, TA read: *Dear TA, After you left with Mr. Kamakura I received a catalog with these two books listed. Since you were on your way to study Japanese maps I thought these books might interest you. With great regard for your talents, Ezekiel.*

TA pulled a stool up to the table and picked up the first book, an illustrated book about Japanese armor. She checked the copyright date; the book was a first edition printed in Edinburgh in 1879. It was absolutely beautiful; tissue paper covers for each hand-tinted and etched illustration and detailed information on each item that made up the costume of a warrior. Evidently a lot of latitude was given to each armorer as the many warriors illustrated toward the back of the book had radically varying equipment.

She studied an illustration of a Samurai in full regalia. Each piece was marked with an arrow and a letter. On the facing page was the name of the item and a brief description. First on the list were the names of the most major pieces with brief descriptions.

The description went on to cover all sorts of smaller pieces of necessary armor such as cheek, neck and throat guards, metal gloves, iron mesh to cover the tops of the feet. It was astounding. All thought out in great detail to protect but allow as much freedom of movement as possible.

There was also a detailed list of clothing worn under or over the armor either for comfort or to identify the wearer in the heat of battle.

Last on the list were items like small banners, flags, tassels and cloak, all again, for purposes of identifying the wearer.

Wow! These men must have been tremendously strong to be able to wear all the armor and still be able to walk, let alone fight.

She set the book aside and picked up the second. It was titled *The Kabuto. The Helmet.* Larger than the first, it would have been a presentation or gift book. She opened it and found that it too, had been published in Edinburgh, in 1899. It was exquisite. The etched illustrations were hand-tinted and protected by tissue cover sheets bound into the book. A limited edition of 500, this book was number eleven and signed by the author, Robert Christopher Anderson.

The first few pages explained how the helmets were made and the various pieces that made up this part of the Samurai armor. All the helmets were basic in shape and most had shade shields over the eyes similar to trucker caps. Some had shields in back to protect the neck; solid molded pieces of metal or many narrow plates attached by rings. But other than the basic shape they resembled nothing TA had ever seen before. They were flights of fancy that carried one into the realm of the mythical.

Primarily made of iron with gold, jewels, and extensions, they were stylized or realistic. Shaped as sharks, bulls, panthers, bats, birds, dragonflies, deer, the list went on. Amazing!

Each page of the book needed hours to study. She checked her watch and discovered it was almost evening. Wrapping the books and card she took them upstairs and set them with her coat.

She found Ezekiel and thanked him profusely. "Can I get you something to eat before I leave?"

"No, my dear. I'm fine after such a big meal this morning. You get going. It's getting dark." Gathering up the books and a paper plate with lox on it, she pulled on her coat and headed out the door. Friend was waiting in the park for his lox.

She ran to catch the bus. Her phone rang as she rode, it was Buck.

"I wanted to give you the day with Ezekiel, but I had to let you know that you're going to be receiving an invitation from the White House They're unveiling the map on Friday. Bigwigs from China and Japan are coming. The governors of New Mexico and California, too. They want all of us there. I'm still pissed off enough about how they hijacked the map that I didn't want to go but then I thought that you'd be there so that changed things." He paused for breath.

"Well," she answered, "at least they're giving us some recognition. Are Moon Child and Fredo and the kids invited? They better be, or I'm not going."

"Yeah, Demetrius, Nathan, the Quintana clan, Fredo, Moon Child and they invited the Gabaldons. They passed. In fact, they want nothing to do with any of it and asked to not be mentioned in any form."

"Not surprising, the way Mr. Gabaldon feels," said TA

The phone was quiet for so long that TA thought the connection had been dropped but then he spoke.

"I miss you so. I never imagined that falling in love would be like this. I thought a person was supposed to be dancing like 'Singing in the Rain' but it isn't. I feel like a super ball. One minute I'm up and the next down." He laughed. "I've thought I was in love before but it was nothing like this. God, I'm so empty and the world is so gray, when you're not here. Tell me you love me. Tell me you feel like this."

She started laughing. "No, not quite like that. Just empty. And yes, I love you. I do. And it is different. You heard me laugh because I feel *such* delight when I talk to you. Do you know when I'll be flying in to Washington and will we be staying at the same hotel? I can't wait to see you." She paused a moment and then out it burst, "I miss you so much. It hurts. Oh nuts! This is my stop; call me as soon as you know anything. No, no, I mean call me lots even if you don't know anything. I kiss at you. Love, bye."

She gathered up her carrying bag, purse, trying to stuff her phone in a pocket and half rose. The phone went skidding down the aisle. The bus driver gave her an exasperated look in the mirror. She shouted sorry as an older woman reached down from her seat and trapped the phone as it slid by. "Thanks", she puffed as she retrieved the phone and practically fell through the door and off the bus.

The bus door slammed shut and it hissed off down the street. Stuffing the phone in her purse she gathered the bag of books and tried skipping toward her apartment. The book bag crashed into her leg; catching herself, she finished her walk at a sedate pace.

She spent the evening alternating between gazing into space with a goofy smile and reading the books.

CHAPTER 33

SAN FRANCISCO

MONDAY, NOVEMBER 6, 2000

The answering machine was flashing when TA entered the shop. The caller identified himself as Ralph Jamison. He asked about maps of South Africa. TA could remember one or two, referenced them from her card file and called him back.

Jamison answered and she introduced herself. "I understand you're interested in maps of South Africa. Can you narrow down what you're looking for? It's a pretty large area."

"Yes." He sounded elderly. "It's a gift for my dear friend and companion of over 40 years. Edward is such a jolly good friend, came originally from South Africa, born near Johannesburg and grew up there. I thought a map of that area would make a wonderful gift and bring back happy memories. I'd like to get it framed and give it to him as a Christmas gift."

"I'm sure we can find something suitable. Tell me a little about Edward. Does he have any special interests or hobbies?"

"Yes. Gardening. He's won many, many prizes for his flowers and we're always on the garden tours. Oh, and old movies. In fact, we have quite a collection."

"I'll pull the two maps I'm thinking of and take a closer look but my card file says we have two maps you might be interested in seeing; one is of the Kirstenbosch National Botanical Garden, near Cape Town. And, believe it or not, the other was drawn for one of the early Johnny Weissmuller movies and has sketches of Cheetah on it. We acquired them recently and I haven't really inspected them but they might be worth a look. Would you like to make an appointment to see them?"

The last couple of sentences were said as Mr. Jamison was exclaiming, "Perfect, perfect. Wonderful! May I come over this morning, say in an hour or so? This is so exciting. I'm so glad I called. Edward will be beside himself with joy."

"Yes. I'll go pull the maps now and look for anything else you might want to see."

Mr. Jamison was still thanking her as he hung up.

She started the coffee, turned on lights and called up to Ezekiel that she'd be down in the workroom pulling maps for a morning appointment. He shouted back that he'd be right down and would cover any calls.

Sure enough, there it was, the Kirstenbosch National Botanical Gardens, nestled at the foot of Table Mountain, in Cape Town. The map was just as she remembered, a detailed map of the garden drawn by a talented amateur watercolorist. There were a few age-related problems, all fixable.

She was delighted to see the Tarzan map was in almost pristine condition. It depicted a part of Africa that had never existed and showed various imaginative flora. Tarzan's treehouse was in the upper right corner. There was a swamp with a pond and a crocodile. A python or some large snake was hanging from a tree branch. A few elephants grazed in an open area – they looked like Asian elephants by the size of their ears, there was a pride of lions lounging in a field with a few zebras hanging around, waiting to be eaten. And yes, there was Cheetah, lying in a hammock sipping from a Coke bottle.

Wonderful! She turned the map over and studied the three sketches of Cheetah in various poses. Super! The map would look great double matted and glassed on both sides. They could hang it with either side showing.

The buzzer rang and the intercom came on. "TA," called Ezekiel, "You have visitors, would you please come up."

"Right there," she answered. She whipped off her smock, ran her hands through her hair, gathered the maps and went up to meet Mr. Jamison.

The visitor wasn't Mr. Jamison. A group of people milled around the shop, admiring the wall maps and setting up cameras. A distinguished looking couple sat by the windows, talking with Ezekiel. They rose when she entered.

The man strode across the room with his hand out. He was dressed elegantly in a beautifully tailored suit. "How do you do?" he exclaimed. "It's an honor to meet you. I'm so glad you are still healthy after all your adventures!"

Ezekiel wheeled up. "TA, meet Chinese Consul Chen Ling and his wife Chen Li."

The Consul shook TA's hand enthusiastically and then his wife joined them. She too shook TA's hand and then gave her a hug. "What a role model you are!" she said. "Come over and sit down. We want to hear all about your adventures."

TA was led to the sitting area and recounted a much-abbreviated version of her adventures. Both the Consul and his wife had questions, some of which she wouldn't be able to answer until the map was translated.

Handing TA an official looking envelope, the Consul explained it was a formal invitation to a reception at the Chinese Embassy. It was on November 11, the day after the White House reception.

"There are many Chinese people flying in to meet you. Many will also be at the White House.

"We have brought you a gift from the people of China." The Consul said a few words to one of the men who had accompanied him. The man stepped forward and handed him a carrying case.

"We will be meeting again in Washington DC but my Government wanted to give you a gift privately in appreciation of your contribution to our rich history."

He set the case on the table and opened it. Inside was a silk-covered box. He flipped the latch and opened the box. The contents were covered in red silk. He lifted the silk and displayed a flat oval-shaped stone with fascinating recesses and carvings.

She looked at him enquiringly.

"This is an inkstone from the Song Dynasty, 90-1279. An inkstone was used by scribes to grind inksticks and add water to create ink. This flat surface has a well at one end. A drop of water is placed on the flat area and the inkstick's end is ground against it. More water is added, one drop at a time, until the desired amount of ink is collected in the well here." He pointed to an indention carved at the end of the grinding surface.

Removing the inkstone from its box and he handed it to TA. The stone looked as if it had been carved from a river rock with crystal ripples of greens and lavenders flowing through it. Except for the work surface it was carved in blossoms and leaves, a smiling dragon winding through the flowers. His head hung over the ink well, his tongue extending down into the well. His shiny black eyes looked up at her.

Mrs. Chin leaned forward. "His eyes are made of jade. The stone comes from the Tao River in Gansu Province.

The door chime rang and a small rotund man entered accompanied by a stone faced Chinese man in a chauffeur's uniform. They paused just inside the second door. TA looked up.

211

"Mr. Jamison, come in," she called. She excused herself and met him in the middle of the shop. "I'm so sorry but it will be a bit before I can show you the maps. Would you mind waiting or perhaps you could come back in an hour or so?"

"I'd be glad to take a walk in the park and return in an hour. Do take your time. I have nothing scheduled the whole day." He bowed to the Chins and left the shop.

TA returned to the Chins. "I'm so sorry. I had an appointment to show Mr. Jamison some maps from South Africa and it completely slipped my mind what with all the excitement. I've never met a Chinese Consul and Mrs. Consul--ever!"

They smiled at her. "We're almost through interrupting your day, my dear. May we take a few photos? You're all the rage in China and people would like to see what you look like."

TA insisted some of the photographs include Ezekiel and one with her holding the inkstone. They also took some of the shop and some of the maps on the walls were also taken. TA cringed at the damage being done by the flash from the camera but held her tongue.

The Chins wanted to see the maps that she was going to show Mr. Jamison and then photos of them were also taken. The photographer loved the sketches of Cheetah and took a few extras of them.

The Chins thanked TA and Ezekiel and left.

Mr. Jamison returned shortly after. He admired the inkstone profusely and then sat down to inspect the maps. Absolutely delighted, he purchased them both and TA promised to have them tidied, framed and delivered by mid-December.

CHAPTER 34

SAN FRANCISCO

MONDAY, NOVEMBER 6, 2000

TA arrived home, laden with groceries. There was a large yellow post-it note on the banister of the stairs. Her name was written on it and *Come to my apartment RIGHT AWAY* Mrs. M. She carried her sacks up to her apartment, stuffed perishables in the fridge and returned to retrieve the note.

Knocking on Mrs. Maisel's' door; it was immediately thrown open and Mrs. M grabbed her arm and tugged her in.

"TA, I thought you'd never get here. My goodness. What has been going on. Oh my. My heart is all aflutter." She gasped, fanning her chest with her hand. "Come in, come in."

"I am in, Mrs. Maisel. What's wrong?"

"This. This is what's wrong, or right perhaps? Exciting, anyway." Mrs. Maisel stuttered in excitement. The TV, muted and turned to a news channel, was behind her with words scrolling across the screen. TA saw MAP FOUND in large letters. Mrs. Maisel thrust two envelopes into TA's hands and waved a folded newspaper under her nose. The largest envelope, made of heavy elegant feeling paper, had an official seal on the back and the return address stated THE WHITE HOUSE, WASHINGTON, DC.

213

"Oh my," said TA, sitting. "It's here." "Do you have a letter opener or a knife?"

Mrs. Maisel hurried across the room to her desk and pulled out an impressive letter opener in the shape of sloth with one long extended claw. She handed it to TA, who sat transfixed by the letter opener. "Where the heck did you get this?" she asked.

"My husband George was down in South America and he brought it back. Neat, huh? OPEN THAT ENVELOPE!"

TA slid the claw under the flap and sliced open the envelope. She pulled out an inner envelop and opened it to reveal an embossed invitation to an official unveiling of the map at 3:00 pm. Friday, November, 10, 2000.

TA turned to the other, business-sized envelope and slit it open. There was a letter folded inside along with plane tickets for first class to Washington on Thursday, November 9, 2000. A suite had been reserved for her in a pricey-sounding hotel. All her expenses, including any food eaten at the hotel, were covered. Any other reasonable expenses she incurred while in Washington would be covered. She was instructed to keep receipts.

The dress for the White House reception was 'afternoon formal.' There would be many official people there, all of whom would want to meet TA. The actual unveiling would be recorded for TV. It went on to say that the other two maps would also be displayed. Everybody who had to do with the map and its recovery, including Herbie, Ruthy and their parents, Nathan and Demetrius from ARF, Buck, professors Alfredo Chen and Ellen Foster would be there. They were all going to be staying in the same hotel as TA.

The return ticket was for Sunday and the suite was paid through that day so that she might avail herself of the various attractions in Washington.

The letter closed with the name of the official that had written it, Maryanne Linwood, along with her phone number in case TA had any questions.

TA sat back and looked up at Mrs. Maisel. "Oh my."

"All right, TA." Mrs. Maisel sat down and flipped open the paper, exposing the front headlines. There was a picture of TA displayed prominently with the words GOLD MAP leading the article. Mrs. Maisel leaned forward, reminding TA of a small dog expecting a treat.

TA, again, told her tale. *I should just record it. I'll never get within spitting distance of the map so I might as well just move on.*

Map to be unveiled on Friday at official White House reception scrolled across the bottom of the muted TV screen.

Mrs. Maisel was delighted with the story and asked lots of questions. In the end it got down to the most important one of all. "What are you going to wear?"

"I don't know. I have a few nice things I bought when I went to work for Ezekiel. Sometimes you have to be really dressy in my job. I'll look through my closet." Her cell phone rang. *Buck.*

"I have to run, Mrs. Maisel, I need to take this call." Rising, she answered the phone as she left the apartment. She could feel Mrs. Maisel following her to the door, trying to hear both sides of the conversation. She pulled the door shut as she left.

"Hi" she said as she started up the stairs. "I got the invitation. Did you get yours? Just a sec, I have to unlock my door and I need two hands. Okay, I'm in."

They discussed the invitations as she put away the groceries and, as she ate a sandwich they talked about their day. His sounded even more interesting than hers as he had been in a class discussing the problems of apprehending underwater treasure hunters invading illegal sites. FBI would be working with Coast Guard and police, both local and state, if the sites were within the twelve-mile limits. Except it wasn't always a twelve-mile limit, some limits were shorter and some extended much farther. Laws were so complicated that sometimes state police would be outside their legal limit before the

US Government limit ended. Arrests had to be made by the proper authorities or they wouldn't stick.

She nestled down into her old recliner. "I miss you so much!" she exclaimed, surprising herself.

"I miss you too, honey. I sit in class and suddenly realize I lost half a lecture because I was daydreaming about seeing you again. Good thing I have a buddy taking the course too, so I can copy his notes. But we'll see each other soon. I'm meeting your plane."

"Oh, I didn't even look at my destination time on the ticket. Just a minute, let me get it." She bent over and tried to reach her purse, which she had tossed on the couch.

"Don't bother," Buck said, "I have it memorized. You get in at 1:45 pm my time. I'm planning to get there early in case you have a tail wind."

They laughed.

After several more minutes of more intimate conversation they signed off. He was three hours later and it was already past midnight. He had to be in class tomorrow at 8:00 am.

Thinking about the time changes she checked her ticket and sure enough, she took off at the ungodly time of 5:45 am her time. Ugh! That meant she'd have to be at the airport at 4:45 am! Oh well, she could sleep on the plane and, since it was first class, she'd have a comfy chair and a fancy breakfast. At least she assumed that. She'd never flown first class before.

She fell asleep going over her clothes in her mind. Wonder what the temperature is there. Cold, I bet.

CHAPTER 35

SAN FRANCISCO

TUESDAY, NOVEMBER 7, 2000

Tuesday morning, no rain, a truly lovely day. TA awoke with a smile, flew through her run with no lurking Asian people in sight, except for a young mother playing with her happy baby. Her bus was on time and everything was 'loverly'. She was humming the song from *My Fair Lady* as she strolled across the park, looking about for Friend. People were out strolling in the warm November weather, enjoying the sun.

Mind busy as she walked, her thoughts bounced between the receptions and visit to Washington and the amazing books Ezekiel had given her and where the heck was Friend. She had his breakfast in her lunch sack.

She was passing Robbie Burns' bust, when she heard a yell and turned to see a man across the park dressed in the armor of a Samurai warrior. He held a short sword; a Wakizashi, she remembered. He wore an elaborate Kabuto helmet in the form of a rearing dragon, mouth open, spitting gold flames. Red ribbons waved from its ridged back. She saw and processed this vision in a moment, as she stood transfixed.

The warrior suddenly charged her, howling what sounded like curses. People all around the park froze in horror. He was running dead out. She held her purse up in front of her like a shield as she dodged behind Robert Burns.

Help appeared from a nearby tree. Friend, all four feet and sixteen claws extended, fur standing straight out, screamingly vocal, launched himself from the upper branches of a Norfolk pine and slammed down onto the helmet of the warrior. He was blinded as the helmet tipped forward. His charge stopped so precipitously that his feet were still pedaling forward while his upper body sailed back. His howls of rage turned to screams of pain and fright as cat and man slammed back onto the cement walkway.

The man's shrieks mixed with Friend's yowls rose to such a high pitch that everyone in the vicinity threw their hands over their ears.

Two policemen appeared, their morning coffee cups flying as they grabbed for their pistols. "Call 9-1-1," they shouted at the by-standers. Several obeyed. Down the men pounced, bravely shouldering Friend aside, they handcuffed the man and retrieved the wakizashi. One couldn't resist brandishing it about until the other said something to him.

Sirens sounded in the distance and then police cars were everywhere. People poured out of shops and apartments to see what was going on. TA considered trying to fading, into the crowd but decided that wasn't a good idea. Several of the by-standers pointed at her as they talked to the police. One of the officers looked as if he were in charge. TA approached him. "I think you might want to talk to me," she said. "I think he was trying to kill me."

The cop gave her *a look* that spoke volumes. Ditsy woman. Wasting my time. "We could talk in my shop, over there, in private. I think you might want to call Lt. Samson. He's familiar with the case." She paused. He just looked at her. She handed him her card, embarrassed that her hand was shaking, and turned to walk away.

"Hey lady, don't walk away until I tell you that you can walk away." She kept going.

"Fuck, Okay. I'll be over there in a minute. Don't go anywhere."

CHAPTER 36

SAN FRANCISCO

TUESDAY, NOVEMBER 7, 2000

It was midafternoon before Lt. Samson, accompanied by D'Angelo, entered the shop. TA was in the basement inspecting some recently received maps.

The intercom squawked and Ezekiel's voice asked her to come up and talk to Lt. Samson.

Samson had already removed his coat and was sitting in one of the padded chairs in the alcove. Ezekiel sat in his wheelchair facing him. D'Angelo was wandering around the room studying the maps displayed on the walls.

Putting a good face on the whole situation, TA advanced with her hand out, "Long time no see."

Samson laughed and rose to shake her hand, "We really have to stop meeting like this." He gestured toward the other chair and she sat.

D'Angelo took his place behind Samson and pulled out his notebook and pen.

Samson took a tape recorder from his pocket and set it on the table. He dictated the Shop's name, address, date and who was present. Then he looked at his notebook, resting on his knee. "Let's see.

The 'perp' is Abe Ryota. He's the brother of Abe Satoshi, deceased. That was the man who chased you on the Albuquerque Tram." He reached out and stopped the recorder for a moment. "You've been busy since we last saw you. I'm looking forward to hearing all about your adventures. Congratulations on being honored at the White House, by the way. Very impressive."

He turned the tape recorder back on and resumed reading his notes. "Mr. Abe flew over from Japan to San Francisco yesterday and he's been a busy boy. He came to avenge his brother. He views his brother's death as your fault. Guess you were supposed to stand there and let him kill you. Anyway, he decided to kill you in 'the true Samurai way'. His words, not mine. Since he landed he's been assembling his Samurai armor." Samson laughed. "His Samurai armor is all rented from a costume company here in San Francisco. I guess that was as true as he could get. The sword was purchased from an armorer and yes, it could have killed you."

Samson drew a deep breath. "But the helmet is the real thing. We put a picture of it on the internet and got an instant hit. It was stolen last week from a private collector in Kyoto. I don't know how Abe managed to get it into the US; probably checked it through. It's worth a fortune and there's quite a reward. We thought maybe you could set up a trust for the cat so he always has food. Seems appropriate.

"We have a lot of legal stuff to go through with Mr. Abe. He's here on a visitor's visa. He hasn't seen a judge yet but he was definitely trying to kill you and he's a flight risk, so he won't get bail. Since he was in possession of the stolen helmet, Japan will want him too. I don't think Mr. Abe will be free for a long time.

"Look, I can't promise you that you're safe now that Abe is locked up. Watch your back at all times and try to stay in areas that have people in them. Be especially careful crossing streets.

He turned off the recorder and pocketing it, he stood. "When you get back from Washington, I'd like to take you out to lunch so you can tell me about the whole adventure. If I may, I'd like to bring my two kids to hear too. It's all pretty exciting."

TA grinned, "That would be nice. How old are your kids, girls, boys?"

"George is twelve and Emma is thirteen. Both think they know everything and I'd like to give them something new to think about. We'll see you then. Stay safe."

He retrieved his coat and he and D'Angelo let themselves out.

After the men went, TA returned to the basement and shut it up for the night, back upstairs she chatted with Ezekiel for a bit and left for the evening.

Cutting across the park with the food she had promised him, Friend met her midway. She sat with him for a bit as he ate. He didn't seem any worse for wear and enjoyed some extra scratching on his back.

It was dark by the time she got home, but the trip was uneventful.

Once in her apartment she called Buck and brought him up to date. He made notes and told her he'd see if he could find out anything else. They spent time with him cautioning her and more time talking about themselves. There was so much to learn about each other.

CHAPTER 37

SAN FRANCISCO/ WASHINGTON D.C.

THURSDAY, NOVEMBER 9, 2000

Thursday morning the alarm went off at 3:00 am and TA sprang to her feet. Her clothes were packed and she was ready fifteen minutes before the taxi was due.

After twitching for ten minutes she dragged the bags down to the front door as the cab was pulling up.

They drove through almost empty streets while she tried to relax.

At the airport she showed her tickets to the sky cap and from there it was an eye opener as to how the ¼ of 1 per cent of the population live. She whisked through check in, was taken to a VIP lounge, greeted by name and offered assorted refreshments and reading material.

TA boarded at 'her convenience' and was ushered to her seat by an unctuous flight attendant, accepted a lap robe and small pillow, and offered a champagne cocktail to keep her occupied while she was waiting for the hoi polloi to be stuffed in the back of the plane. The champagne was not particularly good so she sat holding it. She considered drinking it because it was free and she didn't want to

223

offend the flight attendants who looked as if they would be easily offended. On second thought, not intimidated, she handed it back. It was accepted with profuse apologies and the offer of a slew of other drinks, she declined. The attendant then informed her that breakfast would be served after take-off. "Would you care to see the menu while you wait?" She cared.

After eating she rummaged around in the pocket on the seat in front of her and found an assortment of gifts which she stuffed into her purse.

She spent most of the flight looking down at the spots of earth visible through the clouds and reading her current book, J. K. Rowling's, *Harry Potter and the Chamber of Secrets*. Lunch was offered at noon and she had a turkey sandwich without onions since she would soon see Buck.

An announcement said their arrival time at Reagan International Airport, would be ahead of schedule as they had a tail wind assisting them on the flight.

They swooped in and as they taxied up to the gate she scanned the windows of the terminal to see if one of those tiny heads had hair the color of an Irish setter. She couldn't even see if they had hair. The plane docked and she gathered her things and followed the other first class passengers down the jet bridge to the welcome lounge.

There he was, in front. She resisted the urge to drop her things and run into his arms. When she finally got close he held out his arms and forgetting dignity she dumped everything around her feet and threw herself against him, raising her lips for a kiss.

She felt movement as someone started gathering her carry-on and purse. It was Nathan. He gave her a brotherly kiss on the cheek. "Welcome to Washington, senorita," he grinned. "So glad you decided to drop by" (he waved the carryon and her purse)." Did you check a suitcase?"

224

She grinned and they exchanged hugs. "Yeah, the claim check is in the outer pocket of my purse." She took the purse and pulled out the claim. He took it and handed Buck her carryon.

"I'll go down and find the suitcase and meet you at the terminal door. What personality is it?" he asked.

"Personality? Oh you mean all its identifying particulars. It's an old beat up canvas case, red, white and blue strap around its middle. My theory is the less fancy, the less likely to be stolen."

"Sounds right to me," he said.

They met at one of the many doors and stepped out into a cold but light rain as a limo pulled up to the curb. The driver jumped out and opened the trunk. TA looked around to see who the celebrity might be but just saw various people hurrying about their business. Nathan walked up to the driver and they heaved her suitcase into the trunk. Buck handed them her carry-on and then beat the driver to the rear door and opened it for her.

The drive to their hotel was fun; catching up and discussing tomorrow and pausing occasionally to admire a point of interest.

A doorman greeted them under the hotel canopy and a young man in hotel uniform collected her bags. Suddenly the hotel doors burst open and Ruthy galloped out and threw herself on TA with a big hug. "So glad you're here. This is so neat! Can you imagine? Washington DC. The Capital! And we're going to meet the President!"

Buck herded them into the hotel. TA, with Ruthy hopping circles at her side, checked in. She followed the bellhop with her entourage; just like a movie star of old, she thought. She tried to walk regally with her head up. People were turning and looking. Just as she was preparing to enter the elevator a voice yelled. "TA, you're here. Wait for us." She turned and saw Herbie and Demetrius hurrying across the lobby. All the traffic in the lobby stopped to watch as they exchanged hugs and then entered the elevator.

"Wow!" said TA, as she viewed the suite. Impressed, she tried to look as if she stayed in places like this whenever she traveled. Buck handed the bellhop a tip and as he left she turned to the kids. "Are we all staying in suites this nice? She paused to take in bouquets of flowers, wet bar, large gift basket and even a fireplace with gently leaping flames. It looks like something out of those old 1930 movies. Wait 'til I tell Ezekiel!

She turned back to the children. "Herbie, where have you and Demetrius been? You're soaking!"

Demetrius laughed and pointed to Herbie, "It's his fault. You want to tell her?"

Herbie grinned. "We went to the Smithsonian. Ruthy stayed to meet you. Anyway, we had so much fun. Demetrius knows practically everybody there and they showed us all sorts of things behind the scenes. You've got to go, TA. We even visited areas where they were restoring items. They were reweaving a flag that had mouse holes in it. And we got to see how they treat papers that have been damaged. You probably know about that. But still, it was *so* neat. When it was time to come home he let me pick how we'd get back and I chose a double decker bus so I could sightsee. Oh, and guess what, I got to get on a really old steam engine! Say, did you know they have dental tools from way back when. I thought they just yanked them out, like in the old cowboy movies. It was so much fun, TA." He stopped for breath and turned to Demetrius. "I haven't said thank you. Demetrius, you're the best! Most adults aren't any fun but I'll go anywhere with you. Thank you, thank you."

Demetrius answered, "Just wait. The best is yet to come. We have something really special planned after supper. You'll see." He turned to everyone, "We've reservations in the hotel dining room at 6:30. Herbie, you and I need to change our clothes and TA needs time to get settled. Let's meet outside the dining room." People scattered and soon only Buck and TA were left.

TA, suddenly shy, "What's planned for after dinner?" She wandered over to the gift basket and peeked inside.

Buck followed her and turned her to face him. "Secrets." He pulled her to him and wrapping his arms around her he nuzzled her neck. She lost her shyness and soon they sank into the nearest sofa. Just when things were beginning to get really interesting, the phone rang. Buck reached out and grabbed it from the table at the end of the couch. "Yeah?"

"Oh! Okay. Soon. Thanks." He hung up. "Demetrius, calling to remind us that 6:30 is fast approaching." He stood and offered his hand. She took it and he pulled her upright. "We have 20 minutes to get dressed and down to the dining room."

She laughed. "Just when you were showing me some amazing moves. Okay. Are you far away or on this floor?"

It was his turn to laugh. "Closer than you think." He walked over to an interior door and undid the lock and safety chain. He held up a finger. "Be right back." He went out through the suite's hall door.

A moment later she heard the interior door click and open. Buck walked in, looking smug. "How's that for close?"

TA found herself blushing. "Pretty close," she said, trying to appear nonchalant. To her embarrassment she found herself blushing even harder. Her face felt like she was on fire and she stood awkwardly, not knowing how to act.

Buck was across the room in a second. He gently put his arms around her. "Oh baby, I'm sorry. We'll take things as slowly as you want. The doors can stay locked. I just thought it would be fun to be close but maybe I misread things."

"No, no. You didn't misread. I've had boyfriends before... But, you're different. I feel different. This is more. If I'm wrong, please tell me now." She stood stiffly.

He looked at her for a moment that seemed like an hour. "No, it is different. More. Forever more." He pulled her close, enveloping her with his arms, pulling her against his chest. She could hear his heart as he rocked her gently. Her arms, until now, hanging at her sides, slowing slid around him until they were standing wrapped together, one column.

They broke apart with a laugh. "Later," they said simultaneously. Buck went back to his room and TA bent to open her suitcase and pull out clothes for the evening.

CHAPTER 38

WASHINGTON DC

THURSDAY, NOVEMBER 9, 2000

They all met for dinner in the hotel dining room; glossy wood, heavy linen, sparkling crystal, and general ostentatious ambiance.

The meal was excellent and the conversation lively. When they were finished, Buck tapped his glass with the edge of his spoon and everyone came to attention. "No questions asked or answered, just follow directions please. Put on warm clothes and walking shoes and meet me in the lobby in fifteen minutes."

They trooped out of the dining room were back in the lobby in ten minutes.

Buck, looking smug, raised hand. "We're going on an evening tour of the monuments around DC. We have a special bus and permission to get into certain areas that are usually closed at night. Also, we have a guide who has a PhD in American History and is known as a superb lecturer. In fact, he was a full professor and teaching in Cambridge by age twenty-two." He bowed to Demetrius who bowed back.

"Ladies and gentlemen, our carriage awaits," Demetrius said. He gestured them to the lobby door.

The rain had almost stopped, the streetlights reflected off puddles and dripping trees. A shiny black bus was parked at the curb with a chauffeur standing by its open door. They boarded. The moisture in the air and the heavy clouds seemed to radiate a magical glowing light added to the mystical outing. TA, reminded of the carriage scene in Disney's Cinderella, giggled.

Demetrius stood at the front of the bus and faced them. "I mapped out a circular route with as little backtracking as possible. We'll pass the National Geographic Museum so Herbie can find it later and then the White House." He gestured for the driver to start.

The museum was pointed out and then the bus slowly circled the White House, the Washington Monument in the distance. The White House was lit by lights reflecting against the white paint of the regal building and then radiating up against the heavy moist clouds. The bus moved forward. Demetrius gave a brief history of the lovely building.

The bus continued on and he pointed "Department of the Treasury. The National Theater. Madame Tussuads Wax Museum and the infamous Fords Theatre."

They passed the J Edgar Hoover Building which Buck pointed out proudly. "That's my home office. The FBI building." TA craned to see it as they passed.

They moved along Pennsylvania Avenue and then with a zig and a zag, circled the Capitol Building, looking like a giant wedding cake against the dark sky. Everyone moved to the facing side of the bus.

"Oh, it's so big! It's so beautiful", exclaimed Ruthy. "This is much better than pictures." The bus moved slowly on.

Demetrius spoke, "Here's the National Archive Building. You have to go here while you're visiting. They have the Declaration of Independence, the United States Constitution and the Bill of Rights on display. It's awe-inspiring." Both children turned to their parents and were assured that the visit was on the list.

Passing the National Mall Herbie sprang to his feet and began pointing out various Smithsonian buildings he and Demetrius had visited. Ruthy, bouncing in her seat, requested a later visit to the Air and Space Museum.

The bus slowed to a crawl as they passed the Washington Monument. Demetrius gave a brief history of its construction being interrupted during the Civil War

"It faces the Lincoln Memorial across the reflecting pool." He gestured.

The bus coasted gently along the side of the Washington Monument and Demetrius continued his instruction. "The statue in front of us at the juncture of Independence Ave and 17th St is of one of my favorite people. John Paul Jones, born in Scotland, a rather shifty rascal but he was a great Admiral and he's known as the Father of the American Navy.

On your right is the Vietnam Veterans War Memorial. I lost an uncle in that war."

Naomi raised her hand. "I lost an uncle, also," she said quietly. Her husband pulled her close, in a gentle hug.

The bus pulled into the parking lot by the Lincoln Memorial and the doors opened. "Everybody out. We're going to do a bit of walking," said Buck.

They all trooped out and started walking up toward the Memorial. "One of the most beloved and admired buildings in America," said Demetrius. "Greek Revival architecture and quotations from two of his most famous speeches are chiseled around the room. See if you know which speeches the quotes come from, no peeking."

They walked up the steps and stood in awe in front of the huge statue of Lincoln. Finally, the children broke away and studied the words that ran around the room. Ruthy recited the complete Gettysburg Address by heart, pacing around the memorial and dramatically throwing her arms out. She was applauded by her party and the few other sightseers. The other quotation was properly identified as the Second Inaugural Address.

"All right, now we are going for a short walk," proclaimed Demetrius. He led them back down the steps and ushered them off to the left toward the Vietnam Veterans War Memorial. "We are going to see The Wall."

They arrived and quietly walked its length. Naomi paused to gently stroke the name of her uncle and Demetrius saluted his uncle's name. There was an occasional person or group standing at certain panels, some were motionless, and others knelt.

Their bus was waiting for them near the exit and they quietly boarded. They drove west across the Potomac. Buck pointed out that no way on Earth could Washington or anyone else have thrown a coin all the way across this wide river.

Once across the river they detoured onto the island that held the Theodore Roosevelt Memorial and Nathan delighted them with a list of all the animals that the Roosevelt children had brought to the White House.

Next they paused at the Marine Corp Memorial, commemorating Iwo Jima, of troops raising the flag. It brought enthusiastic comments.

The gate to Arlington Cemetery was opened for them by a soldier in a full dress uniform. They traveled through the cemetery to the Tombs of the Unknowns and their faithful guards. The bus parked and they watched the soldiers as they honored their fallen comrades.

The bus quietly pulled away and the outer gate was opened for them by saluting guards.

Crossing the river again it took them to the Tidal Basin and they admired the Jefferson and F. D. Roosevelt memorials and then back to the hotel.

After many thanks and hugs everyone went up to their rooms.

Buck and TA sat quietly on her couch and shared a bottle of Rose wine from the fridge. It was late and even later when they woke, leaning on each other, slumped on the couch. They moved over to TA's bed and fell back to sleep, wrapped in each other's arms, for the short remainder of the night.

CHAPTER 39

WASHINGTON D.C.

FRIDAY, NOVEMBER 10, 2000

Early in the morning TA heard movement and then a "damn, ow." She flipped on her bedside lamp and saw Buck standing on one foot by an overturned footstool. He was wearing only shorts. He looked adorable.

"Trying to perform the crane position from yoga?" she asked.

He put his foot down, snorted with laughter and then waved two small bottles of orange juice. "Just thought I'd get us a drink. We don't have to be ready to leave for the White House until 2:00 this afternoon. Want an early morning libation?"

She flipped down the covers on the other side of the bed and held out her arms.

They slept late, snuggled under the feather comforter. They called room service for a brunch; enjoyed it at a leisurely pace and then separated to get dressed for the White House reception.

TA bathed with the scented bubble bath furnished by the hotel and then spent an inordinate amount of time getting her hair under control. Tuck a curl in one place and another one sprang out somewhere else. "Damn, damn." It had been so easy when she had

234

practiced under Mrs. M's tutelage. "Finely!" she exclaimed when the elegant chignon took shape.

Hair mastered, earrings in, pearl choker borrowed from Mrs. M around her neck, she slipped on the new faille cocktail dress with a neckline that accentuated her slender neck. The dress was a champagne color that set off her red-brown hair and root-beer colored eyes. With matching shoes and clutch, she felt quite elegant.

She draped the lovely blue wool coat, borrowed from a neighbor, over the back of the couch. By the time the trip date had rolled around, nearly the whole building had gotten into the fun of preparing TA for her big day at the White House. They had even had a fashion show with much applause and a few risqué comments.

Buck appeared at the shared door, his arms wide, looking elegant in a new navy suit (what else for an FBI agent?) But his tie was a joyful paisley of blues and greens. He came to a sudden stop and dropped his arms, the wide grin on his face turned into a wolf whistle. "I was going to give you a big whoop-de-do hug but wow! Hold that pose while I admire you from every angle." He made a big production of circling her.

"Nobody is going to look at the map; they'll just be looking at you." Laughing, he clasped his hands under his chin and staring upward, "To think I spent the night with this most gorgeous of women."

"You dope, if I weren't afraid of my hair escaping again I'd come over and whop you." She laughed. "You know, you look awfully tasty yourself. None of the women are going to be looking at the map; they'll be panting for you!"

The phones in both their rooms rang. It was the desk announcing that the cars were waiting for them. Buck helped her on with her coat and off they went to what TA thought of as 'the great unveiling.'

CHAPTER 40

WHITE HOUSE WASHINGTON, DC

FRIDAY, NOVEMBER 10, 2000

No cars were waiting. There were three limousines, complete with motorcycle police to escort them. Everybody had gathered but the distribution of bodies into vehicles was under vehement discussion. It was resolved with Mr. and Mrs. Quintana and Fredo and Moon Child sharing a limo. Buck and TA shared the second limo with Ruthy who considered TA her role model. 'The men', Nathan, Demetrius and Herbie, shared the third.

They sailed through the White House gate and glided up to the shielded entrance so no lucky photographer could get an early photo. They were greeted by several staff members, including Mrs. (it turned out) Linwood and escorted toward the oval office. Once gathered in an adjoining meeting room, they had their roles explained; they would meet President Clinton and Mrs. Clinton and both the Chinese and Japanese ambassadors. Photos would be taken. The whole party would then adjourn to the room where the map was displayed for photos, the press would come in and still more photos would be taken plus there would be introductions and the press would be allowed to ask questions. They were not to offer to shake hands but if a hand was extended they were expected to shake it. No chit chats among themselves. No interrupting any VIP (very important person) even if that person was giving out inaccurate information. No correcting any of the VIPs in public or to their face but if some piece of information needed to be corrected it was to be done to Mrs. Linwood or Mr. Hafner, who was introduced.

They were escorted into the oval office which was even more impressive in real life than on TV. The room was full of people but there was no doubt who the President was. Introductions were made and President Clinton was indeed as charming as the public had been led to believe. Mrs. Clinton was very interested in talking to TA and her extension, Ruthy. Next they were introduced to China's Ambassador Liu Zhui who was beaming and to Japan's Ambassador Matsuoka Hisashi who looked stern. They went on to meet and greet several other officials and finally they were maneuvered into position for the photo shoot. First, everybody together, all their party and the President and both Ambassadors had an official picture taken. The Ambassadors were then escorted from the room and photos were taken of all of them with the President and Mrs. Clinton. Mrs. Clinton left. Individual pictures were staged with each member of their party posing smilingly with the President. Did he ever feel his face would freeze permanently in his charming grin—doubtful. When all photos were taken they were escorted by Mrs. Linwood and Mr. Hafner to the White House equivalent of the proverbial green room where they could relax and have a drink or snack.

They were escorted out and walked down a couple of halls into a large room where people were milling about. The gold map, spotlighted, was spread on a table that was covered in royal blue velvet. It glowed. The other two maps, framed, mounted and glass-covered for protection, were displayed on easels on either side of the table. Marine guards stood along the back and to the sides of the maps. A draped velvet rope in front of the table kept people from getting too close. It was all quite splendid.

TA recognized several people in the throng: a congressman, a senator, two Supreme Court justices, another congressman. It was an impressive display of power come to do honor to the map.

A man by the large doors at one end of the room announced in a loud voice, "The press is on its way." The crowd in the room stepped back and stood along the walls; the doors opened.

"My," whispered TA to Buck, "it's like the running of the bulls." He laughed. The press secretary, trying to corral the surging herd, frowned. He turned back to the microphone on the podium at one side of the display and tapped it with his pen. "Ladies and gentlemen, *please* control yourselves. You will all have a chance to inspect the maps. A press release and copies of photographs are being distributed. Questions will be fielded by me, *not* the group of people who are responsible for finding the maps. Questions to those individuals will be fielded in one hour in the press room."

Mrs. Linwood leaned forward and tapped TA on the shoulder. "All of you come this way and we'll prepare you for the conference."

"Sorry, we didn't realize the press would be so wild, that's why we changed your question time to the press room. Things are more contained there. This is how it will go. In about thirty minutes we'll take you in and introduce you. TA will be asked to discuss how she found the map and then she'll answer any questions. The rest of you will probably be asked to answer various questions and when your name, is called please come to the microphone. "

Being the main figure at a press conference was like being in a severe hail storm. The only fun part of the whole thing was when the reporters from China carried on a question-and-answer discussion with Ruthy and Herbie in Chinese. TA thought the best part of that was when she noticed the press secretary was practically having a stroke because he couldn't understand what was being said or answered. When Moon Child and Fredo started laughing part way through the questions it became obvious that Ruthy's answers probably had nothing to do with the map. Now, even the Chinese speaking reporters were laughing. The press secretary, coming completely unglued called for a translator to be brought in. He could have requested any number of people in the room to translate but that wouldn't be official, TA supposed. By the time a translator came rushing in, it was too late and that part of the conference was over.

They were ushered from the press room and as soon as the door shut Mrs. Linwood separated the ladies and Mr. Hafner took the males, all to be refreshed and tidied for the up-coming cocktail party.

TA, Ruthy, Mrs. Quintana and Moon Child were escorted into a room with a maid and hairdresser waiting to attend. Hair was redone, makeup applied and they were ready to return to the fray. TA asked Moon Child what had been said in the pressroom and broke into giggles when she learned that Ruthy had said most of the adults present in the Oval Office thought they were better than everyone else and that Herbie had only wanted to discuss the Smithsonian, which he felt was much more interesting than the White House.

The cocktail party was a strain as everybody wanted to ask questions and got snarky with anyone who wanted to ask a different question. It seemed there was a pecking order on who could ask questions and who should just shut up and listen.

After cocktails, some people left and the chosen few who would remain for dinner went on with the questions right up until they were called to the dining room. Even then the questions continued from either side and across the wide table. It was impossible to enjoy the meal or even eat it. Every plate was removed before she had a chance to finish.

Meal over, they all made a concerted move to thank the President and Mrs. Clinton and leave. Their coats were retrieved and they were escorted out to the limos.

Back at the hotel, they all went immediately to their rooms, exhausted. Buck and TA crawled into bed, fully expecting to pick up where they had left off that morning; instead they fell asleep when their heads hit the pillows.

CHAPTER 41

WASHINGTON, D.C.

SATURDAY, NOVEMBER 11, 2000

At 12:15 phone calls summoned the party to the lobby. Limousines were again waiting, this time the chauffeurs were Chinese, but the motorcycle police were Washington DC's finest.

Upon arrival, the party was escorted to a large reception room where they were met by Consul Chen and Mrs. Chen. TA received a warm handshake from the Consul and a hug from Li. She introduced all the members of the party and they were escorted across the room to Ambassador Liu Zhui, a tall distinguished looking man with small spectacles perched on his nose. A matronly woman in a red cocktail dress with an embroidered design of flying birds stepped forward. She whispered something to the Ambassador and then as the Ambassador removed his glasses and slipped them in his pocket she smilingly introduced herself as Mrs. Liu.

The reception, while formal, was more relaxed and less choreographed than the White House event. They were introduced to several important Chinese-Americans from around the country and to the staff of the Embassy. All had watched the news the day before so none repeated the familiar questions. Indeed, Ruthy and Herbie received the most attention and after that, Fredo and Moon Child, who were thanked profusely for the initial work they had done on the map translations.

After a bit, the Ambassador stepped forward and raised his hand. There was immediate silence. "With great thanks and gratitude, the Chinese people would like to present our honored guests with gifts to commemorate the retrieval of the antiquities that have been long hidden from view. We have made an effort to find items that are of interest to the recipients.

"To Professor Alfredo Chan, we present an antique Mahjong Set." He paused while the mahjong set was carried forward by a servant. It was shown first to Fredo and carried around the room for people to view and set on a long table that had suddenly appeared across the room.

"For Dr. Ellen Foster, we have an antique scroll showing a teacher and his students." The scroll was of a teacher standing under a flowering almond tree, surrounded by his seated, busily writing, students. The scroll was marvelously detailed with birds and butterflies attracted by the flowers on the tree. It was displayed and taken to the table where it was draped open on a stand.

'For Mr. Frank Quintana we have chosen a jade desk set." The set consisted of several items in an elaborate gift box. It was paraded around the room to ohs and ahs and then deposited on the table.

TA giggled to herself, as the scene from *The King and I,* where the children were being separately introduced to the new teacher to background march music ran through her head.

"For Mrs. Quintana, mother of these exceptional children, we have chosen a set of hair combs from the era of the map they helped translate." The combs were jade with intricate carvings of butterflies and flowers. They too, were in an elaborate gift box. Around the room they were paraded before joining the other gifts.

"Dr. Demetrius Bean, professor and grand master chess player, there was no more suitable gift than an ancient jade chess set. It is believed that chess originated in China, traveled to India and then

242

to the world. This set is from the Tang Dynasty, which ran from 618- 907. May you always win." The chess set in its presentation box was displayed and placed on the table.

"Dr. Nathan Hale Murillo, polo player, horse lover, we know you raise Andalusian horses, indeed you are famous for your herd, so what could be more appropriate than a Chinese polo pony to add to your collection? We chose a Tang Horse. It is a mingqui, which means tomb figure, of a polo pony and in a ceramic glaze called sancai. Polo has a very long history in China, as I am sure you know." The statue of a horse was brought forward, it was perhaps 15 inches tall, white with a dappled rump and again, in a presentation box. People reached out, as if they wanted to touch it, which wasn't allowed.

"Mr. John Doe, FBI agent, warrior, lawyer. We bestow the gift of a Ming Dynasty dao sword. This dao is a Liuyedao or willow leaf saber. It was the sword of choice with the cavalry and has a single edge. May you enjoy it and may it add to your collection of swords." The sword, in its presentation box looked to be about a yard long and, at least to TA's unschooled eye, lethally impressive. It was shown around the room and joined the other gifts.

"Titania Arial McGovern, treasure hunter of the highest level, we chose an early map from the Ming Period, one that was given to Admiral Zheng He when he first visited India." TA gasped. She hadn't been expecting a gift since she had been given the ink stone by Consul Chen. What was being brought across the room astounded her. It was a map, already mounted and framed. It was of India with mountains, rivers, landmarks and animals, including tiny elephants and a tiger lurking in a forest. Her hands trembled to grab it. The map was marched around the room and set on an easel.

"Mr. Herbert Quintana, your life is before you and may it be long and interesting. Your hero Roy Chapman Andrews led an expedition to the Gobi Desert in 1923. He discovered the first dinosaur eggs and many other wondrous things on that trip and many others.

He was accompanied by a lowly Chinese scholar named Wang Deming; this is a copy, made by Wang's own hands, of his journal of the trip and the finds that were made. Also, we have a dinosaur egg for you. In the words of one of your favorite TV programs, 'May you live long and prosper.'"

This time there were two presentation boxes, one for the book and one displaying the egg which had cracked open and the baby dinosaur was visible inside. Herbie gasped in pleasure. These items, too, were taken around the room and added to the display.

"Ruthy Quintana, we have a special gift for you. We need to go out into the green house," he gestured toward a door at the side of the room and offering her his arm, they led the way. Once in the greenhouse he turned and nodded to one of the attending young men who turned and picked up a carrying case and set it in front of Ruthy. She looked up at Ambassador Liu. He nodded his head toward the case.

"What is in that case is rare and magical. It will give love unasked and will always be at your beck and call. It is gentle and soft to hold but fierce when defending you. Please open the box."

Ruthy knelt in front of the box and opened the latches. Lifting the lid, she let out a joyous squeal. The squeal was answered by a gleeful yip. Out hopped a Pekinese puppy who threw himself with utter delight, into her arms. They were immediately rolling on the floor in giggles and yips, kisses flying in both directions.

TA tore her gaze away from the charming sight to look at Ruthy's parents. It was obvious they had been forewarned and were agreeable. They beamed happily at the pile of child and pup.

It was quite some time before the group was able to tear themselves away from their carefully chosen gifts. The presents-except for the puppy-would be shipped to each of their homes. The puppy would be delivered in a proper carrier just before the Quintanas left for the airport.

With many sincere thanks, they were ushered out and climbed into the limos.

"Wait," said Demetrius, "I have a thought." He leaned forward and tapped the driver on the shoulder. "Wait just a minute, please. I want to consult with the rest of the party."

He jumped out of the limo and walked back to the other two vehicles. They could see him leaning in and talking with each group of people. He slapped the last car on the top and pulling out his cell phone he hurried back and rejoined them.

"Instead of taking us to the hotel, will you please drop us off at the Smithsonian Natural History Museum?" he asked the driver.

He turned to the puzzled group, "I talked to one of my friends and we're going to have after-hours access to the museum. We'll just turn the kids loose!"

The Embassy limos dropped them off right at the door and the drivers offered to wait but were thanked and dismissed. They'd catch a cab.

Everybody enjoyed the different displays, though the men spent most of their time watching Herbie excitedly going from dinosaur to dinosaur. Ruthy, intrigued by the beetle collection, was joined by the women, who chatted softly as she moved rapturously from one shiny, jeweled creature to another.

They were back at the hotel by seven. They enjoyed a late dinner together and then separated to go to their rooms. The Quintanas were staying an extra week and Fredo and Moon Child were going to visit friends in Virginia. The rest of the crew was flying to their various home bases the next day. They agreed to meet for breakfast at 8 o'clock Sunday morning.

CHAPTER 42

WASHINGTON DC

SATURDAY, NOVEMBER 11, 2000

Once upstairs, TA and Buck separated to change. TA, suddenly shy, pulled on her running shorts and a sleep tee with a picture of a bear giving the wearer a hug and over that a bathrobe furnished by the hotel. She had nothing lacy and dainty to put on to make herself alluring and she blushed at the thoughts racing through her head.

Back in the living room of her suite she went over to the bar and pulled down two wine glasses from the rack, then rummaged in the tiny fridge for the bottle of rosé she had seen. Straightening, she heard a gentle wolf whistle and a chuckle. She turned. Buck was grinning appreciatively at her. He also wore running shorts plus an old sweatshirt.

"If we were just a tad farther along in our relationship, I'd have asked you to hold that pose. I want you to admire my restraint and gentlemanly behavior." He laughed.

Suddenly more at ease and feeling in command of the situation, she smiled back. "Well, you certainly strip down nicely," she grinned as she handed him the bottle and a corkscrew.

Gathering up the glasses and treat basket, she crossed the room and curled up on the couch in front of the fireplace. It had been turned on and was giving forth a rosy glow. Buck joined her with the open bottle and soon they were sipping wine and happily digging through the basket for snacks. They discussed the reception and gifts and how much fun the Smithsonian had been.

Buck seemed to be feeling awkward about taking their evening to the next level so TA set her glass on the coffee table. She put her hand on his leg, leaned forward and whispered in her best Hollywood Mae West seductress voice, "Hey, want a kiss, big boy?"

CHAPTER 43

WASHINGTON DC
SAN FRANCISCO

SUNDAY, NOVEMBER 12, 2000

TA woke after an enjoyable night of frolicking, to the sound of a phone ringing. She groped for her bedside phone but when she managed to get it to her ear all she heard was a dial tone. Rinn-nng! It was Buck's room phone. She shoved his shoulder, "Hey, your phone's ringing." He responded with a "Hummmph," rolled over, and pulled his pillow over his head.

Giving up rather easily TA jumped out of bed and ran to his room and grabbed the phone. "Time to get up," said a cheery voice. She wondered fleetingly how you could get a machine to sound both cheery and solicitous at the same time. The voice continued. "It is Sunday, November 12, 2000 and the time is 7 am. Please have a delightful day." There was a click and then a dial tone.

She returned to bed, to cuddle against him for a moment and then rising on one elbow she gently blew in his ear. His reaction was not what she expected. He swatted at his ear and almost took her nose off. "OW, watch it," she protested. He awoke immediately, and turning, saw TA sitting up naked in bed, holding her nose.

"Good grief, not your nose. I'm so sorry. Do you need ice? "

She started to laugh; he was kneeling naked over her. "It's time to get up, but since you already are, we have enough time for a little TLC, if we're quick. "

They were.

At 8 am, they walked into the dining room.

Everyone was gathered around several tables pushed together. The mood was nostalgic and sad. After working together, they were to be parted. Thanks and memories were the main part of the conversation, but, with the children looking forward to a whole week of fun, it was hard for the adults to stay pensive. All too soon the breakfast was over. Hugs and handshakes, promises to stay in touch. Buck again promised to send the map translation as soon as he received it. Their time together was over.

TA and Buck returned to their suites and finished packing. Buck was staying for a couple of days. He'd rented a more modest room in another hotel. A bellhop carried their bags down to the waiting limo, the last of their perks. They were joined by Nathan and Demetrius, who were flying out that day. Everything was loaded in the limo and they went to Buck's hotel to drop off his bag before going out to the airport. He would return by shuttle.

They checked in at the airport and then moved to a coffee bar situated centrally to their gates. Demetrius had business in Maine. Nathan was flying home to the hill country of Texas. TA was going to San Francisco. Demetrius left first, Nathan soon after.

Just before noon, TA and Buck strolled over to her gate and, after a long kiss, she boarded.

She enjoyed the first class seating and arrived in San Francisco midafternoon. She called Ezekiel as soon as she got in and then, met again by a limo, she rode home in style.

As soon as she walked in, Mrs. M came shooting out of her apartment and threw her arms around TA. After a big hug, she helped get the suitcases upstairs and put on the teakettle, ready to settle in for a blow by blow account of the trip. Since TA wanted nothing more than to call Buck, it took all her diplomacy to shoo her sweet landlady out with the promise of being down in an hour to 'tell all.'

Changing into sweats, she made some tea and curled up in her old chair to call. Buck answered immediately and they were soon lost in conversation which came to an abrupt halt when she heard pounding on her door and realized that they had been talking for an hour and a half.

"Coming," she called. It was Mrs. M with the news that everyone was waiting" to hear all about the trip.

They returned to Mrs. M's apartment, crowded by nearly everyone in the apartment complex. All the seats were occupied and the floor was wall to wall people, bottles of wine, pop, cups of tea and coffee, plates of cookies and snacks, everywhere. There were two empty chairs waiting for them.

Everybody had seen the TV news clips and had questions. She finally threw up her hands, "Hush, hush. First I'll tell you from start to finish and then I'll answer questions." She told it all, mostly, the limos, the first class plane, the hotel, the suite, the White House reception and dinner, the Chinese Embassy, the sight-seeing trip around Washington and finally the flight home.

She answered did Clinton hit on her? Lots of laughter. No. What was the Chinese Ambassador's wife wearing? She described her dress at length. Did the guards at the Smithsonian stay late, too, since they were there? Only one. When all the questions were answered; she glanced at her watch. It was evening. "Thank you all for coming and caring. I'm exhausted. Mrs. M, thank you for hosting this lovely homecoming." After a few hugs, TA excused herself and went upstairs and fell into bed.

CHAPTER 44

SAN FRANCISCO

MONDAY, NOVEMBER 13, 2000

TA woke before the alarm. Exercise was far down on her 'want to' list but she rose, threw on her running clothes and hit the chilly streets. She waved at several other runners, ran twice around the park and back home.

She pulled out her laundry bag, loaded it, and took it with her on the bus to the shop. There was a washer/dryer in the basement at work.

She had stuck a can of sardines in her pocket as she was leaving and Friend came running and meowing across the park as she got off the bus. She talked to him as they walked to their favorite feeding spot, under the large tree. Crouching, she opened the can and set it down. He didn't immediately go to it. He wanted to butt her with his forehead a few times and receive scratches. She obliged and crooned to him as he ate.

She dumped the empty can in the nearest trash can and after one more scratch she crossed the street and carried her laundry sack into the shop.

"TA, I'm so glad you're back," exclaimed Ezekiel as he rolled into the shop from his office. "Ever since you were on TV we've had

251

calls right and left. I've set up two appointments for this morning and three for this afternoon. I also called the suppliers, both Dickson & Company and the Herd people. They're sending out some promising maps. Should arrive today."

Hardly pausing for breath, he continued, "Did you have a wonderful time? Toss your laundry down the stairs and come have tea and tell me all about everything. Oh, how could I forget? A package from the Chinese Embassy was delivered this morning. It's on my desk. I've been twitching to see what's inside. Do come!" He almost spun a wheelie in his chair as he turned to lead the way back to his office.

TA hung her coat, tossed the laundry and hurried to follow him. There on the desk was her framed map, wrapped in silk. It must have been hand-delivered by the Chinese Consulate.

"Oh, Ezekiel, wait till you see!" she exclaimed as she carefully untied the package. There was an envelope attached and she opened it. A note inside wished her well and thanked her again for her services. Folding back the heavy silk wrap she exposed the beautiful map. Ezekiel gasped.

There was a display easel in the corner of the office and TA placed the framed map on the stand and flipped on the light that illuminated it.

Stepping back she picked up two magnifiers from Ezekiel's desk and handed one to him. Together they went over the map, inch by inch. She explained its provenance to him as they admired it.

With more time, she was able to see not only the tiger and elephants, but peacocks, a red panda, a snow leopard, a tiny cobra and lotus blooming in a lake. It was almost like looking at a hide-a-picture and finding all the hidden items in a drawing.

The shop bell rang and she pulled herself away. It was a busy day. By closing time, she was thankful to sit in the quiet basement and fold her laundry before stuffing it back in the sack to take home.

She opened a can of cat food for Friend and sat for a few moments while he ate. She had to hurry to catch the bus and would have slept through her stop except the driver knew her and woke her when they arrived.

Soup for supper and a long chat with Buck. Then bed.

CHAPTER 45

SAN FRANCISCO

WEDNESDAY, MARCH 14, 2001

TA woke early, heart pounding; something was going to happen today! What?

Her phone, which she had left charging in her kitchen, was ringing. She sprang up, stubbed her toe and cursed. Limping rapidly into the kitchen, she grabbed it, punched buttons and Buck's beloved voice was on the line.

"TA, wake up! News! The translation is finished. I was just tipped off by a friend. They're trying to keep it quiet because it has things in it they don't want the general public to know about yet. I'm on my way over to the office to try to talk them into releasing all of it to you but you have to promise you won't share any of this with anyone except Ezekiel. If you do, it'll be my head along with yours."

"Oh wow! I promise. When will you know if you can send it?"

"Later this morning. If they agree, I'll take a copy to the airport, and you should have it by midafternoon."

"I love you," he added, and hung up.

TA was bouncing around the kitchen, sore toe forgotten. She couldn't hold still, so she jumped into her running clothes, tiptoed down the stairs and out on the street. She ran until she had to stop and hold onto a light pole. She glanced at her watch, it was 6:15. She caught her breath and ran back to the apartment.

Bathed and dressed, she caught the 7:38 bus and soon arrived at her stop. She met Friend as she crossed the park. Did this cat never sleep? She had brought a fruit yogurt—cherry, his favorite--and opened it for him. He purred loudly while he lapped. Dumping the cleaned carton, she sped across the street and let herself into the shop.

Ezekiel was still upstairs, but she called up to him that she was there and would put on the coffee. She had news. The last bit brought him down promptly, his tie hanging unknotted around his neck.

They sat together at the tiny table in the kitchen, sipping coffee and checking the time.

TA's phone rang. "I have it in a mailing envelope and I'm on my way to the airport. Remember, don't share this with anyone. I'm being sent out to California so I'll see you soon. I'll call when I get it on a plane."

An hour later, the shop open, a customer talking to Ezekiel, the phone rang. "It's on a plane and you should have it by late afternoon. Love you, see you soon, gotta run."

The day dragged even though they had two more customers who made purchases and they received a package of maps from the Herd Company. She was just checking in the contents when the shop bell rang. She jumped up.

"Special delivery for T. A. McGovern. Sign here, please." She was ripping open the shipping envelope even before the door closed behind him. She flipped the open sign to closed and threw the door locks.

"It's here, Ezekiel." She carried the envelope into his office and sat down in the visitor's chair. He leaned forward and turned on the desk lamp. She pulled out a thick sheath of papers. Looking up, she said, "how about we take turns reading it aloud?"

"Good plan," he said, leaning back in his chair.

CHAPTER 46

MAP TRANSLATION

EDITED

This is not a precise translation; certain terms and titles, times and measurements have been changed to English to make them more understandable to the present-day reader. Ming units of measure are: chi=12 inches US, li=1/3 mile US. The Ming years have been changed to modern equivalents. Some of the hyperbole has been left out as it is not pertinent to the 'story'.

A precise and accurate (as possible) translation may be obtained through enquiries sent to the United States National Archives.

My name is Yang Da. I was 47 years of age when I was chosen to be Chief Scribe to Admiral Zhao Huang. All transcribed notes have been lost and I tell this story to the best of my memory, whether it will ever reach China, I know not, but I am a scribe and I will perform the duties of scribe until my death.

The sublime and powerful Zhu Di, the Yongle Emperor of the Dynasty of the Great Ming, in the year 1405, named his favored eunuch, Commander Zheng He, as Admiral to a vast Treasure

Fleet. This fleet was to travel to all countries and through diplomacy explore and set up exchanges of knowledge and trade.

Admiral Zheng He, giant of intellect, height and girth, accepting his Emperor's mandate, separated from the main fleet, five troop ships. Each ship was 6-masted, 220 chi long and 82 chi wide, double hulled, with a balanced rudder, for ease of handling. These ships were outfitted for a long voyage away from all land. Admiral Zhao Huang was chosen as leader of this mighty expedition.

Each ship was fitted to receive approximately 1400 men, including officers and artisans. Enough food and water to last three months was placed in each ship. The ships' double-hulls were used for extra water.

The complement of each ship was approximately 800 sailors, 600 soldiers (archers, swordsmen, spearmen). Included in this number were 100 artisans comprising twenty blacksmiths, twenty carpenters, eight scribes, eight tailors, three doctors, six cartographers, twenty engineers. Also included in the complement were Officers: Army: three Majors, six Captains, twenty-four Lieutenants, Army of lesser grades sixty. Navy: one Captain, six Mates, lesser grades in charge one hundred. Also on board were ten cats. Not included in the official count were infinite rats.

For the fleet at large was one Admiral Zhao Huang with a staff of twenty men, and for the Army, under Admiral Zhao, was one Army General Liu Jianguo with a staff of twenty men.

The ships were named Golden Dragon, Emerald Tiger, Silver Shark, Burning Sun and Shining Star. When outfitting was completed they were inspected by the Emperor with no panoply and launched quietly, with few blessings. This disturbed many of those sailing who felt many blessings were needed for such a momentous adventure.

In the early spring we sailed toward the islands of Japan and passed below the island of Kyushu. We came upon a current that moved NE and sailed within it. On the 30th day of our voyage we were struck by a giant storm, one surely larger than the storm that destroyed the great Mongol Fleet. The storm stayed with us for three days, twisting, tossing and turning our ships, striking us with mighty fists of waves and at the end of that time only four ships remained. The ship Burning Sun was gone but one single mast was floating with us still.

We clustered together to assess our damages, which were great. After checking all the ships our leaders decided to abandon Shining Star, the ship that had the greatest damage. They rescued all the supplies and people and stripped the doomed ship of all moveable equipment. Even the remaining drinking water was pumped out and transferred.

The ships cats, who had all survived, were distributed between the three remaining ships and there was much betting when the new cats met the resident cats, as fights ensued. Every effort was made to leave the rats with the sinking ship. It was somewhat successful. All cats survived the swelling of their ranks.

On the 67th day we saw land. There were many tall pine trees and a giant mountain with snow on its peak. Rains started and continued. It was cold and there seemed nowhere to dry out, on land which was muddy or on ships which were dank. There were natives along the shore and we stopped and traded with them. They offered dried fish and fresh greens, and shellfish which they were happy to trade for a few sharp knives and beads. We offered silk but they were more interested in the knives and a few simple ceramic bowls. We sailed away with both sides satisfied with the transactions.

We continued southward down the coast. The rain followed. Occasionally we would see natives and we were able to trade with a few. We found many sea lions and seals. Dolphins and whales accompanied us on our journey. The men fished from the sides of the ships and were successful. Our cooks prepared many fish dishes but it was difficult to dry or smoke the fish because of the rain. Once we were able to trade for the carcass of a giant deer-like creature. It had wide webbed antlers and a large nose with a beard on its chin. There was enough meat for the officers and a few men. The cooks made a tasty broth of the bones for the sailors and soldiers.

We continued on for many days as we would travel only a short distance and then put down anchors and investigate the coast. After twenty-five days we came to the opening of what appeared to be a mighty bay. We sent in reconnaissance boats. They came back with the information that it was one long bay with a narrowing at the middle. There were marshes all around the bay and the marshes were full of many types of waterfowl in prodigious numbers. Both ends of the bay would accept large ships but the one to the North had a mighty river flowing into it. The water was pure as if it had just fallen from the heavens. The river looked deep enough to accept the ships' small boats to send exploration parties into the continent toward the mighty mountains that were visible in the distance. There was also evidence that people inhabited the area and there were areas suitable for camping. No people had been seen but much wildlife was present.

With great care the captains guided the ships into the bay and turned north. They dropped anchor off the estuary of the great river.

The officers ordered all the archers to go ashore and then allowed the other men to draw lots to see who would accompany them. One thousand men, mostly soldiers, and most of the cooks disembarked. They spread out over a wide area and hunted birds for the cooks to prepare.

The cooks dug deep pits for cooking the birds. When the birds were piled up I was ordered to make an official tally. I brought the other scribes to help and together we counted, the number is approximate: 900 cranes, 6000 geese, 3000 ducks, 400 swans, 5500 herons. There were a few birds that I could not identify. The men also brought otters. The whole crew gathered to pluck the feathers from the birds. Every effort was made to save the feathers for bedding. All were gutted and cooked on coals. After such a long voyage it was wonderful to eat meat. Many men ate so much that they threw up but then they went back and took more food.

The officers allowed most of us to sleep on the ground and not return to the ship. It was pleasant to lie on solid earth again and to breathe the scents of plants and soil.

The following day, the naval officers inspected the ships and decided they needed at least a month to repair the effects of the trip. They met with the army officers and it was decided that to keep the men who were not working on the ship busy they would send out search parties in many directions.

Most sailors and artisans would remain with the ships. Two hundred soldiers with their officers would remain to guard the ships.

Six boats from the ships were outfitted to carry search parties. Two of these boats would row up the mighty river and investigate. Lumber was needed for repairs and they would look for forests plus they were to make and take soundings of the depth of the river, to explore any large tributaries that they came to and try to meet and befriend any tribes of natives. The other boats were to circumnavigate the giant bay, looking for natives, rivers, and anything else of interest.

The rest of the available men were divided into approximately thirty exploration parties which comprised fifty men plus officers. They were to be sent in a fan shape from the position of the ships. All were charged with looking for any natural resources, meeting and befriending natives, and making a general map of the topography of the area that they were exploring. They were to return to the ships within 25 days.

It took four days for the parties to assemble their supplies. They started off with much fanfare, each shouting to other parties that they would find the most interesting things. And then, all was quiet and they were gone. The remaining officers set tasks for all the men and then there was noise again, hammering, sawing, shouting, cursing and laughter.

It was decided that most of the work would center on the two ships that were in the best condition. The other ship, Silver Shark, would have little work done on it until the search parties returned. If they were able to find the proper type of wood the third ship would be repaired but if no proper supplies could be found the third ship would be sacrificed to complete the repairs on the two, more-able, ships. One problem that had yet to be solved was that any new wood would have to be aged to prevent warping and that would take time.

The cooks began experimenting with cooking native plants. They had used cattails before but they tried various berries, nuts, grasses, mushrooms and shrubs. One plant with a lacy leaf killed the cook that cooked and ate it. After that they were more careful. They caught some ship rats and fed them the different plants. They kept drawings of the plants and made careful notes about the survival rate of the rats.

On the 22nd day of the expeditions the first party returned. All fifty-two members of their expedition returned safely. They reported they had visited vast forests of trees that were so tall their heads were not visible and the forest floor was so dark that it was difficult to see to walk and was so thick with needles that all sound was deadened. The mighty trees were so big around that it took thirty men holding hands, arms extended, to encircle one tree's trunk.

On the 23rd day of the expeditions, twenty-four parties returned. It is difficult to remember in what order the parties returned and what happened to each party so I shall lump them together as best I can. Most parties encountered vast forests with mighty trees. One party encountered a bear-like creature that was twice as tall as the tallest man and it had a large lump on its shoulders. It killed eight men and despite being filled with arrows and piercings from spears it ran away. The men were buried and the expedition continued. Deer and giant deer, far bigger than the regular deer, were encountered. More bears, some large with a hump and some smaller, were fishing. They stand in the water and use their large paws to bat the fish onto the shore. Mother bears teach their cubs how to do this.

A large lion without a mane attacked and began to devour one of the men. The lion was killed by a lucky spear thrust and the skin was brought back to the ships. The lion was cooked but it was not pleasant to eat.

Many birds of infinite types were seen and some were killed and eaten. Most were tasty.

One party reported being stalked by wolves. The wolves attacked but were driven off with torches and arrows. They followed the party for several days.

One of the parties that searched along the ocean reported prodigious sea lions, seals and an otter-like creature, larger than our otters. They floated in the harbors and wrapped themselves and their babies in kelp. When they grew hungry they swam to the bottom and picked up spiny sea urchins and a large rock. They would then swim up to the surface and float on their backs with the rock balanced on their stomachs and hit the sea urchin on the rock to break it open and then they would eat. Some men were walking along the edge of the cliff overlooking the beach when the cliff gave way and they fell to their death.

One party that came back missing seventeen men reported they had met a group of friendly natives but when they tried to trade for the natives' women a great fight ensued. The leader reported that eighty-two natives were killed but I doubt this.

Another leader reported that two of his men got in a fight and he had them both executed.

Several expeditions reported they visited with natives and some were friendly and willing to trade but many held back or disappeared into the forests.

There was evidence of forest fires in several areas; some recent and some were already reforested and were covered in red flowers.

One party that had traveled along the coast of the mighty ocean described beaches covered in the trunks of downed trees that had been uprooted during storms, washed out to sea and then floated back to land. They saw the skeleton of a whale but all that was left was bleached bones.

Of the two parties that had gone up-river in boats, one did not return, the other returned and said they met friendly natives who fed them and traded. One of them offered to trade a necklace of gold nuggets on a leather thong. He accepted a spear and a knife. The necklace is very heavy and the smallest nugget is perhaps the size of a cherry and the largest the size of a hen's egg.

Five expeditions did not return but 5 days after the date they were supposed to be back two men came from one of the parties. They were ill and one died soon after he returned.

The next day Admiral Zhao Huang called a meeting of all officers. The meeting started early and went into the night. It was held on the ship Emerald Tiger and no one, even personal servants, was allowed on board.

The day following the meeting it was announced that Colonel Wu Aiguo would lead an expedition in three days' time. The time until the departure would be used to prepare supplies and select men to accompany him.

There was no announcement as to what the destination was but the whispering within the ranks was that they were going inland to find the source of the gold. If the expedition was successful great honor would be given to all who participated and perhaps some of the gold would accidently fall into the pockets of those who were members on this great journey.

The large party led by Colonel Wu Aiguo and mixed Army and a Navy officer comprised a group of seventy-five men and was accompanied by six of the sturdiest of the exhausted men from the party that had brought back the gold necklace, left on the third day.

We did not to hear from them for sixty-six days.

263

The remarkable Colonel Wu Aiguo returned with all his men and they reported there were many traces of gold in the south fork of a large river. They had followed it up stream into some large mountains to the east. There, while investigating along a river that was in a deep canyon they came upon a layer of gold, shining in the sunlight. The layer was the height of a standing man and extending many feet in length before it dipped back into the mountain at both ends. The gold was is in veins within white quartz rock. The recovery estimate is very high. Colonel Wu says he will know more when they start removing it.

Admiral Zhao Huang again called a secret meeting with all his officers. At times they would call for food and drink but more interestingly they also called for various men, not officers, of skills such as blacksmiths, engineers and cartographers. Finally, they called for me, Chief Scribe Yang Da and I was instructed to write down all their decisions.

Boredom was creating a large problem. Since the landing of the ships in this harbor with approximately 5600 men we have been subjected to the following (rounded): Illness and accidents 1000 men, loss from the exploratory exhibitions 300; executions because of fights, thefts, and assorted other illegal acts 270.

Solution: The men will be divided into three groups as follows: Ship repair; Mining, smelting and casting the gold; Exploration- five parties to be sent forth for a period of one year of which two thirds of the time will comprise going forth and one third returning.

Admiral Zhao assigned superior officers to head the various sections of the plan and soon all the major decisions and assignments of officers were determined.

The group of men that stayed with the ships and did the repairs were led by Naval Captain He Jiayi. His work force was 1500 men, the majority from the Navy.

Army Major Don Jiang was put in charge of mining and smelting the gold as he had experience with working in metals. His work force was 1000 men, mixed Army and Navy. He was also given two ship's boats.

The rest of the men were to be sent out on the yearlong expeditions. The five groups which were sent would go, one each; north, northeast, east, southeast, south.

Each exploratory group would be under a Major or Captain with several other officers and would comprise approximately 300 men of mixed army and navy. The staff would also be drawn from both services. Artisans of various trades, but in particular doctors, scribes and cartographers were assigned. There was much complaining by the scribes, tailors and doctors who felt that people of their professions should not be sent walking on long trips. Their protests were ignored.

After six days of outfitting the five expeditions left our camp. The camp became much quieter.

The Gold Mine

Major Don had been preparing his separate expedition to go east to mine the gold. He discussed his plans and needs with Admiral Zhao and divided his men into several groups. The two boats were loaded with some of the heaviest equipment and started almost immediately to the canyon with the gold. A large group of his troops paralleled the boats on the banks of the river. Several of the men who had been in the original exploration accompanied them. The remaining men packed the rest of the heaviest equipment, such items as iron, heavy tools, etc. were transported by using wheelbarrows that the carpenters had made for them. The plan was that as soon as the boats arrived at their destination they would unload and return to pick up more of the heavy equipment being carried by the second group of men. Later, we heard that this plan worked well and that soon all equipment and men were making up a semi-permanent camp at the mine site.

Major Don's first action was to make shelters for his troops. They cut trees and built simple longhouses. Fire pits for heat and cooking were put down the center of each house. The mine was in the mountains and the nights were already turning cool. Wood was collected for burning and building. Hunters were designated and it was reported that they ate well.

Natives contacted the group and occasionally they would hunt together. The natives showed our cooks what plants and nuts and berries were good to eat. They were much interested in how the longhouses were built and the process of mining the gold.

Major Don designated who would remove the matrix that contained the gold. The removing was to be done by using black powder, picks, sledgehammers and chisels. When a pile of the quartz/gold rock was created it was hauled by wheelbarrows down to a rock crusher site.

The rough gold bearing rock was placed in a circular pit. The pit had a flat, tamped bottom paved in flat rocks. The pit had a center post placed in a sleeve so that it could rotate. Two arms were attached to the center post. One arm was at chest level to a man and extended out on both sides well past the pit edge. The men would power the milling process by pushing the arm. The lower arm, which extended to the edge of the pit, had drag lines attached to large flat-bottomed stones, used to crush the rock. There were many of these pits.

When the rock matrix had been ground to a coarse consistency it was shoveled out and put in a long open chute which had cross pieces set into the bottom. Water from the river was diverted through the chute and the heavy gold became caught in the cross pieces, while the lighter quartz rock was washed away.

The gold was collected in large piles on pieces of sail cloth and when a load of these bundles was accumulated it was transported by boat downriver to the site of the ships. There it was smelted. We had one crucible with us, and the fires were kept lit day and night.

When the gold was melted a stout branch was run through the handle of the crucible and it was carried to the beach. Using the wet sand as a mold, the gold was poured into oblong bricks and left to cool. When the bricks were cooled, the sand was brushed off and the gold was stacked, much like a brick wall, along the edge of the beach. Guards stayed with the 'wall' day and night.

Winter was late but harsh; Major Don was driven and his men were still removing gold when the year was up and the expeditions had returned.

It was late Fall when the expeditions started out. Not the best time of year to travel but Admiral Zhao was eager to separate and remove the men from the main camp. As ordered we did not hear from them until the year rolled over and again it was Fall.

To the east

After they had crossed the first mighty mountain range, the leader Major Song Hai had separated the expedition into three parts; he led the main group and Lt. Hu Jian took a group a day's march to the north and paralleled Major Song's group. Lt. Shen Lei took a group to the south and also paralleled Major Song.

Major Song's group angered a tribe of natives and the leader called up a herd of giant brown cow-like creatures, taller than the tallest man. They had large heads and curving horns and a hump on their shoulders. Thick curly fur covered the animals' shoulders and heads and the rest of the creature had short smooth hair. The natives lit fires and drove the herd of animals over the expedition. The stampede went on for two and a half days and only one man lived to tell what happened.

Lt. Shen's men came to an area of cliffs that had bones of giant dragons falling from it. The bones were so old they had turned to stone. He sent two messengers to tell Major Song that they had found dragon bones. One skull was as long as a man is tall and was full of teeth as long as the foot of a man. The messengers came upon the bodies of the eighty-seven dead men, their remains smeared across the earth. Wolves were fighting over the corpses. The messengers led the surviving man back to tell Lt. Hu who then sent runners to tell Lt. Shen to return. It was unfortunate but Major Song had kept all the skilled men with him and the expedition was left with only two cartographers. Together, Lt. Hu and Lt. Shen, decided to continue the expedition.

Lt. Shen related how his party had found a vast lake of water so salty that no fish could live in it.

They continued traveling together toward the east and crossed grasslands with grass so tall it came to their chests. They were overcome by a blizzard and despite sheltering along a stream bed with high banks they lost half their men to freezing.

They came to several native villages which were surrounded by stockades. The natives were not friendly so they continued on.

They struggled on and crossed mighty rivers and then they came to an immense sea of fresh water. The sea extended north so Lt. Hu followed the west side of it and Lt. Shen went up along the east side. Their plan was to meet at the end of this sea but there was no end. Finally, each group turned back and met at the camp where they had started. Lt. Shen, reported that when he had turned back he had followed along the side of more fresh water but whether it was the same lake or a new lake, he knew not.

They turned toward the west and crossed the mighty rivers and vast plains. While on the plains they saw a gigantic dark cloud and as they watched it grew a black moving column that touched the ground and everywhere it touched grass and trees and even animals were swept up in it and whirled around. The men prayed to the gods and hid in low areas and they were spared. As they continued they met friendly and/or curious natives along the way.

Coming back they dropped down south slightly to learn new things.

They came to an area of dry mountains with flat tops and while investigating them they found many deserted villages and small groups of houses that were built into caves under the overhanging cliffs. The houses were deserted, some with bowls and implements still in them, but there were no people. The architecture was remarkable and very well done, the houses were made out of flat rocks and some extended three or four stories high. Why the people had left they did not know, perhaps because they did not have enough water. It was very arid. The houses were a great wonder.

Continuing west they came to the rim of a grand canyon that had a large river in the bottom. The canyon was at least three li deep and they did not try to descend into it.

On farther they came to another canyon that was full of many spires of rock. The spires were of marvelous colors and very high and it took many days to thread their way in and out and around the spires and finally to leave the canyon behind. They found another river, perhaps the one from the original canyon but the river was going south and they proceeded west toward the Ocean.

Finally they came to the ocean and followed it north to find the bay that the ships were in. When they arrived at the ships the expedition that had traveled east eleven and one-half months ago with 265 men had eighty men remaining.

To the northeast

In late Fall Navy Captain Yao Jan led his men up into the mountains northeast of our encampment. They traveled for several days wending through tall peaks and by rushing rivers. They came to a beautiful blue lake, high in the mountains. The water was so clear that you could see down many chi. They set up camp by the lake, surrounded by high peaks, already snow-covered. The clouds came in and it started to snow. It snowed for three days and when it stopped and the sun came out the group of 265 men was reduced to

137 and the snow was so deep they could not walk without sinking above their heads. One of the surviving men had come from the land of the great Mongols and he made round wood sandals that extended out on all sides of the wearer's foot. When the men saw these they made pairs for themselves and wearing these sandals they were able to walk on top of the snow and out of the mountains down into barren warm land.

There was little to eat and they struggled to cross this land for many days until finally they came to forests and high plains and there was a wide beautiful river, the grass by it was still green, huge trees stood nearby and big fish swam in the river and large and small deer and antelope creatures grazed on the grass.. The men rejoiced.

On they traveled, sending out scouts in a fan in front of them. The scouts that had traveled slightly south came back and told of a great forest with plains of snow- covered grass beyond. There were large lakes and rivers teaming with fish. In all of this, with drifts of snow all around, were ponds of mud colored in reds, yellows and browns, steaming in the cold air. As they watched in wonderment the ponds threw up bubbles of thick mud which fell back to the surface in splats that then reabsorbed into the pond. The mud was too hot to touch without pain.

The party wandered in this strange place. Sometimes it was difficult to see as the steam rose from vents in the earth. They came to a deep pond of clear water the color so blue it rivaled the sky. It was so hot that if a man fell in he would be cooked in minutes.

In areas there was steam and hot water shooting from the ground and over the eons the minerals in the water had built up columns and wondrous shapes which were constantly growing as the water spilled over them.

Everywhere between all these hot water wonders, streams wended in grassy area where different types of deer and gigantic shaggy cow-like creatures grazed.

Captain Yao led all the men to this marvelous place and there they camped, within the warmth, until the trees budded and wildflowers grew. They shared their sanctuary with the animals and three groups of natives. All mingling together in peace, sharing songs, wrestling, holding archery and spear throwing contests and teaching each other simple words and phrases.

When summer came Captain Yao led the men east to visit a 'medicine wheel' site that one of the natives had told him about. It was high in the mountains and the men found it difficult to move rapidly without getting out of breath. There were many paths that led to the wheel. It was built high on a flat-topped mountain and was of great interest to Captain Yao. It was made of large stones and was 48 chi across with twenty-eight arms extending from the center. He said that it showed north, south, west and east and though he could not wait long enough to be sure he thought it also pointed to the winter and summer solstice and to some of the star systems.

After visiting the medicine wheel the expedition continued NE across great plains filled with the large dangerous cow-like creatures but were never threatened. In late summer they turned back toward the west. Hoping to avoid the high mountains that had been their downfall at the beginning of their exploration they went directly to the coast and then followed it down to the bay where the ships were waiting. They arrived back with approximately 126 men.

To the north

Army Major Wei Chen divided his troops into three groups. He led the center troops, comprising 88 men straight north toward the unknown. On his left, west, he sent 88 men under the leadership of Navy Captain Yuan Jian and on his right, east, he sent 88 men under the leadership of Army Captain Peng Chao. He ordered Captain Yuan and Captain Peng to make drawings and

271

notes and to meet with him after 50 days. After 30 days he would leave markers showing his trail every 200 paces so they would be able to find him.

When they met by a long lake, 50 days later, Captain Yuan confirmed what the previous exploratory parties had reported, many great trees, rough coasts, plentiful sea lions, otters, seals and whales. Captain Peng reported running into blizzards and great snowdrifts. He had lost men to the inclement weather. He also said they had come across great areas of volcanic ash and he had seen dormant volcanos in the distance. He brought back some samples of volcanic glass. Major Wei had also lost some men to the mighty rivers they had crossed. He had seen great forests but not the giant trees that were growing along the coast.

They rested by the lake for a month as hunting was good. After a month they again split and continued northward to meet once again, but in 60 days.

When next they met it was by a great river, too deep and too fast to ford. Again, Captain Peng reported volcanic activity and he pointed north and called attention to pointed mountains across the river that were high, snow-covered and ominous with smoke rising from their slopes and tops. He also said that much of the way there had only been short pines and then arid rough ground. They had found a high cliff of volcanic glass colored black with streaks of orange.

Captain Yuan had traveled up the coast. The beaches were narrow and covered with driftwood in the shape of huge gray trees. They had forded many rivers and seen many seals and sea lions. They had met with natives, most of whom were interested in trading. The natives had a way of dry smoking fish that was delicious he said. He brought a sample of the dried fish and of the type of wood that was used to prepare it.

Major Wei reported that he and his men had traveled through forests for many days and that he was glad that they were now out in the sun. Perhaps he should not have spoken because the next day it began to rain and it rained for 22 straight days.

Major Wei took all the men west along the river and when they neared the ocean they came across a native village. They traded knives as they had brought many for that purpose, and the natives, who had long boats, ferried all of them across the river. Since Captain Yuan had never seen such a boat, he made numerous measurements and sketches. The boats were long, some longer than 60 chi and wide enough to carry many people and their belongings. They were made of slats of wood and painted with wonderful designs.

After crossing the river they still had to ford many smaller rivers and streams. They came to an enormous rain forest. The trees were huge, both around and tall. There were ferns as tall as a man and it was easy to get lost as all sound was damped in just a few chi. The men stayed together and it rained for days as they walked north. Finally they came to the ocean and turned east to get away from the rain forest. It was not to be. After traveling for over a month along the coast and having to travel east and then south, they realized they had been on a gigantic spit of land and that they were now back where they had started.

Again they traveled east and followed what turned out to be a huge bay. They were sure it was the bay where the ships had first touched land. They followed the bay along its edge until they could turn north again and then they had the wonderful luck to come upon a village of friendly natives. The people lived in long houses of prodigious proportion. Several families or extended families lived in each house and there were several of these houses. The people welcomed the men and fed them new meats and berries.

Major Wei set up a camp for the men on the outskirts of the native village. He warned the men that if any dared to offend the natives in any way he would have them immediately put to death.

The natives invited the visitors to go hunting with them and Major Wei sent Captain Peng and a group of 50 men to accompany them. There was much sadness for those who could not go. The chosen men came back with stories of many strange animals and there were pine trees over 300 chis high that had soft needles and many different varieties of berry bushes.

While the hunting party was gone small groups of men wandered the forest and along the shore. One group came back with berries and a story of sharing picking berries with a small, perhaps 2 chi in length, animal that had a black mask and a black striped tail. It had a pointed face and paws so nimble that it used them like hands and sat and picked berries with them. It then ate them like a person. They came across another of these animals that was feeling in the water of a stream and as it felt it looked forward, not at what it was searching for. Then it found a little fish and it washed it in the stream, just like a man, and then it sat and ate the fish. They reported that they could not kill it, as it was too amusing to watch.

When the hunting party returned there was a huge feast of animals from the forest and shellfish from the ocean.

The next morning they were awakened by much noise coming from the village. The village was tearing down their houses and loading their boats. After just a day of labor they were packed and left. They went upstream on the widest river.

Major Wei tried to question the natives as to where they were going. All he could understand was that they were going to catch big fish. He sent a group of men to follow the villagers but they soon lost sight of them and though they traveled on for several days they saw no evidence of the villagers and finally returned to the main party.

Major Wei gathered all his troops together and continued north for the space of a month. They went through thick forests of trees but came to no new native villages. Finally, as summer was ending, they turned back.

They retraced their steps and finally came to the big river that they had needed help crossing. There were no natives there and their village had disappeared so the party turned east and followed the river toward its source. As they traveled they became aware of activity in the water of the river. It was full of huge red fish, six or seven chi long, with a hook on their noses. The men were able to catch some of the fish and they grilled them over the campfires. They report that they were delicious. Finally, after several days, they came to a native village. All the people were busy catching fish and smoking and drying them along the bank.

After much haggling the villagers agreed to break off from the fishing and to ferry all the troops across the river. It took many knives, spears and bows and arrows as they were reluctant to stop fishing.

The party continued south but they ran into an early snowstorm and then another and another. Several men became ill and died. They were buried and the party continued on.

Illness continued to plague the troops and several more deaths occurred before the party finally reached the bay and the ships. Only 109 men returned.

To the southeast

Army Captain Tan Guang, leader of the exploration to the southeast chose Navy Captain Liang Dong and Army Major Shen Ling to assist him. Going southeast they were lucky to get over the mountains just before the first hard snow of winter. Dropping down off the mountains they found themselves in an extreme desert region and rather than trying to cross the desert they headed south, along the base of the mountains. After several days of hard marching they were still flanked by the desert so Captain Tan sent some of the best runners toward the east to find watering spots across the arid landscape. Water was found and Captain Tan led his troops east.

Ironically, the next major obstacle to their travels was water. They came to a large river, however, since it was fall, the water level was down from its summer levels, attested to by the markings on the banks and cliffs where it ran, they were able to cross with only the loss of seven men who made foolish choices and panicked as they tried to cross and paid for it.

Once across the river Captain Tan divided his troops into three groups. He chose to take the center path and sent Major Shen off to his north and Captain Liang to his south. They were to travel parallel to each other at a distance of one day. Every ten days Major Shen and Captain Liang were to send runners to report on any interesting finds. They were to draw pictures and make maps.

Major Shen and his group came upon a mighty canyon. It was many li deep. They followed it along its upper rim going east, after several days they were able to continue freely as the river went almost directly north.

They traveled along the side of tall cliffs colored a deep red and then beside cliffs in colors of cream, red, blues and greens. He later said it looked as if a muted rainbow had fallen across the earth.

Some of Major Shen's scouts found two groups of houses which were abandoned. Major Shen, upon hearing of this find proceeded to the discovery. It consisted of two large open-sided caves that had sheltered many people. Both still had houses made of sandstone rocks and the houses were several stories high. One cave was over 450 chi high and 370 chi across; the other was smaller but had more rooms packed in. Major Shen took some measurements and had sketches drawn. All this was reported to Captain Tan.

Major Shen continued on his exploration and came to a rapid river which they were able to ford and continue on their way. They soon came to another abandoned settlement. It was as if all the people had one day, long ago, decided to walk away from their homes and farms.

Across the river on the south side was another larger settlement. It had many rooms on several floors and in front was what remained of a large round room, set part way into the earth that had probably been used for ceremonies. There was another such room in the living area and several small round rooms partly buried around the open area. There were signs that it had suffered a great fire. The signs led Major Shen to believe that all this had happened many years ago.

One party that was ranging out from the second settlement came back and said they had found a road. It was very wide and though it looked like it had not been used recently it was still in good repair. It led directly south.

Since Captain Tan was south, Major Shen gathered all his troops and followed the road. He was amazed. It was 40 chi across, well graded and laid out. When the road makers came to a cliff they either made steps or ramps.

They traveled for a long time when in the distance they could see men traveling toward them. When they got closer they saw that it was Captain Tan. They met with much laugher and rejoicing. All in all, the road was approximately 135 li long. Captain Tan said that it was built on an exact line north south from a large house in another settlement that they had found. This settlement had many rooms but no one had lived there for a long time.

They camped for several days in the area and many sketches and measurements were taken. There were several settlements in the area, all deserted. The architecture was of much interest. Each outer wall consisted of two load bearing walls made of large sandstone bricks held together with a mortar of mud and the interior of these walls was filled with rocks and dirt. Many walls still had an exterior veneer of small rocks set in mud.

Captain Tan sent runners to Captain Liang in the south, telling him to come to meet the main group. After a few days Captain Liang and his men came and looked with wonder at the giant complex of houses. He had many interesting things to report. His troops had found several multiple houses built in caves on the side of a canyon. All were deserted. Next they had come to a forest of stone trees. The trees had been huge and when they were turned to stone they had fallen down. It must have been mighty magic

277

as they were still shaped like trees but had turned to crystals and red, white, yellow and blue stone. They lay in pieces all over a large area. He had brought several samples and they were a great wonder.

Next his group had crossed a large area of rough lava, long cooled, but still twisted and lumped. It had ice caves in it and lava tubes.

Still moving SE they had come to a mighty mountain with a flat top. People were living on the mountain and farming on the plains below. They would not let the troops up to visit and they did not want to communicate in sign language.

Captain Tan broke camp and led all the men southeast. After many days of traveling across arid earth with few places to drink they came to a large river, lakes and swampy areas. People were living there and they were friendly. Captain Tan managed to negotiate with the people and through trade we were given food and an area to camp.

The food was interesting. There were gourds and a plant that came in kernels which had to be crushed to make patties that were then cooked on hot rocks by the fire. It could also be soaked and boiled.

After resting a few days Captain Tan sent Major Shen and a group of 40 men north to follow the river upstream. He was to return in two months at the latest. Captain Liang was sent south along the river with the same instructions. Captain Tan kept all the ill and crippled men with him to rest for the trip back.

In two months Captain Liang returned and told of seeing sand dunes, marshes with many birds. There were geese and cranes in such number they could not be counted. He had met a few wandering groups of natives but again, some were friendly and some ran away. There had been no large settlements, either empty or occupied.

In two months and five days Major Shen returned. They had followed the river and found several small settlements of natives. Most were shy but friendly. They had followed the river north through some steep canyons, sometimes traveling on the land above the river. They had come to a mighty complex of buildings but this time people were living in it. There was a tall mountain at their back and broad plains in front. The people were friendly but cautious. They had visited with them for three days. Major Shen said that the people indicated there were no more settlements in the north for many days so he turned back.

When everyone was rested they started the long trek to the coast. They went directly west and after weeks they came to the ocean and followed the beach up north until they came to the bay that held our ships.

To the South

We waited, but Captain Luo Cheng and his men never returned.

Back at the Ships

While the expeditions were out we had not been idle. After assessing the ships and the supplies it was decided that rather than try to age lumber and transport it to our site we would cannibalize the Silver Shark. All went well and the two remaining ships, Golden Dragon and Emerald Tiger were repaired above the waterline and below.

With time on his hands, Admiral Zhao decided to have a sheet of gold poured and on it would be engraved a map of all the places the exploration parties have seen and all the animals they discovered. When the voyage was completed and all the information incised, the map would be given to Emperor Zhu Di. I was picked to transcribe all the information brought back and indeed, all the information about our whole trip. The map would be poured flat, in the lost wax method we had been using to make the gold bricks. Fu Bai, another scribe who enjoys working in metal, was picked to make the map's case. He drew many designs before Admiral Zhao was satisfied.

The creation of the sheet of gold took several days of pouring and re-melting and re-pouring. We were not able to make it thin enough so one of the engineers devised a set of rollers made from smooth logs and was able to press the sheet enough and in the correct configuration. It was transferred to a flat board that had been cut to extend on all sides. It was to lie on the board until all the transcriptions were completed and then it would be rolled and inserted in the tube of the map case. Small pegs were driven into the board along the sides of the gold sheet to keep it from slipping.

Once the gold sheet for the map was made for the Emperor, Admiral Zhao decided that he needed to take something to Admiral Zheng He who had sent us forth. He decided that he would have an anchor cast in gold in the exact dimensions of our existing anchors.

To do this a real anchor was hauled up on the beach. The anchor had four arms so two were removed to be cast separately. The shaft and attached cross arm was sunk in the wet sand to make a mold. Our engineers and blacksmiths cautioned Admiral Zhao that the gold would not retain its shape without a reinforcing bar so after an initial pouring an iron bar was laid on the main shaft of the anchor and one on the lower cross piece. The blacksmiths created a loop of iron to reinforce the top of the anchor. All these iron pieces were welded together and laid on the already poured gold and another layer was poured on top of the first. The mold had dried and the top pouring had to be filed and buffed to make it acceptable. The removed cross arms were cast separately; they too, had reinforcing. When all pieces were cool they were attached and the whole anchor was smoothed. It was very impressive and would make a fine gift for Admiral Zheng He.

The gold anchor was extremely heavy and it took great effort to lift it into a specially made box and then to place it in Emerald Tiger's hold. The gold map and its board and case were placed in Admiral Zhao's cabin on the flag ship Golden Dragon. I will be working on it under his direct supervision.

After all hope had been given up on the return of Captain Luo Cheng and his men, Major Don Tiang and his men were recalled. The last of the gold bearing rock was smelted and loaded. Supplies and fresh water and all men were boarded.

All the scrolls of written information from the exploration trips to the north, northeast, east, and southeast were collected and brought to Admiral Zhao's cabin. I had already begun transcribing the illustrations to the gold. It was time to leave. I will etch the descriptions while we travel.

In the spring of the new year of 1407 our two ships set sail on the tide. We picked up a strong current to the south and followed it down the coast of this vast land. Just as we were passing a group of small islands the lookouts started shouting and pointing. I ran up on deck and was astounded to see the land in front of us heaving and shaking, trees toppling, cliffs falling, rocks sliding into the sea. The small islands between us and the land were lifting and twisting. It was a terrible sight. Suddenly I heard our captain screaming and turning I saw him pointing out to sea. Far out on the horizon the sea itself was rising and moving. A giant wave was coming toward us. It was then that I realized we were facing a Tsunami. The captain was shouting orders and looking to our left I could see that the captain of the Emerald Tiger was shouting also.

All the maneuvering in the world was not enough, at the last minute our captain managed to turn our ship toward the giant wave that towered over us but the captain of the Emerald Tiger was not as skilled. We rode over the wave but the Emerald Tiger was caught broadside and as we watched it was lifted up on the crest of the wave and over the top of the nearest island it sailed, first upright and then on its side, spilling everything, equipment and men alike out onto the wave as it broke over the island. The wave continued on to strike the mainland and wash across it, picking up anything it could rip loose and carrying it inland. Suddenly all was quiet except for the sobbing of a man standing next to me, his arms tight around the railing.

281

Then the water started backing out, swirling with trunks of trees, bodies of animals, back into the bay, back across the island, depositing death and debris and carrying everything it could out toward the setting sun.

The Admiral seemed frozen, unable to think or act. The Captain, on the other hand, was everywhere; thinking, directing, reassuring. He lowered boats and sent search parties to the islands and to the mainland.

When the search parties returned the information was bleak. The Admiral sat and listened but it was obvious that he did not understand, so the Captain again took charge and listened to the reports. Pieces of the Emerald Tiger were on the far side of the island. Several bodies were scattered among the stumps of broken trees. The shore of the mainland was scoured bare. The captain sent a burial party to the island and when they returned they reported that they had buried 16 men and that small foxes had come out of holes and were already eating the dead men. They had shooed them away but could not bring themselves to add more death by killing them.

We anchored for the night and the next morning we sailed on. Within a week we hit a current that carried us west, toward home.

I had been tracing a map on the center of the gold leaf; I called it that because it looked like a giant gold willow leaf. After the loss of the Emerald Tiger, Admiral Zhao had stayed in his cabin, windows and doors closed. He insisted I work by his side and had a work area created in one corner. After a week or so he ordered me to stay in the cabin with him day and night. We ate in the cabin and I served him as no one was allowed in. I could not go out even for a walk in the fresh breezes.

Day by day I observed his intellect and essence escaping from his body like the steam from the spout of a kettle. He has quit speaking and sits brooding, watching me. I changed my work position so that I could always face him.

All the papers from the expeditions sit around him in piles. I have been illustrating the map by copying the drawings the expeditions brought back and have traced the paths that each expedition traveled.

I started etching the opening declaration on the map and I have read all the information written down by the leaders. As I read accounts of each trip I carefully tied the precious papers together and set them back by Admiral Zhao's side. I planned to refer to each stack again when I started the actual transcription.

Admiral Zhao watched silently. When I had replaced the last stack of papers he suddenly spoke, telling me to go out and walk around the ship. He said he was tired of watching me.

I gladly went. I breathed in the fresh air and reveled in the sky and the clouds. It was wonderful to speak to people and to carry on conversations.

I don't know how long I was gone but suddenly I heard a shout. "Fire, fire." The most feared word on a ship at sea. I ran toward the voice and saw smoke escaping from cracks around the door of Admiral Zhao's cabin. Men stood in front of the door afraid to break it down. Admiral Zhao had ordered no one to enter or to knock. Our food had been set by the door and I had taken it in when I had become hungry and then I had served the Admiral, though he ate little.

I screamed to open the door or we would die. Finally, the captain himself took an axe and chopped through the door. The Admiral was a pyre and the cabin was filled with flames. All the scrolls had been consumed.

We put the flame out and the Admiral lived for seven long days before his death. He raved the whole time. The responsibilities and the deaths had been too much for his mind. It was a blessing when he passed.

I immediately went back to work on the gold map, it was my monument to the Admiral. I moved all my belongings into the fire-blackened cabin and worked day and night on the beautiful gold map. It was been difficult to remember exact details but I think I have remembered a great deal.

I hear voices. Land is on the horizon. At last, we will be home to our wonderful green land. I have missed the noodles. I will go up on deck to enjoy the view.

Japan

I am Deng Huiqing, junior scribe; we were attacked by wreckers along the coast of Japan. Nearly everyone was killed. Our ship that had served us so faithfully was beached in one of the many bays. I am allowed to finish the story of the journey but then I too will be killed. I do not care. No one is left.

I am Kawagushci Atsushi, mighty warrior. I have claimed this map for my family.

I found the golden map when I entered the ship. I ordered a lowly scribe to tell the final end of the vessel and then I put the map in its beautiful case and spirited it off the ship that we had conquered. I will not share and have brought it to my home in the mountains of Kyushu Island.

* * *

TA and Ezekiel, the story of bravery and tragedy completed, sat quietly looking at each other, stunned.

CHAPTER 47

SAN FRANCISCO

TUESDAY, MARCH 27, 2001

TA was at work in the basement when her phone rang. She was surprised to see it was Buck. He usually waited for her to get home before he called.

"Hi," she answered.

"Hi back at you. Guess what, I'm flying toward California as we speak. Well, I'm in the airport lobby getting ready to fly. Unfortunately not to San Francisco. I'm going to Oxnard. The powers that be think they've figured out where the Green Tiger sank. It's by one of the small Channel Islands. San Miguel. It's part of the Channel Islands National Park group. There're some salvage vessels there already and Nathan and I are going to be there to be sure there's no hanky panky with any gold bars; if they find any. The island they'll be working on is pretty rough, so we'll be camping out–fun.

"Are treasure hunters gathering like a pack of jackals?" asked TA.

"Not yet, but they're expected. All the map information hasn't been released but people will be able to put two and two together and come up with TREASURE. The Coast Guard is deploying several ships to cruise around the area. Hopefully we can keep control, but you never know.

"The rest of the translation is going out Monday, April 2. They were going to release it on Sunday until they realized that the 1st is April Fool's Day.

"Anyway, be thinking about coming down for a few days. If they're successful for sure you have to come down and see 'what you've made happen. As soon as I know anything, I'll put you in for a travel expenses paid trip; no 4-star hotel, this time.

"Oh, oh. They're calling my flight. Hope to see you soon. I love you." He was gone.

She dropped her tools and ran up the stairs to tell Ezekiel. He was busily going through a new shipment of assorted maps one of the suppliers had found in the back of a decommissioned library in Massachusetts. He looked up, "The library that had these maps has been closed for several years. They took only the new books when they moved and left pretty much everything else on the shelves; just locked the door. Now the city wants to recycle the building so everything is for sale. Our supplier found a treasure trove of old plot maps plus a bunch of maritime maps, all from the 1800's. Bet he didn't pay much. Unfortunately he's not passing his savings on to us." Ezekiel spun around in his chair and looked at her over the top of his spectacles. "Now, what were you saying, my dear."

She related the little she knew from the short phone conversation.

"My, that's exciting. You know, TA, I've been thinking, we could use some more help around here. What would you think about putting some ads out at the Universities and Colleges in the area. Goodness knows there are enough. We ought to be able to find several students interested in doing work studies. We could pay above minimum wage but maybe they could also get credit at their schools. If it works out it would take away some of your guilt. Yes, I know you feel guilty leaving me to manage alone. But you shouldn't. I do need help, but you need to have a life and I can see that all this might open up opportunities for you.

"Yes," he continued. "Let's make up a job description and send it to some of the schools in the area. They'll probably have to check us out to be sure we're reputable and not some white slaver organization," he laughed.

They sat down and hammered out a job description and emailed it out.

All the information was accepted by the schools. On Wednesday, April 4, from opening to closing they interviewed a steady parade of young applicants. After closing, they sat and narrowed the selections down to four.

Their first pick was a young man, a jock who played soccer. Ned was an over-achiever. Had a double major in the history and archaeology of North America and was already working on his masters. He planned to teach and loved maps. The next was Maya, a young woman, in art school, where they had not advertised, but the word had gotten around. The final two were Helen, an older student who loved geography and a young freshman named Nadia, a prodigy in chemistry.

TA felt comfortable about all of them and looked forward to teaching them the exciting things that went on in the basement restoration area. Ezekiel was thrilled to have all these young minds interested in the same things as he.

CHAPTER 48

CHANNEL ISLANDS

MONDAY, APRIL 23, 2001

Early Monday morning TA's phone rang. "Hi," said Bucks excited voice. "We hit gold yesterday. I had to hitch a ride to the mainland to call you or I would have called last night. We don't have any reception on the island.

"Anyway, you need to get down here as soon as possible. I want you to see what you're responsible for finding. The project will pick up your plane tickets and food." He laughs. "Your food will be what we're all eating at the mess tent. Bring warm clothes, it's chilly here and you'll be roughing it, so bring jeans and sweats, best to put it in a pack, not a suitcase. Oh, bring a flashlight, bug spray and sunscreen. Email me; one of the ships is able to get our emails. Anyway, tell me when you'll be arriving and I'll have someone meet you at the airport and get you out here. I love you. Got to go, my transportation is here."

TA rolled out of bed and after several phone calls she was able to book a one way commuter flight to an airport near Oxnard. She'd be leaving at 10:00 am and needed to be at the airport by 9:00. She phoned Ezekiel and let him know what she was doing and that she'd no idea when she'd be back and to please, please, get one of the new kids to feed Friend. He promised he'd see to Friend and wished her luck.

The San Francisco to Oxnard flight was crowded. Checking out the seat pocket she found a familiar face grinning at her from the front of a magazine, extolling Las Vegas.

"No way!" she exclaimed, as she grabbed it. Her row mate looked up from his computer with a disapproving look.

"Sorry," she mumbled as she flipped the magazine open. Yes, there she was in all her Elvis glory, her partner on her flight to New Mexico. It was Elvas Priestly, without her baby bump. She had a double page spread talking about her grand opening in Las Vegas on Friday, June 14th.

TA's eyes unfocused on the present and she remembered back to her flight, Kamakura in first class, TA in 'last class,' she grinned to herself. Elvas had dropped a soggy little Elvis in TA's lap while she stuffed her guitar in the overhead. TA recalled how excited Elvas had been to be going for an audition in Nashville. She had shared her dream of having an Elvis act that included her Mother, her baby Elvis and any other babies, all to be named Elvis.

TA snapped back to the present. Evidently the second baby had been a boy and was called Elvis Two. The article explained that baby Elvis, the one TA remembered with such horror, was now strumming back up to his mom. TA blinked, he had only been around ten months old when he was dropped on her lap the end of October of last year. A year and a half now. Wow! He was either a prodigy or they didn't have a mic on him. Elvas's mom was part of the act too. She looked like she had lost some of those fifty pounds she was trying to lose and she looked pretty sexy in a Rubensesque sort of way. Evidently Elvis Two was part of the act. He was wheeled on the stage in a baby carriage shaped like a guitar.

The article showed Elvas in all her sexy glory, standing on stage with her guitar. Evidently she was playing to sold out audiences in Nashville. TA laughed and carefully tucked the magazine in her back pack.

A couple of hours later she found herself climbing into a helicopter at the Oxnard Airport and was soon on her way to San Miguel Island.

Just as Buck had said, it was cold and windy. There were three other passengers in the copter and all were excited when they realized TA was the woman they had watched on TV. The map lady. She was embarrassed by their attention. The three people enthusiastically questioning her were all tops in their field of oceanography. As they flew, talking eagerly about the sunken ship, even the pilot started asking questions. They landed at a cleared, leveled area on a hilltop not far from a tent city.

Wind, heavily laden with the scent of salt, gulls swooping and screaming, machinery clanking and men shouting. Buck grabbed her in a hug with a big kiss. This was applauded by several people who had hurried to unload the copter. TA blushed but Buck just laughed and pulled her down the hill toward the largest tent.

"Look," he said excitedly, lifting the flap covering the entrance. Rows of tables were lined up, all were covered in artifacts separated as to type. Ceramics included whole bowls, platters, spoons and some tea pots. Bins held broken pieces of dishes. One area was just for metal objects, most unrecognizable but she could see armour and tools. On one side were bins holding bones. Another part of the tent had high stacks of gold bars with guards in attendance.

Worktables were scattered about, some with scales, photographic, and other unidentifiable equipment. People were working all around the tent.

They heard excited shouting and running feet. Everybody jumped up and exited the tent. Buck grabbed her hand and they joined the rush of people running toward the beach.

One of the dredge ships was tipping to the side, its arm extended over the water, obviously stressed by what it was raising. Everybody on the ship was peering over the side. All the people on the beach were leaning forward, watching intently. Quiet fell as all the watchers waited. Gulls and the sound of the straining dredge motor could be heard across the water. The cable was feeding back onto the reel. Suddenly, its load broke the surface of the water and rose, dripping, covered in coral and barnacles, TA turned to Buck. "Is that one of the ship's anchors?"

"No," he replied. "It's way too heavy. It must be the gold anchor." He turned to her, "The bars are cool – lots of cash – but this? There's nothing like it in the whole world. A gift to one of the greatest Generals of all times. It's Zheng He's anchor!"

The End – The Beginning

BIBLIOGRAPHY

Clapp, Anne F. *Curatorial Care of Works of Art on Paper.* New York: Nick Lyons Books, 1978

Dolloff, Francis W. and Perkinson, Roy L. *How to Care for Works of Art on Paper.* Boston: Museum of Fine Arts, 1985

Hucker, Charles O. *China's Imperial Past, An Introduction to Chinese History and Culture.* Stanford: Stanford University Press, 1975

Kliban, J. *I Love to Eat Them Mousies* song

Rand McNally Road Atlas 2017

Yamashita, Michael. *Zheng He.* Vercelli, Italy: White Star Publishers, 2006

Wikipedia

ACKNOWLEDGEMENTS

Thank you to my husband Bob and daughter Beth for all their patience and son Mike and his wife Laura for their interest from afar; to Marie Trump, editor extraordinaire and her husband Bruce for his knowledge of physical editing and to the entire Fountains writing group, especially Barbara-the slasher. Last, to Helen 'Hebi' Mattison whose enthusiastic encouragement launched the effort that resulted in this book.